CATTLE STOP

KIT OLIVER

PARROT CAT PUBLISHING

For Mr. Russ
Forever our number one

CATTLE STOP

PROLOGUE

THE FIRE POPS, Whit grins, and far off in the pasture, a cow moos, low and long. Cooper blinks and Whit's still smiling, and Whit never smiles.

"Easy there," Whit says, and that's more how he normally sounds, bossy and sharp.

"Just looking for a beer," Cooper says, but instead of finding a bottle, his fingers meet a slush of melted ice in the cooler and he drops heavily, gracelessly, onto a hay bale.

"Another?"

"I want one," Cooper says, but really he wants to know why Whit's smiling.

Cooper reaches up two wet fingers to press to the fullness of Whit's bottom lip. Whit's tall. Cooper is too, but he's sitting and Whit's standing and the fire's sending up sparks into the glitter of stars in the night sky.

"What's so funny?" Cooper asks. Whit's mouth is soft and his hand is warm and strong around Cooper's wrist.

"You." Whit pulls Cooper's hand away to sip from his own beer.

There should be more bottles, the cooler full when they'd dragged it out here to the pasture as the sun set and

Drew lit the brush pile. But the pile's smaller than it was, the glow of sunset has long faded, and the world spins a little whenever Cooper closes his eyes.

"Where'd you get that?" Cooper asks, but when he reaches for it, Whit draws the bottle away.

"It's mine."

"Give it."

"No." Whit settles next to him on the bale. He's warm. Whit's warm, not Cooper. His hands are cold and he tucks them into his armpits, clumsy and tired. He should help Penny and Drew drag brush from the edge of the field onto the fire, but instead he hugs himself tight and yawns.

Whit's throat works as he takes a drink, tendons flexing against skin burnished a deep brown tan from the summer sun. The rim of the bottle presses a divot into Whit's lip and Cooper wants that more than he wants a sip of beer, wants that curve of Whit's mouth. He leans in and Whit's smiling again—and that's really something, isn't it?—straight teeth and those lips that were so soft to touch. They're soft under Cooper's mouth, too. And there's the sharp taste of beer and the fire-warmed skin of Whit's cheek and the smell of him, all woodsmoke and clean sweat.

Whit pulls back, and Cooper chases after him. Slumps with the motion, into the curve of Whit's shoulder.

"You've had enough to drink," Whit says. His hand is nice on Cooper's chest. Firm as it braces him. Warm, too. And big.

"M'fine," Cooper mumbles.

"You won't remember this."

Cooper's mouth is wet. His hand is too. But cold, unlike his lips.

"I will," he says and come dawn, and the dew wetting his clothes and glittering on the grass, and the smolder of embers, Cooper rolls over, a throb going through his temples with the glare of sunshine and the thought, *I did.*

Whit's already tossing hay bales down from the loft of the barn and the cows are milling around their pen and the pigs are kicking up a ruckus. Cooper presses the heels of his hands into his eyes. *I did remember,* he thinks, *I did.*

PART 1

———————

APRIL

PRESENT DAY

CHAPTER ONE

"I'M HERE!" Cooper jumps down from his truck into the muddy sludge of the barnyard. Silence meets his shout and he cups his hands around his mouth to call, "Drew? Penny?"

But Two Pines Farm is quiet, even the cows in the barn only glancing his way as they chew over their cud. The frozen puddles don't answer him and neither does the tractor, nor the stray chicken who clucks to herself as she strolls past the barn. Cooper tosses the truck door closed with a thump that echoes across the empty plane of crusty snow on the fields and the trees' bare branches.

The only movement from the house is Sadie wagging her tail where she's sprawled on the porch. It takes her a long, slow heave to get to her front feet, and longer still to drag her hips under her. Cooper jogs across the slush in the driveway before she can totter down the porch steps on her short legs, and bends to rub behind her drooping ears.

"Hi, sweet girl." Once, her back leg would've started going as he scratched the tawny fur beneath her collar, though now he only gets a huff against the cuff of his sweatshirt, a gentle lick of a kiss, and her deep brown eyes turned up to him. *Matching blonds*, he's said to her more than once. He bends down to press his cheek to the top of her head.

The door's unlocked, like it always is. The swell of dry heat from the woodstove tells Cooper he missed a bigger welcoming committee by no longer than it takes a log to catch on the coals. He peers around, shoving a handful of hair behind his ear, but the room's empty except for Sadie waddling toward her water bowl.

But even still and silent, the kitchen is the same as ever, the scent of woodsmoke and fresh bread, that perpetual note of hay from the chaff caught in the cuffs and hems of the jackets hanging on their hooks. As always, the boots are lined up against the wall. Whit's, the largest pair, Drew's in the middle, and then Penny's shoes she wears for work as a bartender, the smallest.

There's not really space for Cooper's boots, so he kicks them off and nudges them toward the heat of the woodstove. At least they'll be toasty when he leaves later that afternoon.

And then he lets out a happy, long breath. Back again and it feels oh so good.

The whiteboard hangs on the wall where it always has, Drew's cheese-making schedule written in his scrawl, Penny's bartending shifts at Murry's in her far neater print, and Whit's cursive of the cows' due dates and hay deliveries. Apparently, it's Penny's night to cook and—*perfect*—Whit's day off from his job here on the farm, which gives Cooper a couple hours to visit with Drew, and no dour and dreary Whit to bump into. Plus, if Cooper can finagle it, maybe some lunch.

"Drew?" he calls again as he makes his way into the living room and then up the steep, creaky stairs.

Drew's room, the master bedroom, sits empty except for the laundry spilling out of the hamper and the unmade bed, a single pillow against the headboard and the sheets kicked back.

"Where you at, bud?" Cooper asks, but Drew's socks don't answer him.

Just down the hall, Penny's door is half-ajar. Cooper taps his knuckles against it, waits, and pokes it open with one finger, but her room is as empty as Drew's.

At the other end of the hallway, Whit's door is closed and entirely too tempting.

He shouldn't, but Cooper still eases the door open. *Just curious where everyone's gotten to*, he thinks and peers inside. He takes a step in. And then another.

The room smells like Whit. Like the soap he uses and the smell of his skin. *Just looking for Drew*, Cooper thinks as he picks up one of the picture frames on top of the dresser of Whit and Penny, their heads tipped together and arms around each other's shoulders. *Cousins*, Cooper had eventually learned, nearly a decade ago when he'd first met them when they were all teenagers, with their dark hair, dark eyes, and olive skin, and the same quirk to their mouths, Penny's smile wider than Whit's ever is. Cousins and best friends with Drew, and now that Drew's uncle has moved to Florida and left the farm to him, roommates.

Jealous, Cooper's caught himself thinking more than once. Penny and Whit tied together by their family, their parents and grandparents and Penny's sisters living not that far away, and their trips back to Mexico to see cousins and aunts and uncles. And the two of them getting to live with Drew here at the farm, Whit working here each and every day, ending more often than not with long evenings gathered at Murry's, hanging out together. Hell, the three of them got to go to high school together, too, while Cooper only got to visit upstate New York during the summers to see his grandparents, got dropped off here at the farm for a way to while away the time, and then it was back to Brooklyn for the school year. Then, like now, he just drops in to say hi, before he's off again.

Whatever. If Cooper spent more time here, he'd have to see Whit and no fucking thanks. A visit to see his best bud, Drew, say hi to Penny, and then get the hell out of here sounds far, far better.

He puts the picture back down, trying to get it in the exact right spot. There's no mark of dust to tell him where it precisely sat, though he's sure Whit will somehow know Cooper's been poking around.

But he's just looking to see if anyone's home, not snooping through the drawer of the nightstand between the two twin beds, checking out what Whit might keep there.

Though, he could.

No, he tells himself, even as he reaches for it.

From the hall, the stairs creak.

Cooper pulls in a breath and holds it, listening. That's not the sound of Drew's footsteps. Please, *please*, let it not be Whit.

"Cooper?"

"Penny? Oh, thank God."

She pushes open the door and laughs as he picks her up, swinging her in a circle, her ponytail long enough to dance over his forearms. "Fuck you. You gave me a heart attack, but I thought that was your truck."

"I thought you were out," he says as he sets her back down.

"I was in the cheese room. And I thought you were up north, not breaking and entering."

"Just finished up a winter job in Maine and next stop: Oregon. Figured I'd swing through before I head out west, say hi to my moms down in Brooklyn, and I could surprise Drew on the way."

"By hiding in Whit's room?"

Cooper slips past her into the hallway. "Well, I told Sadie I'd check in there just to make sure. Where is everyone?"

"Drew had to go to the hardware store for some Tyvek, and I got the dubious honor of giving him a hand flipping the Brie." Penny flexes one arm, pointing to her bicep. "You're welcome, cheese eaters of New York, 'cause I thought my wrist was going to fall off salting each and every one of those little bastards."

"Tyvek? Is he finally building Sadie the dog palace she needs and deserves?"

"You haven't talked to him? Come up and look."

Cooper follows Penny up the attic stairs, which squeak like they always have. He and Drew used to take turns locking each other in the attic during weekend sleepovers, when Cooper's grandpa needed a break from watching him and he'd been thrilled to terrify himself with the cobwebs and dust and hair-raising creaks of the centuries-old house. Even now, some of that good old terror sparks up his spine, though this time it's at the sight of the roof.

Fucking *yikes*. "What the hell?"

"I guess a family of squirrels spent all winter digging into the siding and window trim, and we got a hell of a lot of snow this year. It all melted, and yeah, Drew's not too thrilled."

Cooper follows the stained and pockmarked rot of wood across the attic's ceiling until he's standing right over the room he normally stays in. The damage travels down the wall to the floor, and he takes a careful step backward. "Wow."

"You think this is a mess, you should see Drew. He's not exactly—how should we put it?—in the best of moods."

"He didn't say anything. We talked the other day and he—"

"Is low-key panicking and probably was in the middle of one of many nervous breakdowns? Welcome to my and Whit's life these days. Please start visiting more often than every six months, we can't actually handle him." Her head tips. Cooper hears the rumble of a car outside, and then Sadie barking. "Ah, the grump himself."

Cooper jogs down the stairs and nudges Sadie aside with his foot to throw open the door. Sure enough, there's Drew, his arms spreading wide as he sees Cooper.

"I knew that was your goddamn truck!" Drew nearly lifts Cooper off his feet with his hug.

"Miss me?"

Drew smacks him on the back with one meaty hand. "Of course, I fucking missed you."

"I can't breathe."

"I love you, man. Where the hell have you been all winter?"

"Working." Cooper tries to heave in a breath, but Drew just squeezes him tighter. "Go do something useful, milk a cow."

"They only like Whit," Drew says, "and you and I both know it. Hi, you fucker. Thanks for the warning you were stopping by."

"Hi, yourself. Did you shower in the last six months? 'Cause all I can smell is cow shit." Cooper looks him over, Drew's mop of red hair, the length of his winter beard, and the freckles over his nose and cheeks, stark against his pale skin. "You look good, though."

"You look scruffy as shit." Drew smacks him on the shoulder again. "Come in, you asshole. Pen, go slash his tires so he can't leave."

"I can't stay. I told the mom squad I'd stop by and then"—Cooper shapes his fingers into guns and points both at Drew—"grand adventures await. Can I get a hell yeah?"

"You can get your butt in a chair and tell me how your winter was. You fucking promised you'd come down to visit and here you show up and it's already spring."

"What can I say? I lead a life of mystery."

"You lead a life of refusing to plan more than five minutes in advance."

"Enigmatic intrigue."

Drew snorts a laugh. "Is that what you tell all the boys?"

Cooper winks at him. "We don't do much talking."

Drew sets out Brie, Camembert, and cheddar, and pulls a dish towel off of a lump that reveals itself to be freshly baked bread. Cooper settles into one of the mismatched chairs around the worn kitchen table and leans back into the heat of the woodstove, idly scratching at Sadie's ears when she totters over. The kitchen always seems like something out of an old-time museum, wood beams in the ceiling, quaint curtains over the window above the soapstone sink, and a refrigerator nearly buried in magnets. It's like Drew's aunt and uncle should walk back in at any moment, given how it's frozen in time since they retired and left Drew the house and the farm. But only Penny appears, pulling a sweatshirt over her head.

"Well," Cooper says, "I'd ask how your winter was, but I saw the attic."

Drew points a jar of jam at the ceiling. "The attic? That old thing? There's nothing wrong at all, except if you thought you were going to stay in your usual room and wanted, you know, walls between you and the great outdoors."

"Good thing I'm only swinging through town to put a smile on your face and a twinkle in your eye," Cooper says.

"If you touch the plaster in there, it just"—Penny wiggles her fingers and makes a fizzing noise—"crumbles. It's kind of cool, actually."

Drew grabs a knife and an apple and brings them to the table too. "Very cool, complete with the fact that we're being harassed by a team of squirrels intent on tearing down my damn house."

"So, it was a great winter, then." Cooper pops a piece of cheddar in his mouth and closes his eyes as he chews. There's a lot of cheese in the world, but none like Drew's. Fucking brilliant idea, back over summers during high school when Drew had first been messing around with the idea of trying his hand at mozzarella and ricotta. Then, Cooper had just enjoyed it as a snack after an afternoon helping around the farm, and now, it's an entire business.

"I think we should just hire the squirrels to fix the house," Penny says, slipping into the chair next to Drew. "Trade them acorns, make peace in the neighborhood, put this entire disaster behind us."

"They'd probably do a better job than I would." Drew slices the apple with a whack of the knife. "Or maybe at least they can give Whit a hand with the damn cows so I can make some progress on the house."

Cooper grins and reaches for a slice of apple. "You didn't hear it from me, but I would bet the squirrels would be better at farming than Whit is."

"Whit, our esteemed farm manager, you mean?" Penny points a piece of apple at Cooper. "Drew has him running the farm this year, you know."

"Yeah, I gotta focus on this damn house. I asked him to pretty much take over the cows," Drew says.

"The poor cows," Cooper says.

"He's helping with sales too," Drew says.

"Poor customers," Cooper says.

"Oh my God, the two of you," Penny says. "Whit's not even here, and already you and him are going at it."

"I'm just here to say hi, eat cheese, and give a true and honest assessment of Mr. Whit Morales's skills."

"Of course you are. But look, I really think I'm on to something here. I've got work at the bar, Drew has, you know, cheese stress, which leaves only Whit to get the farm ready for the spring, so what I'm thinking is an entire army of squirrels helping him. Like maybe a rehabilitation program for them, give them a satisfying goal to work toward so they stop trying to take apart the house."

"I like this idea," Cooper says. "Can they give Whit a performance review, too? I'll set them up with little squirrel-sized clipboards and a checklist."

A chill gust of cold air slices across Cooper's back, followed by the echo of heavy footsteps.

Oh.

Fucking great.

He twists in his chair and there's Whit in the doorway, pressing the door closed with a broad palm to seal it against the frame.

Cooper tugs at his sweatshirt. The grease stains worn into the gray fabric and the raggedness of the hem seem suddenly more obvious. That and the fact he hasn't shaved in a couple days or gotten a haircut in much longer. It's like Whit can somehow tell Cooper's socks don't match through the mud-splattered cuffs of his jeans, despite his feet being tucked beneath the table. Fucking hell, he'd been so sure he'd be able to get in, see Drew, and avoid Whit's cool appraisal.

Cooper curls his toes. "Hey."

Yeah, that was casual and easy, and like he doesn't even give the tiniest of shits. He still can't believe he *liked* Whit. Had that burning, awful crush on him, back when they were teenagers and Whit seemed so damn cool.

Has, his brain supplies, and Cooper frowns and grabs a piece of apple.

Had, he thinks firmly and sets a slice of cheddar on top.

The cheese slides off and falls to the table.

"What checklist?" Whit asks.

Cooper doesn't have to look to know Whit's hanging his coat neatly on the far left hook, like he always does. Cooper should've shucked off his own sweatshirt and hung it there, just to mess with him.

"Cooper's here," Drew says. "He came to bear witness to the last day this house is standing before the squirrels come back armed with screw guns and crowbars."

Cooper picks up the slice of cheese and sets it back on the apple. It falls again, and he sighs. "Thought you were out."

"I came back," Whit says. "Hi."

Cooper pops the apple into his mouth. "Hi."

"Coop's gonna help me train the squirrels to work on the farm," Penny says.

"That was the grand idea I just walked in on?" Whit asks.

What an ass. What an unfortunately gorgeous asshole. Especially since the shape of Whit's chest beneath the thin fabric of his T-shirt, the perfect curls in his dark hair, and those deep brown eyes of his make Cooper want to do stupid shit like stare at him. How fucking treacherous to be back here on the farm. Every single time Cooper spends too long around Whit, that damn crush crops up again, unwanted and stubborn and overwhelming.

All the more reason to ignore it. Not to let it get a foothold in his mind again, and to focus on his irritation with Whit, that familiar annoyance with him that keeps those feelings at bay.

"I know you're allergic to new ideas, but it was a good one." Cooper has half a mind to kick away the empty chair next to him before Whit can take it, but Sadie's in the way, so he just grimaces as Whit sits. "How you been?"

"Fine." Whit neatly sandwiches a piece of cheddar between two thin slices of apple. "Does this mean you're staying?"

"I've got a job to get to, actually."

"You got a job?"

"Surprised?"

"You should stay for a bit, Coop," Drew says.

Whit takes a neat, tidy bite of his perfectly constructed, stupid snack and glances at Cooper's cheese still on the table. "You always ask Drew for a reference. Figured I would've heard if that'd been the case."

"Well, I'm working on getting a job." Cooper grabs the last slice of apple before Whit can. "It's a real awesome farm out in Oregon, and I'm driving out there soon as I say hi to you lot. New life on the West Coast, see you never."

"Think they know about squirrel training?" Penny asks. Across the kitchen, the kettle whistles and she pushes her chair back. "Want tea, anyone?"

"I'll have some, but sit, stay, I'll get it." Drew stands. "What kind of farm?"

"Goats, and they've got a real sweet setup."

"Oh," Whit says. "Goats. I hear you love goats."

Drew points from Whit to Cooper and back again as he

fills Penny's favorite mug. "It's been all of five minutes. Play nice. And I want to hear about the new job."

"We always do love to hear the latest career move," Whit says.

At least I haven't worked at the same place my entire adult life, Cooper could snap. Though it wouldn't be worth it, because Whit's not even looking at him. No, he's just slicing a piece of bread for himself and covering it with Brie. Same old Cooper coming up with a retort just as Whit's already coolly, drolly brushing him off.

So no, nothing around here has changed. For the better in so many ways, like a worn-in, well-loved life Cooper can slip back into, but the stillness of time means Whit's the same as ever: achingly handsome and his attitude already grating under Cooper's skin.

"I was going to hit the road to get down to Brooklyn," Cooper says. "I wanted to see mother number one and mother number two before I head out for the sunset."

Drew sets Penny's mug on the table. "Okay, but counterargument, I will feed you cheese until you burst."

"Squirrel training, squirrel training," Penny chants, slapping the table in time with the words. "Come on, Coop, stay tonight at least. I'm off work, and Whit's here too, so we can all hang out."

"Yeah, and you can see the true state of dilapidation this damn place is in," Drew says as he roots through the cupboard for another mug.

Cooper frowns at Drew's back, the joking in Drew's voice too faint beneath what sounds like genuine exhaustion. Beneath the table, Penny kicks at Cooper's ankle.

"What?" Cooper asks.

"Sorry." She kicks again and Whit looks up at her. "Dile que haría una gran diferencia si se queda hoy, de todas formas necesitamos la ayuda."[1]

Whit neatly, precisely spreads jam over his Brie.

"Tell him," Penny says.

Whit sighs. Sets the knife down and wipes his fingers off. Then, he leans close to Cooper, close enough the hairs rise on the back of Cooper's neck, and Whit's breath ghosts over his ear as he whispers, "Penny says it'd make a big difference to Drew if you stayed tonight."

Cooper jerks away.

"It would," she says. "Tell him the other part."

"No."

"Tell him."

Whit leans close again. Cooper tenses, his eyes straight ahead as Whit's arm brushes his. "And we need help with work, too."

"So, yeah?" Penny asks. "What d'ya think? Stay, would you?"

Whit's here, Cooper so wants to say. He wants to rub at his ear.

Drew pours hot water into a mug and a couple drops miss, splattering against the nicked and worn wood of the counter. There's still the circular burn-mark where, years ago, Cooper'd set down a pot straight from the oven, and afterward, he'd tried frantically to wipe the scorch away before Drew's aunt saw.

She'd noticed it—but, Whit'd been the one giving him a look cooler than she ever had or would. How fucking typical.

Drew stares down at the water. He sighs and wipes it with the cuff of his sweatshirt, then stares at the wet mark, like wherever his mind is, it's far away from the cause and effect of blotting and damp fabric.

Yeah, Cooper could spend the day here, help Drew out, and take off in the morning. Surely, he could manage twenty-four hours without wanting to strangle Whit.

Or wanting to kiss him. Again.

Cooper blows out a breath. "Ok, one night."

It's worth it, to see the grin spread over Drew's face and how Penny punches both fists in the air. And even more so, the flex of Whit's cheek as he tightens his jaw. Well, this is just the first of many annoyances Cooper can heap on Whit during this visit, 'cause he's got the rest of the day now and maybe, if he works hard enough at it, he can get Whit's eye to start twitching, too.

CHAPTER TWO

COOPER LEANS against the kitchen counter, his cellphone pressed to his ear. He pictures the landline ringing in the tiny galley kitchen of the apartment he grew up in, the view of the neighboring building's cement wall outside the window and the flicker of fluorescent lights. It'd be something if his mother answered the phone for once. Bothered to tear herself away from her computer. Let alone if she'd actually been planning to make it to dinner tonight instead of preferring the allure of yet another work meeting.

"Langdon residence," he hears as the receiver's picked up and *of course* that's not Mom.

"Stepmother?" he asks.

"Stepson, hello," Terry says and then louder, "Linda, Cooper's on the phone!"

Don't bother, he thinks. "I'm just calling to tell you I'm gonna stay at Drew's tonight."

"Never mind, Lin, it's not Cooper, it's someone offering a lower monthly car payment if I just give them our social security numbers, address, and bank info!"

"Too bad you barely even drive," Cooper says.

"Shush, you. How's Drew?"

"Yeah, good." From the attic comes a clatter that sounds like lumber falling and then footfalls on the stairs in time with Drew's cursing. "Less than good, maybe."

"I hate the fucking attic," Drew says as he jogs down the last steps. "I'm pretty sure the squirrels are running a rotation to make sure they maximize their daily damage."

"Medium bad," Cooper says. "Listen, I'll text when I know I'm heading down your way, okay? I gotta fight some rodents before I'm done here."

"The more you tell me about farming, the less I understand. Love you, Coop."

"You too," he says and taps his phone to end the call. "Drew?"

"Fucking fuck!" Drew shoves his fingers into his hair. "Was that your mom? Can I move in with her and forget cows exist, let alone this damn house?"

"Is that a hint you want help with chores?" Cooper asks.

"I want to have cut the board to the right length the first damn time." Drew cups his hand around his mouth and shouts toward the ceiling, "And it's a hint to the fucking squirrels."

"Measure once, cut fifteen times. And excellent communication skills. A bit more of that and I'm sure the squirrels'll be packing their bags." Cooper laces up his boots and frowns at Whit, who's zipping his coat neatly up to his chin. "What're you doing? Isn't it your day off?"

"You can't do chores by yourself. You haven't been here in six months," Whit says.

Cooper pushes past him out into the chilly wind in the barnyard. "I think I can figure out how to feed a bunch of damn cows."

"And pigs."

"Oh, we already have pigs for the season? A shocking

notion, feeding a pig. I wouldn't have thought I'd need supervision since they're, well, pigs."

"We?"

"Next you're going to tell me something else surprising, like we're expecting calves anytime this spring."

"*We* are expecting calves any day now."

Cooper walks quicker, which is always a losing battle because Whit has a couple of inches on him, and it seems to be all in his legs.

The barn's the same as always. The watering trough by the fence, the hose coiled and hanging, the pitchforks set against the wall—everything where it's been since that first summer day Cooper's grandfather dropped him off, back when Cooper was still in high school and Mom had judged him too rambunctious—*Cooper, I'm working, please*—and had shipped him upstate to his grandparents. *The worst,* he'd thought with Grandpa promising he'd be back in a couple hours, waving to Drew's uncle and reminding him about their weekend's golf plans. Cooper had stood in the barnyard, skinny and full of his early adolescent awkwardness, with no clue about cows or pigs or chickens.

But Drew had been there to show him the ropes. And Whit to critique him, every damn step of the way.

What joy, Cooper thinks as Whit trails him down the barn's center aisle. The spigot set into the wall rattles as Cooper turns it, letting out a hiss of air. A far-too-weak stream of water flows from the end of the hose.

"You still haven't fixed this?" Cooper asks.

"Sorry, I didn't know there'd be an inspection this afternoon."

"I told you: clipboards and a checklist." Cooper sets the end of the hose in the watering trough. "You might be able to find the time, if you didn't have to stand around waiting for this to fill all damn day."

"If that's what you're planning to do, I'll let Penny know not to hurry with dinner," Whit says. "Wedge the hose so it stays and feed out the hay while the water's filling."

Cooper throws his hands up. "Oh my God, you just stumbled upon the secret of farming, thank you so much for sharing that with me."

The hose tips out of the trough and dribbles across Cooper's thighs. He turns a shoulder to Whit and reaches down to grab it. There's a bracket in the wall and a dirty mark on the hose where Whit must push it in every morning and evening.

Cooper has to try twice to get it set just right, and he can feel Whit watching him like a burn across the back of his neck.

"Should I tell Penny about dinner?" Whit asks.

"Thanks for giving you a hand, I think you mean. You're welcome."

Cooper climbs the ladder to the loft quickly, his jeans sticking to his legs where the denim's soaked. How lovely it would be to go back down there, yank the hose out, and accidentally-on-purpose drench Whit's pants too. Though it probably wouldn't be nearly as satisfying as he imagines, what with the trickle of water the broken spigot lets out.

Or, he could go down there, throw off years of nerves and worry over Whit's reaction and blurt out, *I'm so fucking into you.* He snorts a soft laugh to himself. It might be worth it, just to see the look of disgust on Whit's face. The exasperation he has in spades for Cooper and the horror of the thought that Cooper could be anything more than the irritation of a rock wedged in the sole of his shoe.

Though that soft, hurt spot in Cooper's chest would ache, the one it's better to shield with thoughts of poking back at Whit's ire with him by being a pest in his own right, than having to hear once and for all, out loud and forever imprinted in his memory, that Cooper will never, not ever, be good enough for him. Too impulsive, too distracting, too rash, talks too much—Whit probably keeps a list of what he dislikes about Cooper and adds to it every time Cooper swings by the farm.

Socks, the barn cat, lounges in a weak beam of spring sunlight. His ears prick when he sees Cooper, the end of his tail flicking and his claws flexing. He relaxes when he sniffs Cooper's fingers, then butts his forehead against his knuckles, trying to get Cooper to rub his neck. Well, at least someone likes Cooper. Drew, Socks, and Sadie—what a crew of best friends. Cooper'll take it. Spend his time petting Socks's long fur, rather than have to deal with Whit for another minute, but he takes a look around at the hay bales and—no. Just no.

"Socks," he whispers, chucking the cat under his chin. "What the fuck is Whit doing to this place?"

But Socks just purrs and Cooper calls down, "Whit?"

"Cooper."

"You're feeding the cows these bales?"

"Do you see any others up there?"

"These bales are tiny. How many of them do you have to feed out a day? Ten? Fifteen? What happened to the round baler, or do you just enjoy wallowing in misery and driving yourself nuts doing this?" Cooper grabs the nearest one, hoists it up onto his hip, and then drops it into the aisle. The bale lands a couple feet from Whit, showering him in chaff. "Wow, this actually, literally, hurts my soul to feed an entire herd of cows like this."

"The baler broke."

"Ah, must be on the list to fix after you get to the spigot."

"So we used the old one and only have these smaller bales."

"Drew really stands for schlepping these damn things all day, every day?"

"Drew's making cheese."

"Lucky Drew."

Cooper tosses two more bales down before he just gives up. He'll drive the tractor into the barn, set a pallet on the forks, and load it up with bales so he can bring enough down for tonight and tomorrow morning. The rest, he'll leave to Whit, who can sling bales by hand to his heart's content once Cooper leaves.

When Cooper jumps down the last rungs of the ladder, Whit's already pulling the baling twine off the bale, which is just absurd, because then Whit has to carry the flakes to the cows one armful at a time. It's easier to grab the entire bale by the strings, toss it into the feeder, *then* cut the twine with a pocket knife. But Whit's Whit, and he ignores the fact that Cooper's finished with three bales by the time he's done with one.

He just does things his own way, Drew had said once, years ago. Not bad, or worse, just different. Cooper had brushed Drew off then and would do it again now, already shoving a handful of baling twine into his pocket and asking, "Pig grain?"

Whit carefully folds the string he's holding. "Scoop and buckets are outside the cheese room."

"Scoop and buckets?"

Whit folds yet another length of baling twine in half and then in half again. "You scoop the grain into the buckets, unless they do it differently in Vermont."

"I was working on a farm in Maine this winter."

"Sure."

"Can you not get yourself a damn grain bin? Or is hauling buckets of grain part of your master plan to keep yourself busy while the water fills?"

"The water system's fine." Whit tucks the twine into his pocket and straightens his coat. "Why don't you help Drew with the house? I can handle this."

Cooper opens his mouth, but Whit wipes his forehead with his sleeve. It pulls the hem of his jacket up, and with it, the bottom of his T-shirt. Cooper snaps his eyes away to where a cow's chewing a mouthful of hay, because otherwise, he's going to look at how Whit's belt and waistband sit against the flat plane of his stomach just so, beneath the jut of his hipbones.

Yeah, helping Drew is a good idea. A better one than being here in the too-quiet barn with Whit already bending down to pick up another bale, his bicep curving against the canvas of his coat.

In the backyard, Drew is bent over a sawhorse and a stack of lumber, his pants coated with a fine layer of sawdust.

"Hey, Drew," Cooper yells over the whine of the circular saw. "Whit sent me to see what I can help you with. He said I did so well in the barn, he doesn't need me anymore."

"Is that what he said? Yeah, you can grab the wrenches and take apart the bed in the guest room," Drew says. "We gotta get all the furniture cleared out. Sorry I don't have anywhere better for you to sleep."

"We gonna snuggle tonight?" Cooper asks.

"Only if I get to be little spoon."

"Nah, I'll share the couch with Sadie, in that case."

"She snores."

Cooper pokes a finger into the side of Drew's nose. "So do you."

The shop's as cluttered as it ever is, the combination of Whit's organization and Drew's whirlwind leaving a neat pegboard on the back wall labeled for each individual tool, yet most of them hanging empty. Cooper sorts through the handfuls of screwdrivers and hammers Drew dumped on the workbench, but wherever the wrenches are, they're not hiding beneath that pile nor on their appointed peg.

Across the barnyard, a hay bale falls from the loft and lands in the aisle of the barn. A second one follows, puffing up dust, and then boots swing onto the ladder, pants neatly cuffed above them.

Cooper cups his hands around his mouth and shouts, "Do you know where the wrenches are?"

Whit carefully picks his way down the last rungs of the ladder. Cooper sighs. Whit can hear him, even if he isn't bothering to answer.

"The wrenches," he calls again as he jogs over. He has to blink against the dimness of the barn, his eyes straining after the brightness outside. Socks yawns at him, his pink tongue curling and one paw dangling off the edge of the loft. "They're not in the shop."

Whit doesn't even bother to look over. "They're in the truck."

"Which truck?"

"The truck," Whit says again and bends down to loop his fingers through the baling twine.

"Your truck or the farm truck?"

"The truck." Whit points with his chin toward the barnyard.

Cooper breathes in slowly through his nose. "Okay."

"I'm using them," Whit says.

"It looks more like you're feeding the cows."

"I've got to get the fences fixed before we start grazing." Whit has his weight on one leg, the bale on his hip, his shoulders bulging against his coat. *Don't look*, Cooper tells himself, and then looks anyway at that swell of muscles. "Don't take those wrenches."

"I just need them for a second."

"Don't," Whit calls after him.

"A minute, tops," Cooper calls back. Four wrenches sit in the cupholder of Whit's truck. Cooper raises his hand and shouts toward the barn, "Thanks!"

"The two of you," Penny says when Cooper pushes open the door to the kitchen. "I can hear you and the windows aren't even open."

Cooper salutes her with one of the wrenches. "Whit missed me, what can I say?"

Penny sets the heavy cast-iron Dutch oven on top of the stove. "Of course he did."

Upstairs, the room Cooper normally stays in is chilly, like the heat's been off all winter and the door left closed. Cooper touches the brown watermark on the wall near the window, and sure enough, the plaster gives.

Well, it's a good thing he didn't visit over the winter, then—trying to survive any length of time in Whit's presence aside.

Cooper kneels and fits a wrench to a bolt in one of the bed's legs, though he pauses at the stamp of feet up the stairs. He doesn't need to look over his shoulder to know Whit's standing in the doorway.

"I'm using those," Whit says.

"Actually"—Cooper gives the wrench a quarter turn—"I am."

"The gate in the back field needs to be replaced and I—"

"Took every single wrench on the farm while you were feeding out hay? Isn't it your day off?"

He can nearly hear Whit cross his arms. "I had to stop back in, so—"

"And you figured you'd work all damn day? Hey, quick question, the gate you're fixing, isn't that the one the cows break every single year? Maybe—" Cooper twists the bolt free with a grunt. "Maybe this will be the year you convince them not to use it as a scratching post, tear it down in their itchy glory, and then escape onto the road to the delight of the neighbors and our enduring embarrassment."

"Can I have those back?"

"M'nearly done."

"You aren't."

"Well then, give me a hand, why don't you?" Cooper lies down, scooting under the bed so he can reach the far leg. The floor's cold where his sweatshirt rides up and takes his T-shirt with it, his back bare against the floorboards and now gritty with dust.

"Can't this wait?" Whit's feet move closer. He's got his boots off, Cooper sees when he glances down the length of his own body. Trust Whit to neatly unlace them and leave them by the door downstairs so he doesn't track mud all over the house before chasing after Cooper.

Cooper shoves his foot at Whit's ankle. "No, 'cause Drew's going to try to do this all himself, and he's got enough on his plate."

"And here I thought the point of you staying tonight was to spend time with him."

"I'm pretty sure it was just to annoy you. Drew calls me up special for that. I've got a certain touch."

Whit's feet shift. He must only be able to see Cooper's legs from where he's standing, maybe the bottom of his stomach where his shirt's hitched up above his belt. Cooper tugs his shirt back down, though it rides up again when he reaches to fit the wrench around the bolt.

He must paint those on, Cooper'd grumbled once about Whit's abs, shirtless and sweaty, as Whit heaved a sledge-hammer overhead again and again. Cooper's in good shape too. Great shape. He yanks at his shirt once more. He just doesn't need Whit staring at him, probably appraising all the sit-ups Cooper could be doing to achieve the perfection Whit holds himself to.

Whit steps closer and then kneels next to Cooper's thigh. Cooper freezes, fumbling at the wrench, but all that happens is that hands wrap around the bottom of the board he's loosening.

"You're going to drop that on your face," Whit says.

"Then won't all the boys be sad." Cooper loosens the bolt and spins it free the rest of the way with his fingers. He's not used to Whit being so close to him. *Breathe,* he tells himself. What was Whit even going to do, bending down like that—touch him? Hell, if Whit doesn't always stay as far away from Cooper as he can. Cooper clears his throat. It's too quiet in here, so he adds, "The ladies, too."

"Didn't know you were so equal opportunity."

"I'm not, but they're welcome to look." He scoots forward, crawling out from underneath the bed and forcing Whit to shift aside. Still, their shoulders bump, and Cooper tugs his shirt down his back before scrambling to his knees. Even with the bolts gone, the two of them have to wrestle the board free, the wood held together for so many years that it doesn't want to budge.

Whit reaches for the wrench in Cooper's hand. "Can I have that back now?"

Cooper holds it away from Whit, like he used to do to Drew that single year that Cooper was taller. "Yes, taking the first board off of the bed frame was my entire goal for the day."

"The gate—"

"Oh Lord, someone alert the cows that their favorite farmer is five minutes behind his schedule for the afternoon. There's going to be a riot. A stampede, if you will."

Whit's eyes flick toward the wrench, though he doesn't grab for it. Cooper taps the wrench against the headboard of the bed and raises his eyebrows. Maybe if he pokes at him enough, Whit really will lunge for it, though won't that go against that image he so carefully curates? All precise control and thoughtfulness, where he's got to consider every damn word and action ten times over before he can commit to anything.

Cooper stretches another few inches, waving the wrench in the air. "What were your big plans for your day off?"

"I was with my parents."

"Ooh, fun." Cooper draws the words out and wiggles the wrench again. "What'd you get up to?"

"We were in Albany."

"And what were you doing in Albany?"

"Why do you care?"

"Jesus, never mind." It's never worth trying to have a conversation with Whit, 'cause doesn't it always end up like this, ire flaring hot through Cooper's chest. A good little reminder that his lingering adolescent crush aside, the two of them would never actually work. He gets his toes under him and shifts his weight to his feet, standing so he's at least taller than Whit for once, with him still kneeling. "Forget I asked."

For one blindingly brief moment the summer Cooper'd come out to Drew, and therefore effectively to Penny and Whit, he'd thought there'd be...well, something between himself and Whit. If not the fruition of his daydreams of tanned, brown skin and Whit's muscled chest to press up against that he'd been nursing, at least a comrade-in-arms, us-against-them, fist-bumping, shared-jokes sort of queer collegiality.

Instead, Whit had just clammed up all the tighter until he'd largely given up speaking in Cooper's presence at all—and Cooper kissing Whit certainly hadn't helped. No, Whit hadn't talked to Cooper for ages after that. And maybe Cooper prefers that to the type of annoyance he and Whit stir in each other these days, like prodding at a sore cut even though he full well knows it'll only end in a dull ache.

Well, Cooper wasn't the one who'd started that frosty silence. Whit'd been the one to shove a distance between them as wide as the tractor bucket all those years ago. They could've been friends, instead of the most stilted of acquaintances, held together only by a herd of cows and Drew's good cheer.

Cooper points the wrench toward the door. "You can go. I'll put these back, cross my heart."

"You can't do the rest of this yourself."

"I think I can take apart a damn bed."

"No, I just meant—" Whit shakes his head. "Never mind."

"What?" Cooper calls after him, but Whit's already gone, the floorboards in the hallway creaking and then the stairs. He can hear Whit's and Penny's voices for a good long while before the kitchen door squeaks on its rusty hinges and then shuts again, Whit apparently done complaining about him for the time being. Back to work for the rest of his damn day off.

Cooper sets the wrenches back in Whit's truck as the sun sinks toward the tree line with the orange glow of early spring. He's got grime all over his hands from the worn bed frame, and he wipes his fingers on his pants before shutting the door, sure that Whit would notice stains on his truck.

For a moment, Cooper stands there staring at his reflection in the shiny door, the loose fit of his sweatshirt and the smudges of dirt on his knees. Then he grins, and quickly, he pulls the length of baling twine from his pocket, opens the door again, and ties the wrenches up in a neat little bundle. He finishes it off with a bow and sets them in the middle of the driver's seat. Maybe Whit'll sit right on them and bruise his ass.

Cooper rounds the house already calling to Drew. "Furniture's done, and Whit and I had a grand old time, as always—"

But Drew holds up a finger, then points at the phone pressed to his ear.

"Sorry," Cooper whispers loudly.

"Thanks for letting me know," Drew says, nodding as if the other person can see him. "Nope, should be just fine, yep, okay, bye."

"Everything all right?"

Drew tosses his phone down onto the pile of lumber. "The farmers' market closed."

"Shit, it did?"

"Oh my God, I'm not going to sell a single ounce of cheese, the squirrels are going to pull down the rest of the house, and knowing my luck, the cows are going to put up a 'for sale' ad for themselves and move out to Ohio."

"Ohio?"

The kitchen window screeches open, and Penny leans against the screen. "Cooper, don't let him start."

"And then all the wheels will fall off the farm trucks, and none of the tractors will start, and the damn grass won't even grow this year."

"What's wrong with the tractors?" Cooper asks.

"Nothing's wrong with the tractors," Penny calls out the window.

Drew covers his face with his hands. "Where the hell am I going to sell cheese?"

"The squirrels?" Cooper asks.

"Drew's having a moment." Penny shuts the window halfway, then calls through it, "One of many. Bring him inside, please."

She closes the window the rest of the way, and Drew drops his hands. "I'm fine."

"Yeah, you seem real fine. Did that market have good sales?"

"It was the busiest one, and the only one we even went to last summer." Drew picks up his phone and stares like it'll give him different news if he just watches it long enough. "It's fine. The guy who runs it retired, but it's fine, it's—" He blows out a long breath. "Oh fucking hell, I'm going to have a heart attack."

"Beer?"

Drew nods and jams his phone into his pocket. "Beer."

Whit's already inside, washing his hands at the sink. It pulls his shirt against the muscles in his back, and Cooper spends too long studying the bottles of beer in the fridge. When the faucet shuts off, he finally pulls two out, waving one bottle toward Penny, who nods, and then Whit, who shakes his head.

Cooper grabs a third and shuts the fridge with his elbow. "Drew, is the real problem that you won't have your line of admiring local ladies lined up to sample cheese this summer? Whit, the farmers' market closed. That's the big news."

Whit dries his hands in a way that does far too much to flex the tendons in his forearms. "I know."

"Right. Cool." Cooper holds out a beer to Drew. "Whit already knows."

"And the real problem is the lack of sales," Whit adds.

"Whit's also real clear on the fact that we sell cheese at said markets."

Whit wedges the towel back on its hook and mutters, "We."

Drew presses the bottom of his bottle to his forehead

and slumps in his chair. "I should've figured something like this would happen."

Penny points a wooden spoon at him. "Drew, there's no way to have guessed this, okay?"

"Hey." Cooper pokes him in the chest. "Let's cheer you up, yeah? Sadie, come over here and give Drew some love. Look on the bright side: it's more time to work on the house, if you're not hauling yourself to a market every week."

"But we still have the pasture gates to finish." Drew leans down to rub the top of Sadie's head. Her tail thumps against the floor, and she squirms closer on her stubby legs. "And I gotta do the cheddar tomorrow, that'll take all day."

"No problem. I'll do the gates," Cooper says.

Whit pulls a long knife out of the knife block as Penny slides a handful of onions toward him. "I'm doing the gates."

"I'll do your half of the gates, Drew," Cooper says.

Drew straightens a little. "You'd stay tomorrow, too?"

Oh, wait, no. That's not what Cooper meant, because he's gotta see his folks and then start the drive out to Oregon. But Drew's looking at him, a hand on Sadie's head and something too hopeful around his eyes. Cooper scratches the back of his neck and risks a glance toward Whit's back where he's carefully slicing the onions.

"Sure," he says, dropping his arm as Whit turns around, before Whit can catch him fidgeting. Doesn't matter anyway. If Mom couldn't make dinner tonight, tomorrow's probably no different. "Yeah, I can stay a bit longer."

What about that job? he can nearly hear Whit ask, but he just turns back to his cutting board. *Be responsible, grow up, Cooper, act like an adult,* would probably follow that question.

Well, Whit can have whatever damn opinion about him that he wants because Drew grins. Really, actually smiles and starts scratching Sadie's ears. "Cool," he says.

"Cool," Cooper echoes.

"Cool, now come help chop," Penny says.

"I thought it was your night to make dinner," Cooper says.

"It is, but as established by farm rule thirteen point six, section A, those who work on fences also chop all the veggies. I've already taught Whit how to make a mean mixed drink, so I know he's good for helping. M'keeping my eye on you, Coop." She tips her beer up, swallowing as she starts rooting through the kitchen cupboards. "Besides, it's gonna take me all evening to find the cards."

Whit stops with his knife halfway through an onion. "No."

"Yes." Penny takes another drink. "It's a fine night for a bridge game, I do believe."

"It's my day off," Whit says.

"So sorry, but how often does Cooper visit us?" Penny closes the drawer and opens another one, shifting through the years of detritus within. "Though we'll go easy on you, Whit. You two don't have to be partners."

"Of course, it is more fun when they are," Drew says.

Penny holds her bottle up in a toast toward him. "Oh, hell yeah, it is."

I won't be down until late tomorrow, Cooper texts Terry as Penny drops a bowl of potatoes in front of him. *Think Mom'll be around then?*

I'll try to make sure she's free. Does this mean the rodents are winning? Terry sends back, and Cooper snorts a soft laugh, tucking his phone in his pocket and trying to ignore the half step away Whit takes as Cooper starts chopping beside him.

Later, the glow of a hockey game on TV fills the living room, shining on the litter of cards and empty bottles. Drew, slumped in the corner of the couch, doesn't even stir when the stairs creak. Whit, it must be, because Penny's footsteps were much lighter when she finally hauled herself up to bed. And yep, that's him, probably coming downstairs for something wholesome and boring before he falls asleep, like a cup of warm milk. Cooper nudges the beer bottle out of Drew's loose grip.

"Go to bed, you old man," Cooper says, tucked deep into his sweatshirt and yawning into his own shoulder.

"M'awake."

"You're drooling." Cooper props his foot against Drew's hip and gently kicks him. "Go. You're in my bedroom."

Drew rolls halfway upright, yawning and rubbing at his eyes. "You want to come upstairs?"

Cooper claps his palm to his chest and gasps as dramatically as he knows how. "Andrew. I thought you'd never ask."

"I'm serious." Drew stands and yawns again, stretching his arms over his head. "You're not really sleeping down here, are you?"

"I'm keeping my girl Sadie company. And thanks, man, but you've got a double bed. You're cute, but get a queen mattress, and I'll think about it."

"There's a joke in here about you jumping into bed with anyone who even casually identifies as male."

"Yes, thank you, but you don't have to say it out loud."

"And then not ever calling them again."

"Good night, so great to be visiting you, sleep well, asshole."

"Just saying."

"Look, if it's embarrassing-your-friend hour, why the hell aren't you and Penny a thing yet? That'd free up an entire bed for me, thank you very much."

"Fuck you," Drew says, his cheeks red. He tugs Cooper's hood down over his face, and by the time Cooper's brushed it back, Drew's jogging up the stairs, the back of his neck flushed.

Ah well, Drew's too easy. Low-hanging fruit, his life-long crush on Penny. Cooper yawns, stretching out his back. He should put sheets on the couch, at least. Get a decent blanket if nothing else. It's weeks until the weather warms, and despite the woodstove in the kitchen, the house is entirely too damn drafty.

"Cooper."

He looks up at Whit's voice. "Whit."

"Drew really is glad you're here."

It's hard to look at Whit straight on. Silhouetted against the light from the kitchen, he looks taller than normal, his shoulders wider. His sweatpants sit low around his narrow hips, and his shirt falls loose around his stomach.

Cooper sets his elbows on his knees and shrugs. "Well, yeah, it's good to see him."

"I mean it. It makes a difference to him, you helping out."

"And you're here to let me know I'm not actually being helpful?"

"I wasn't going to." Whit pulls his sweatpants up an inch, though they just slip back down, revealing the elastic band of his boxers.

Not that Cooper's looking. He frowns at the mess on the coffee table and scratches his fingers into his hair.

"You can come upstairs," Whit says.

Cooper jerks his head around. "What?"

"I have that second bed."

A laugh bubbles out of Cooper's throat. "You're not serious."

Whit takes a step toward the stairs. "Suit yourself."

"I will, thank you."

It's quiet when Whit goes back upstairs. Drew's sink

runs for a couple minutes and then shuts off again. Across the kitchen, Sadie sneezes. *A blanket*, Cooper thinks again.

He's got another sweatshirt in his truck. A hat and gloves, too. He hauls himself off the couch and shoves his feet into his boots, not bothering to tie them. Outside is still and silent, frost settling over the ground. The air nips at his cheeks by the time he gets to his truck and roots through his duffle bag, filling his backpack with a change of clothes and his toothbrush.

Back inside, he looks up toward the ceiling at where Whit's room is. The two of them, sharing a bedroom. Maybe one of those wrenches hit Whit on the head.

Cooper'll be fine down here. Chilly, uncomfortable, and smelling like farm dog and stale beer, but he's slept in worse places over the years.

Whit's room was warm, earlier, he thinks and immediately frowns.

The stairs are as creaky as they ever are as Cooper slowly climbs them. And Whit's light is still on, a halo shining around his closed door. Gently, Cooper taps his knuckles against the wood.

"I hate that you had a good idea," Cooper says as he eases it open.

Whit's cross-legged on his bed. And he's taken his shirt off. Oh Lord, this is a mistake. The lamplight shades Whit's skin golden, and the shadows only throw into relief the straight lines of his collarbones and the curves of muscles in his arms.

Cooper squeezes his backpack tight against his chest. Just one night. Cooper can handle the mire of annoyance and attraction for one night. And it's better that Whit just glances at him and then turns back to the book balanced in his lap, because Cooper can slip into the bathroom and shut the door between them.

The shower has drops of water clinging to the curtain. Viscerally, suddenly, Cooper can picture Whit in there, water sliding over his body, his arms shifting as he rinses his hair, soap suds sliding down to—

Fuck. Fuck, fuck, fuck, this is a bad idea. Cooper grabs the sides of the sink and doesn't look up into his own reflection, just quickly scrubs at his teeth with his toothbrush. His mouth tastes like Whit's toothpaste, and his skin pricks with the knowledge of where he is.

It's even worse when Cooper opens the bathroom door. Whit turns a page in his book, his back rounded as he bends over it, and his ribs moving lightly on his breath.

He's gorgeous. A total jerk. But a really pretty one.

"Uh, thanks." Cooper plucks at the quilt on his bed. It's made so painfully neatly that he feels a little bad pulling the covers back.

Though there's a piece of hay in the middle of the pillow. Oh, nope, that came from him. A second piece wafts gently down, landing next to it. He quickly pulls off his sweatshirt and an entire shower of hay rains onto the bed. Whit's watching this, he's suddenly sure.

Cooper fumbles for the knob on the lamp for way too damn long and finally switches off the light.

Whit's book snaps closed. "Guess I'm done reading for the night."

"Sorry."

Cooper's not, even though now he can't see to sweep the hay out of his bed. Though at least he can strip down to his boxers and T-shirt in the privacy of the darkness, and if Whit heaves an annoyed sigh, he can focus on the itch of chaff under his cheek as he slips into bed.

It's just the one night. He'll be fine.

CHAPTER THREE

WHEN COOPER WAKES UP, the sun is cutting into the room in a harsh glare, shining on Whit's empty bed. The bathroom door sits ajar, the door to the hall closed, and Whit's book is on top of the stack on the nightstand.

Cooper would think he'd been entirely alone, except that he'd dropped his backpack next to Whit's dresser last night, and now it's sitting by the foot of his bed.

Whit's bed, rather. Or Whit's extra bed. Whit who's twenty-seven years old and sleeps in a twin bed because he's just that cool.

Well, fucking noted about where Cooper can and can't set his obviously inconvenient backpack.

Downstairs, the coffeepot is already half-empty, and Drew's favorite mug sits in the sink, so he's probably elbow-deep in cheese curds. And wherever Whit goes first thing in the morning, it's thankfully not loitering around the kitchen.

Running, probably. That'd be like Whit, to jump out of bed at the first sign of dawn and pound out a couple miles before he starts work. Cooper grimaces as he pours himself a cup of coffee. Classic Whit, filling his day with every ounce of misery possible.

Cooper pushes his feet into Drew's tall muck boots, not bothering with socks and letting his sweatpants bunch up around the top. Bleary-eyed and still yawning, he hunches into his sweatshirt as he makes his way across the barnyard. Only Socks is out there, tail lashing side to side as he studies a tall tuft of grass, some hapless critter likely burrowed inside.

"Is it a squirrel?" Cooper asks.

Socks flicks his tail, his butt wiggling as he shifts his feet under him.

Cooper nudges the cat with his toe. "Scram. Let it live another day. I doubt it's the guilty party."

Cooper sips at his coffee and scratches cows' noses as they sniff at him. Whit must've already fed them, because instead of the clamor of a hungry herd wanting their breakfast, they root into fresh, fluffy flakes of hay. He probably did it while Cooper was still asleep, just to avoid him.

Good, Cooper thinks and tickles the soft fur under a cow's chin. "Between you and me, let's not tell Whit he's so damn slow that chores take him two hours longer each day than they actually need to."

Cooper fiddles with the spigot, the metal cold in the morning chill. Probably the only way it'll ever get fixed is if it breaks completely. If the temperature drops too low in here some winter night and the spigot freezes solid, or if a wayward cow uses it as a scratching post and knocks it clean off the wall. Maybe that's the best present Cooper could give Drew while visiting: take the end of a shovel and give the spigot a few whacks so there'll be no choice but to replace it.

Though probably, if he stands here and messes with it

long enough, the thing's so old that just touching it will accomplish the same through sheer accident. Cooper sets his mug on an overturned bucket and spins the handle back and forth. There has to be some plumber's tape kicking around so he can fix whatever part of it is leaking. And if not that, he can make his way to the hardware store and just pick up a new spigot, install it, and then be on his way down to Brooklyn.

Especially 'cause there's apparently no need to hurry, if his mom can't seem to make the time for him anyway. He blows out a breath. How annoyingly typical.

"Cooper."

He jumps and snatches his hand from the spigot.

"Where're the cows?" Whit asks, silhouetted in the barn door, his hands on his hips.

Cooper slowly points at the cow closest to him. "Um?"

"Not these cows, the other cows. Did you try to move them?"

"What other cows? I didn't move anything. I got a cup of coffee and came over here and—"

"The cows that were in the back pen."

"Oh, of course, the back pen." Cooper stands and grabs his mug. "What back pen?"

"The—we put it up the other—never mind." Whit holds up a finger. "Do not tell Drew."

"That you lost his herd? Or that you're setting up secret pens? Did you ask the squirrels where they went? I'll give you a hand with the interrogations. Can we put up a corkboard that has thumbtacks and red yarn connecting the suspects?"

Whit rakes his eyes over Cooper. "You're not even dressed."

Cooper looks down at himself. Already there's hay clinging to the knee of his sweatpants. "I'm dressed, it's not

44

like I'm naked. I mean, I am, under all my clothes, but—hey, where're you going?"

Cooper jogs around to the passenger seat of Whit's truck. Whit's sure to just take off without him, leaving him in a squeal of slush, and Cooper hops into the cab quick enough coffee splashes over the cuff of his sweatshirt. He wipes it on his sweatpants before Whit can see.

"What—" Whit shifts onto his hip and feels around beneath himself.

The wrenches, Cooper remembers. He grins. "Morning, roomie. Aren't you glad we get to spend this quality time together?"

Whit sets the wrenches neatly in the cupholder. "What a delight."

"Well look at that. We finally found something to agree on."

Whit doesn't return his smile. Doesn't even glance over, just shifts the truck into gear. Ah, same old Whit, same old farm, same old everything. It's as comforting as it is hilarious, that Cooper can swing back through here and slip right into how things always were.

Cooper sips at his coffee as Whit pulls out of the barnyard. "How do you know the cows even went this way?"

"Don't spill that."

"Don't drive so damn fast." Cooper takes a loud slurp. "Do they always head down the road? Say hi to the neighbors? Pick up the morning newspaper on the way?"

"Can't you just pour that out and get another cup when we get back?"

"I'm almost finished."

"You've nearly spilled half of it all over my truck."

"Don't worry. One happy day of working with you, and I'll be out of here. You be careful, you might just miss me."

"Right, because you have that job."

"Hey, consider this our big chance to catch up. What's new, how's life, anything exciting happening these days?" Cooper means it as a joke, but curiosity wells up in his chest. *Don't*, he tells himself. *Don't, don't, don't, don't* —"Seeing anyone?"

Whit's eyes cut toward him. "Why?"

"Why would you be seeing someone? See, Whit, when two people love each other, or, you know, just want to get it on, they—"

"Why do you ask?"

"Wait, are you?"

"There they are." Whit jerks the wheel to the side so hard Cooper's coffee really does spill.

Cooper wipes his hands on his sweatpants as Whit jumps out of the cab, like the cows are really going anywhere, not just idly exploring the poor neighbor's lawn. Because, sure enough, there they are, a dozen of them, sleepy-eyed in the morning mist and making a mess of things, oblivious to the trouble they've caused.

"Caroline?" Whit calls, a hand cupped around his mouth.

From her porch, Caroline waves, her long gray hair tied up on top of her head and the hem of her nightgown wet with dew.

"They came over to say hello!" she calls back.

Whit claps his hands together, trying to shoo a heifer as she sticks her head into Caroline's flowerbed. "I'm so sorry," he says.

Three more cows round the corner of the house, where they must've been investigating the backyard, and jogging behind them, his arms outstretched—

"Brad?" Cooper asks.

He has to stare for a long moment to be sure, because that doesn't look like Brad. And what the hell is he doing over here instead of at his own farm, clear across town? Though it has to be Brad, just without the mess of his usual scraggly beard. And, apparently, he's been hitting the gym this past winter. He looks...different. More put together, with jeans that aren't covered in cow manure and a plaid shirt that doesn't have tractor grease all over it. Even his brown hair is combed, not the messy mop Cooper's used to seeing. Probably still just as irritating, though.

"Coop?"

Brad smacks a cow on the flank to urge it toward the road and then comes over to give Cooper a handshake that turns into a back-clapping hug, as if they haven't seen each other in ages. A year it's been, maybe. Though, Cooper can't remember going down to Brad's farm last season, since that would have involved actually seeing Brad. So maybe it was the year before he last saw him, or even two years? Pity to break the record.

Cooper squirms free of Brad's grip, but Brad just slaps his shoulder again and snaps a piece of gum in his mouth, loud enough Cooper can hear it. "Good to see you, man."

"What're you doing here, Brad?" Whit asks.

"Came by to chat with Travis. Wanted to catch him first thing this morning. He just took off back to Manhattan, and the next minute," Brad tips his head toward the cows. "These ladies showed up."

"Travis? He's in town?" Cooper steps away from Brad under the excuse of ushering another cow away from a stand of hydrangeas. Travis, Caroline's son, who back in the day used to tag along behind Drew and Cooper, though he was still a couple years too young to be of any real use. Travis and Brad: damn. They sure do round out the list of folks besides Whit who Cooper didn't want to deal with during this quick visit to Drew.

"He was just here for the day," Brad says. "I swung by

to set up an appointment with him, but I didn't know you were here too."

"Doesn't Travis sell real estate down in the city these days?" Cooper asks.

"Yep." Brad snaps his gum again.

"Yep?" Cooper echoes. Next to him, a cow sniffs over the lawn and huffs a breath, dissatisfied with the brown grass of early spring. "Are you—an appointment? What'd you come all the way over here to see him about?"

"Sold the herd." Brad grins and shrugs, holding his hands out wide. "Yeah, I know, right? Sent 'em on over to Ohio."

"You sold them?" Brad's family had been milking cows since—well, since before Drew's uncle and probably before Drew's grandfather too. "All of them?"

"All of them." Brad laughs. It's an annoying sound, Cooper remembers all over again. There's a reason he hasn't seen Brad in a good long while. "Drew's gonna have to hold down the dairy tradition in these parts, 'cause I'm out."

"You're selling your land, too?"

"Thinking about it."

With Travis's help, apparently. Travis, who's all grown up and selling off dairy farms. Fuck. Maybe Penny and Drew are right that only stopping by every six months instead of spending entire summers here is leaving him in the dust when it comes to the neighborhood news.

Brad claps his hands to usher another cow toward the road. "I was just telling Drew the other day, we've got some equipment we're getting rid of. Come by if you want to take a look."

"You sold your herd," Cooper echoes softly, and Whit looks over at him as he tries to coax a cow away from a stand of lilacs. He probably heard Cooper muttering to himself like that. "Really?"

"The equipment? Yeah, really. I'll give you a good deal. I just want it gone at this point." Brad catches Cooper's eye and snaps his gum again. "It'd be good to catch up too, you know?"

Cooper doesn't know, but Brad's still looking at him, so he nods.

"The cows, Cooper," Whit says. "Let's get them back to the barn. Thanks for your help, Brad. We're all set, though."

"Well, we could use a hand—"

But Whit steps between Cooper and Brad, his shoulder knocking Cooper's to steer him toward the road. "We're good," Whit says, shooing Cooper across the lawn like he's another damn cow.

With Whit calling for them and Cooper following behind, the herd shuffles back up the road, past Whit's truck, where he leaves it parked in Caroline's driveway, and toward home. The cows would've probably made their way back anyway, after giving the neighborhood a good sniff and finding no grass growing. But Whit hurries them along all the same, chasing down a straggling heifer and urging them faster when they'd rather loiter on their morning stroll. When the farm finally comes into view, Cooper can dimly hear the whine of the saw, so Drew must be back at work on the house again.

"What the hell?" Cooper glances toward the sound and lowers his voice, as if Drew could possibly hear him clear across the barnyard. "Brad really went belly-up?"

"Milk prices are down."

"So he just called it quits?"

"Either that, or eventually have the bank take the entire business and the land too."

"That sucks. To have worked all those years and watch your farm go under."

"Brad seems relieved."

"I think Brad's got a screw loose." It's probably telling that Whit doesn't argue the point. Cooper chews at the corner of his mouth. All those cows just...gone. Living their lives out on some other farm. "Well, at least Drew's still here."

Cooper pushes at the haunch of a cow that stops to sniff at the tip of a daffodil bulb poking through the crust of snow with all the greenness of spring hope. Brad's farm would be completely empty of the busyness of spring right now.

He pulls in a deep breath, looking around. Drew's farm is so pretty with the hill cresting behind the barn and the fields spreading out from the house. Tired and old and in need of some work, but far more gorgeous a setting than Brad's farm. *Stunning*, Cooper used to think, shaking off the grayness of the city, the subway, and the cracked sidewalks outside his apartment, and jumping out of Grandpa's car and racing toward the barn and a summer afternoon of adventures with Drew.

"For now."

Cooper drops his hand from the cow. "What?"

"That farmers' market closed, and like I said, milk prices haven't been good."

Cooper waits for more, but Whit just urges the herd toward the back of the barn. Sure enough, there's a new pen back there, strung together from mismatched fence panels and a gate lying in the crusty, snowy mud, where the cows must've pushed past it to begin their morning escape.

"There are other farmers' markets around," Cooper says slowly as he bends over to pick up the gate.

"If it'll even make a difference."

Cooper stops with the gate halfway off the ground, the metal cold and gritty against his hands. "What does that mean?"

"Drew didn't tell you?"

"Tell me what?" He wants to shake his head to clear it, sure he's not hearing Whit right. "Yeah, that the market's not running? I know, I was here yesterday too."

"Drew's thinking about selling the farm."

Cooper drops the gate and it lands with a metal clang. "What the hell?"

"After this season, depending on how everything goes."

"No, he's not."

"That's why he's so bent on getting the house fixed."

"Well, there's a hole in the roof." The words sound stupid falling out of his mouth like that, weak and uncertain. "He didn't say anything."

"It's not like you're ever around."

Cooper grabs Whit's arm. "Bullshit, we talk all the time. He would've told me."

Whit looks down at Cooper's hand, where he's gripping tight enough his knuckles whiten. "Apparently not."

Something this big, this important? Cooper tightens his hold on Whit's arm. "He would have."

"Well, seems like he didn't."

Whit pulls away and shoos the last of the cows into the pen. Cooper lets his hand drop and watches Whit walk into the barn. He comes back with the hose and sets it into the cows' trough, where it dribbles its slow, feeble stream of water.

"You gonna shut that?" Whit asks.

Cooper looks down at his feet, where the gate's still lying in the mud. Right. He bends down and picks it up again, fitting it against the fence post. The only thing to secure the gate is a twist of wire. No wonder the herd got out, if that's what Whit's using to keep them in.

No need to invest in improvements if Drew's selling the

place off, he can nearly hear in Whit's voice. With numb, wet fingers, Cooper wraps the wire over the rail of the gate.

"I'm going to go get started on the fencing," Whit says and he walks away, leaving Cooper there, cold mud pressing against his boots, and his sweatpants doing little against the morning's chill.

CHAPTER FOUR

IN WHIT'S BATHROOM, Cooper rinses mud and grit from his hands, warming his fingers under the hot water. *Sell the farm* rings through his head, too loud and harsh.

He picks up the mug of coffee he set on the edge of the sink, then sets it down again without taking a sip.

Work clothes. He came up here to get dressed, so he needs to put on his jeans and hope the dew and cow snot on his sweatpants dries before he leaves.

Right. 'Cause he's leaving. Though he just slowly strips off his sweatpants and stares down at his legs, winter pale and now goosefleshed in the chill of Whit's room, trying to swallow the fact that he might never, not ever, come back here.

He sets his sweatpants down. Picks them up again, lays them over the foot of the bed, and plucks a piece of hay from the fabric. Someone else would live in this house if Drew sold the farm. Mow the fields, work in the barn, tend the flower bed that Drew's aunt used to weed every summer, dirt up to her wrists and her huge, floppy hat bobbing among the blossoms.

Or no. Maybe whoever buys this place will tear the

front yard up. The fields too, subdividing the land for a housing development. There'll be tiny quarter-acre lots dotting the hills and a paved road cutting through what's now stone walls and tumbling creeks.

But that's impossible. It's Drew's farm. His uncle's before him, and his grandfather's before that. Cooper takes a bite of the toast he brought upstairs with him for his breakfast. The butter's warm and the sweet peach jelly's made from the fruit of the trees that line the backyard. This is Drew's place, just like Caroline's is Caroline's, and Brad's is Brad's.

Was Brad's. And isn't, now.

"What the hell are you doing?"

Cooper looks up slowly at Whit. "I thought you were working on the fences."

"It's going to be warm out today, so I came to get a different shirt." Whit glances over Cooper, in his sweatshirt with his legs bare where his boxers end mid-thigh. "Though you're apparently dressed for the weather, I see."

Cooper looks down at himself too. Work jeans. Socks. He should get on that. Instead, he takes another bite of toast and frowns as he chews, his stomach knotting. Sell the farm. What an awful set of words to string together.

"Are you eating up here?" Whit asks.

Cooper looks down at his toast, jelly smeared over his finger, and a drop of melted butter pooling on the plate. "Is that a trick question?"

"There'll be mice."

"Drew's really selling the farm?"

"Can you not get hay all over?" Whit asks and with the side of his foot, pushes a couple pieces across the floor, away from his own bed. "I told you, he's thinking about it. Mice added to the squirrel issue might seal the deal, though."

"He can't sell it."

Whit picks up a shirt off the floor and shakes it out. It's Cooper's, clearly, a size too small to be Whit's. One autumn when he'd swung by on a visit, Cooper had mixed up their jackets and found himself swimming in Whit's, the cuffs falling past his hands and the shoulders too roomy. *Unfair*, he'd thought at the time, like by virtue of also living a life working outside all damn day, Cooper should have the same build to fill out clothes like Whit does. Now, he just stares at the shirt as Whit throws it on top of Cooper's sweatpants.

"Thought you were heading out to your new job." Whit turns his back to Cooper, grabs his own sweatshirt by the back of the neck, and hauls it over his head, taking the long-sleeved shirt underneath with it and leaving his back bare.

Oh man. Shifting muscles in the morning light streaming through the window. The narrow taper of Whit's waist and the breadth of his shoulders. Brown skin that doesn't pale like Cooper's does over the winter, just looks smooth and soft over the sharp jut of his shoulder blades and the long dip of his spine.

Cooper would never see Whit again. He shifts a step back, dropping his toast onto his plate. He'd stay in touch with Drew. But Whit? No, if Drew sells this place, then when Cooper steers his truck down the dirt lane that leads away from the farm, that'll be that between him and Whit. All those years of getting under each other's skin, of bickering and annoyance and—and that kiss.

"Drew can't sell the farm." Cooper grabs for his jeans. There's stiff, dried mud on the cuffs and it falls in dusty clumps onto the floor. Whatever, he'll deal with that later. First things first. "We'll get those gates fixed, and I'll talk to Drew when he's done with the house today."

"I've talked to Drew, and he—"

"And I'll get that back pen fixed, too, so it's not an entire summer of chasing cows."

"Cooper."

"Look, you do you. But I'm going over to Brad's to get some new gates."

"Brad doesn't sell gates. Cooper, the financial reality that Drew's facing is—"

"You know, you might have a more positive attitude if you didn't clear out of here at dawn o'clock and bothered to sleep more. Brad sold his herd, so ergo, Brad has no use for the gates he has. It's a hell of a lot cheaper than going to the co-op. Closer, too. Money saved, that's how you do it."

"You're going to just take Brad's gates?"

"I'm going to ask Brad nicely for his gates, and then I'm going to come back here and talk to Drew and get this entire situation fixed."

Whit puts his hands on his hips. It bulges out the muscles in his shoulders. Cooper doesn't let himself admire the sight of Whit's pecs or the flat line of his abs, just jerks on one sock and then the next.

"You're going to just fix it? Just like that?"

"I'm going to do something more than putter around like everything's the same as it always is. So yes, I'm going to Brad's, and you can sit around here with your thumb up your butt, doesn't matter to me."

Whit sighs loudly and grabs a shirt from his dresser. "I'll drive."

On the shady side of the street, snow sits under the trees and in the shadows of the houses they drive past. Cooper turns away from the window so he doesn't have to look at those tidy, neat little lawns with their swimming pools and basketball hoops and swing sets.

"Have you been by Brad's place since he sold off his herd?" Cooper asks.

"You could've just called Brad, not dragged us across town."

"This is so much more fun." Cooper waves a hand between them. "When else would we get to spend such quality time together?"

"I'm serious."

"Oh, I know, 'cause being serious is what you're best at." Cooper shrugs and turns back to the window. "Don't worry. One blaze of farm-saving glory, and then I'll be out of your hair, so you're welcome, bud."

And Whit can go back to his life without Cooper. The second Cooper drives away after each visit, Whit probably comes up with a damn laundry list of complaints for Penny and Drew, complete with a presentation and handouts laying out all the reasons Cooper shouldn't be allowed back next time.

Next time. Cooper touches his fingers to his stomach, frowning at the houses that whizz past the window.

The domed tops of the silos come into view over the trees first, and then the roof of Brad's barn. It's a pretty spot. The house peeks out of the forest and an old lichen-crusted stone wall runs along the driveway. Cooper's always thought so, the handful of times he's dropped by, though without cows sticking their heads out of the barn, it just seems lonely. Quiet too, when Whit turns off the truck and Cooper jumps down to the muddy gravel of the driveway.

The door to the house opens and Brad waves. "Cooper!" he calls, both arms held out. Cooper gets hugged again and the smack on his shoulder is just as hard. Whit just gets a lift of Brad's chin and Cooper's shoulder smarts in jealousy. "Whit. Hey."

"Morning," Whit says.

"Didn't know you'd both be coming," Brad says. He's got gum in his mouth again and he snaps it loudly.

"Well, two's a party," Cooper says and puts on a smile. This was a shitty plan, not dragging Drew along and getting stuck with these two, of all people. "Thought we'd take you up on your offer to look at some equipment."

"Anytime, Coop."

"We're looking for some new gates," Cooper says.

"We're repairing the gates we have," Whit says.

Cooper waves a hand. "Same thing."

"I sold off most of our fencing," Brad says. "A couple guys from Pennsylvania came and took it all down."

Whit steps back and jangles the keys in his pocket. "We should just go, then."

"We'd love to take a look at anything you've got left," Cooper says.

Whit sucks his cheek in, like he's chewing it between his molars. "I have work to get to."

"We all have work to get to," Cooper says.

Though, not Brad, maybe. But Brad's still smiling as wide as ever and he snaps his gum again. Well, smiling at Cooper, because nobody in their right mind would turn a smile on Whit, not with that pinched glower on his face.

"You can leave Cooper here for the morning," Brad says.

"No." Whit releases his cheek to shake his head. "It's fine."

Cooper leans towards Whit as they follow Brad across the barnyard. "Why don't you like Brad?" he asks quietly.

"I like him fine," Whit says, his words sharp.

"He's annoying, you can say it." Cooper raises his eyebrows. "Wait, I know, did he turn you down? Did you ask him out for a romantic evening of hauling tiny hay bales and folding baling twine and he offended your delicate pride?"

Whit brushes past him, into the dark mouth of the barn. "I have better taste than that."

Cooper snorts out a soft laugh. No, Brad probably

wouldn't top Whit's list—and besides, interested in men or not, Brad's not dour enough for Whit, who'd choose a guy as bland and forbidding as himself. Brad, with all of his enthusiasm and gusto, would just grate at Whit. *A second thing we see eye to eye on*, Cooper could say, but it's no use trying to joke around with Whit, so he just follows him into the barn's dusty, dim interior.

"Not gates," Brad's saying to Whit as Cooper picks his way over to them, past the pieces of a disassembled rototiller and the shanks of a rusted plow. The snap of Brad's gum is loud in the dark space. "Cattle stops."

"They look like gates," Whit says. He sounds as waspish as ever. "And aren't they called cattle guards?"

"I worked at a farm down south that used them," Cooper says. Grids of bars as long as Cooper is tall, laid flat on the ground and just as effective as a gate for keeping cows in a field. Stock gaps, the farmer he'd worked for had called them, though Cooper turns to Whit and says, "Cattle stops, that's the right term."

"It's not."

"Is," Cooper says. "Brad, you're getting rid of them?"

"I meant to get them installed, then never got the chance before selling the herd off," Brad says. "They're perfect for our pastures. You dig a ditch, drop the grate over it, and you can drive right over them. The cows won't go across it."

"We'll take them," Cooper says.

"We won't," Whit says. "We need to ask Drew if he even wants cattle guards."

"Cattle stops," Cooper corrects. "And what does he care? He's busy with cheese and the house."

"The cost?" Whit tips his head and gives him that look.

Cooper sighs. It's the same look he used to give Cooper when Whit was on one side of twenty years old and Cooper was on the other, like Cooper, perpetually two years younger, was some kid Whit had to put up with.

"Fine, let us know what you want for them, Brad, and we'll be back for them after we talk to Drew."

"We might be back for them at some point." Whit's got his keys out of his pocket already.

"You're welcome to stay for a bit," Brad says. "I've got some coffee on. Coop, I haven't seen you in ages."

"We have work," Whit says before Cooper can answer, already heading for his truck.

He'll probably leave Cooper behind and have a good time doing it if Cooper doesn't hustle, so he gives Brad a wave and follows Whit.

"Another time," Brad calls after them. "Hey, Coop, let me give you my number at least."

"Oh." Cooper shrugs. "I can just stop by again."

"Or I'll take yours," Brad says. He's still smiling and once more snaps his gum.

"We have work, we can't stay," Whit says again.

"Yeah, okay," Cooper says and recites his number for Brad.

"Cooper," Whit says before Brad's done typing it in. Cooper turns, half-surprised that Whit isn't also tapping his foot.

"I'm coming," he says and opens the truck door as Brad smiles at him again.

"I'll call you, so you have mine," Brad says.

"Now?" Whit asks.

"Can I get a printed itinerary," Cooper says, "if the schedule's really that tight?"

Brad waves to them, still grinning. Whit's lips purse, and he twists the keys in the ignition hard. Any harder and he'd probably snap the key in half, and then where would they be? Stuck here with Brad and his gum and his empty farm that's slightly creepy with no cows milling around.

Cooper waves back, just to annoy Whit. "Those cattle stops could be good, if you don't get your undies in a bunch over them."

"It's Drew's decision."

"Those stops are easier than a gate. The cows won't walk across them, 'cause with the hole beneath the grate, they think there's a cliff, when really—"

"I know how cattle guards work," Whit says with a snap to his words that makes Cooper raise his eyebrows.

"Okay," he says slowly, drawing the word out. *Cattle stops*, he could add, though for once he doesn't.

Whit stares out the windshield as he drives. Once, his mouth opens, but he shuts it again before saying anything. Cooper turns to the window, ignoring him and the silence in the truck. Whit never did like Brad. Well, whatever. Whit can be peevish if he wants to be. Probably wants to sit there and mull over his ruined day, what with cows escaping and having to see Brad. Just Whit's luck that the only other farmer in these parts who, according to the scuttlebutt, is out and isn't Cooper, is Brad of all people.

Well, it's not like the lack of romantic options around here matters, 'cause Whit's a loveless recluse who sleeps in his twin bed every night and wouldn't know a date if it bit him in the ass. Always has been and probably always will be.

"What'll you do if Drew really sells the farm?" Cooper asks.

"You can't just go around making decisions about the fences and gates without asking him."

"If he does sell it, what're you going to do for work?" Cooper tries again. Though if Whit's not talking, he's not talking. Whit's like a cow that won't walk into the barn when she sets her mind to it, feet dug in and head thrown back, clammed up good and tight with a stubbornness that would make even the most ill-mannered heifer in the herd seem sweet and docile.

"I'm serious," Whit says. "Drew's got the farm set up the way he wants it. You can't just show up here and change it all around."

"Drew has only ever worked on his own farm his entire life, which sounds exactly like someone else in this here pickup truck. He doesn't even know how other farms out there might be doing things better. The systems his uncle set up years ago aren't the be all and end all of farming."

Whit makes a low noise in the back of his throat. "Then it's just so fortunate you're here to save us from ourselves."

When they reach the farm, Cooper jumps out of Whit's truck before he's even shifted into park, tossing the door closed behind himself with a loud slam. Ass. Giant, fucking, unremitting asshole. Cooper shoves his hand into his hair and blows out a long breath.

The one he draws back in is cool with the chill of spring. He takes a long look around at the familiar shape of the barnyard, breathes in the scent of cows and hay and melting mud. Behind him, Whit neatly parks his truck in the exact, precise spot he always does, the tires retracing their own ruts in the wet slush.

"You don't want to leave, do you?" Cooper murmurs to a heifer. She arches her neck so he can scratch it, her tail flicking lazily in the spring sunshine. *Fuck you*, he thinks toward Whit as Whit softly closes the driver's door. Cooper will fix this, thanks very fucking much.

He finds Drew washing his hands in the cheese room at the back of the barn, his shoulders bent and his head down.

"Hey," Cooper calls from the doorway.

"You taking off already?"

"No, no, I—" Cooper scrunches up his nose. The words don't even feel real. "Whit said, uh, the farm? That you're not, maybe, going to keep it?"

Drew scrubs harder at his hands. "Whit said that?"

"It's true?"

"What's truer is that I told him to keep his damn mouth shut." Drew turns off the water with a hard twist. "It's just a thought."

"You want to talk about it?"

"You just got here. I wasn't going to dump this on you."

"You could've called. I've got this newfangled thing called a cellular telephone, real fancy like."

"You never work on farms that have service. And besides, it's not a big deal."

Cooper licks at his lips. Selling the farm is a hell of a big deal. Five generations it's been, and if Drew ever settled down and had a family, it'd make six.

"You okay?" Cooper asks.

Drew waves toward the house. "Absolutely. What about the giant hole in my attic isn't fine?"

"Drew..."

"You guys get the cows back all right?"

"Whit didn't want you to know about that."

"Kind of obvious when a dozen cows sprint by the window and then you and Whit chase after them."

"Well, Whit did a shitty job on their fencing."

"Whit's done a lot to take on the farm so I can focus on the house and having some damn cheese to sell to a farmers' market that now no longer exists."

"Yeah." Cooper scrapes his foot over the threshold, leaving a mat of manure and hay that he kicks away. "I— sorry. I do want to help with the gates. We went to Brad's, he's got some stuff that could be useful." Cooper squints down the hall toward the rest of the barn. He can't see them from here, but he can hear the cows shuffling through their pen and there, over the low murmur of the milk pump, Whit's voice as he talks to one of them. "Drew, you can't sell this place."

Drew closes his eyes. "It's not like I want to."

"I can stay." Cooper hears the words before he's really thought them through. "At least for a bit, until the cows go out on pasture and the season's underway, if it'd make a difference."

"You don't have to do that."

"I want to."

"Coop, that's, no. I can't—I can't even really pay you much, so it's not a good—"

"Pay me what you can. The rest? Compensate me in cheese, my man, you know I'd do anything for you." *In it to win it*, he thinks. What had Drew said to him? Never planning more than five minutes in advance? Well it's not like this is the first time Cooper's pivoted on a dime. "Plus, you know how much cheese I can eat when I set my mind to it, and that's the one thing in this good world I ever want."

Drew stares somewhere to the left of Cooper. "Don't you have a job to be getting to? Oregon, right?"

"I only interviewed with them. I haven't even heard back yet, but don't tell Whit that, it'd make him too happy."

Drew gives a weak sort of smile. "Where would you sleep?"

"Fuck." Cooper lets out a laugh. "That's just details. Is that a yes? Want a hand for a bit?"

Drew shakes his head. Then he steps forward, crushing Cooper in a too-tight hug. "I'm not going to say no, you jerk."

Cooper hugs him back. "We'll figure this out, okay?"

"Okay," Drew says, and maybe it's what Cooper wants to hear, but he sounds a little more certain.

Cooper leaves him to his wheels of cheese and tank of curds, making his way back to the center aisle with his hands in his pockets.

"Whit?" he calls. Maybe Whit's already halfway out to the fields, intent on fixing the same fences that'll just break in the same place they always do each summer. Time after time, the cows so well versed in the weak spots in every field that they just saunter out whenever the fancy strikes.

Though, no, there's Whit crouched down next to a cow lying in a bed of straw and breathing in hard huffs. She grunts once, then settles as Whit strokes her haunch, his voice low as he murmurs to her.

"Whit," he says again, leaning against the wall of the cow's pen. "How's she doing?"

"Fine," Whit says without looking up. He keeps petting the cow's rump, his hands as gentle as his voice as he talks to her.

Cooper braces his hand on the post next to him, rubbing his finger over an old nail worked into it. He and Drew carved their initials just up there, one summer long, long ago. Where would the herd go if Drew sold the place? Auction, most likely. Some other farm, somewhere else. Maybe they'd follow Brad's cows out to Ohio. Most of these girls were born here, and their mothers before them. Cooper presses his lips together as the cow heaves herself to her feet.

She turns in a circle and huffs out a breath. Beyond her, the rest of the herd chews through their breakfast. It's the same every morning and evening for these ladies, and soon enough their calves too. They spend their days concerned with the choicest bite of clover each summer, and through the winter all they care about is getting a prime spot at the feeder, where they can stuff their mouths with hay cut and dried from the season past, and as the weather turns come spring, they get ready to do it all over again.

The cow stretches her neck and lets out a bleat that rings in Cooper's ear, her eyes wide.

"I told Drew I'd stay for a few weeks, help get the season started."

Whit's shoulders rise, though he keeps his eyes on the cow. "How great."

You don't mean that, Cooper could say. Though the fight drains out of him when the cow calls out again, her cry pealing through the barn.

"I can take some of the work off your plate." Cooper pushes his hands deeper into his pockets. "And help Drew with the house too."

Whit pets over the cow's back and flank. Her udder's full, ready for the little one inside of her. They both watch as she pushes her calf out, and it lands on the straw with a quick inhale and a bleary slow blink of its brown eyes.

"Welcome," Cooper says softly.

"Well, this makes it officially spring," Whit says. "Hi there, sweet thing."

The calf rises to its feet, nosing until it finds where to drink. It's a girl, Cooper can see now, and her birth will mean plenty to do this afternoon and tonight. Check the calf over, get the cow some fresh water, her own flake of hay, and move her to a smaller pen, away from the herd until the calf's gotten her bearings. There'll be more calves tomorrow, too, if not tonight, and soon enough an entire herd's worth of them on skinny, too-long legs as they race each other up the length of the barn and back again, heads tossing and hooves kicking.

"Um." Cooper shifts his weight, poking at a piece of straw with his foot. "So, can I maybe crash in your room a little longer?"

Whit finally looks up at him. Oh hell, this is a bad idea. Cooper can feel that truth as certainly as spring in the air, the season crashing down on them no matter if they're ready for it. The last time Cooper spent more than a couple weeks here on the farm, it ended in firelight and his mouth against Whit's.

Cooper turns away, staring at the milling herd. How fucking embarrassing that he did that. And how clear a response on Whit's part, to never, not once mention it again, his firm *no* to any interest from Cooper coming through that silence loud and clear.

"I'll try not to, you know, drive you too crazy."

Whit just watches him with soft dark-brown eyes. His work pants are stretched across his knees from how he's crouching, the cuffs neatly folded up above his boots. Fucking hell, this is going to be torture.

Cooper clears his throat and shifts his weight again. "I know. I get it that you don't like me, but I swear I won't be a total pain in the ass."

"I don't not like you."

Cooper lets out a huffed laugh before he knows he's going to do it. "Well, that's news."

"You can stay, if you're really going to help."

Of course I'm going to help, Cooper wants to snap. He swallows the words. "Anything for Drew."

Including rooming with you, he thinks and when he looks back at Whit, he's entirely sure the same thought is written on Whit's face, too.

PART 2

———

MAY

CHAPTER FIVE

"I DUG A HOLE," Cooper says. "That's what I did today."

"I bet it's the world's best hole," Terry says. "Linda! Cooper dug a hole! Coop, send us a picture, I want to show your mom."

"Just imagine the ground, right? And then picture that some of it's missing, ta-da." He lifts his hat, wipes the back of his wrist against his sweaty forehead, and sets the hat back on his head. He imagines actually snapping a picture and sending it, his mom eagerly crowding over the phone to ooh and ahh. Then, he pushes that idea away. Of course she wouldn't look, not over the allure of all the damn emails in her inbox. "Um, what else? I fought a spigot and lost."

"Like the ongoing squirrel battle?"

"Please, squirrel war. We're losing battles and may still be under siege, but we're not giving up yet."

"That's the spirit, kiddo. The type of stuff every parent dreams of their progeny achieving. I'm going to brag about you tonight at cook group, but of course, I do that every night."

"Thought tonight was book club."

"Please, that's next week. Keep up with our busy and thrilling schedules."

"Is Mom going?"

Terry sighs into the phone. "She's got to work."

"Yeah." Cooper tips his hat back, rubbing at the sweat stinging his eyes. "Course. Well, I'm on my way out to the bar as soon as I finish this, since we already lured Drew there with the promise of fries, so sorry if I actually know how to have fun."

"Live life on the edge, Mr. Coop. Love you, kid."

"Love you too, and so does Sadie." *Tell Mom I say hi*, he nearly adds, though he could tell her himself if she ever bothered coming to the phone. "Catch you later."

"Bye, gator."

From her spot in the shade of an oak tree, Sadie's tail thumps at the sound of her name. She stretches, her toes flexing before she relaxes again, her eyes drooping shut.

"That's a good fucking hole," he tells her. Not that there's anyone around to agree with him. Or argue. It's longer than he is tall, nearly half again as wide, and deep enough that if he jumped into it, he'd have to climb back out. This hole's better than the first one he did that morning, and probably better than the second one, too. He rolls his shoulders forward, stretching out his back. A twinge of pain's settled there from so many hours in the tractor, and it aches as he wipes at his face again.

The gates he took down are an awkward fit in the tractor bucket for the drive back to the barn, the metal bent from wayward cows and a winter sitting out in the snow. It doesn't help that the ground has yet to firm up from the spring's melt, no matter how the sun shines down. All that warmth does is leave a humid stick to the air as puddles begin to dry. Cooper picks at the sleeve of his T-shirt where it clings to his arms, one hand on the steering wheel of the tractor, and Sadie sauntering along beside him.

By the time he makes it to the barnyard, the sky's lit up with sunset, glowing over the maple tree's new leaves. Cooper tugs off his hat and rifles his fingers through his sweaty hair, lifting it where the ends curl against the back of his neck and behind his ears. There's nobody around to even admire the gates he dumps behind the barn. The farm's deserted except for the cows, their jaws working over their cud and the rooster strolling past with his head bobbing. Whit's truck is gone, and the spaces where Penny's motorcycle and Drew's Jeep should be are empty too.

Well, Penny's at work, and for once, evening has come without the whine of the saw or hammering as Drew stomps around the attic. And with Whit gone, Cooper could enjoy some blessed alone-time upstairs, take a shower without the certainty Whit's probably timing his use of the hot water, and sprawl on his bed like he has a room to himself.

And it'd work, as long as he doesn't look across to the other bed and see Whit's dresser, Whit's books, Whit's neatly hung shirts in the closet, Whit's towel on its hook, like even in his absence, Whit's determinedly reminding Cooper of whose space is whose.

So tempting. He could oh-so-casually leave a stray sock on Whit's side of the narrow aisle between their beds too, just for the fun of the pinch in Whit's forehead when he discovers it later. But Cooper hauls himself up into his truck, whistling tunelessly and draping an arm out the window as he shifts into gear.

When he pulls into the parking lot of Murry's, Drew's Jeep is there, parked next to Penny's bike. It's dark inside, compared to the sunshine still clinging to the evening, and Cooper pauses in the door, letting his eyes adjust. Penny's working behind the bar, leaning on her elbows and chin in her hands as she chats with Drew.

"Beer?" she asks when she spots Cooper.

"Please." He pulls back the barstool next to Drew and then freezes when he spots who's on Drew's other side. "Whit. I thought you were at your parents'."

"I'm here."

"Obviously." *Oh shit*, he really means. Well, Whit was going to find out what Cooper's been up to at some point, and maybe it's better that it's here at the bar and not in the cool, steely silence of their room. Whit's room. Whatever.

Cooper claps Drew on the shoulder, drops onto the stool next to him, and says, "Consider your gates fixed. Almost fixed. About to be fixed."

"You got all that done today? Out in the back fields?" Drew asks.

Cooper takes the glass brimming with beer from Penny and clinks it against Drew's. "I'm good, what can I say?"

Whit straightens on his stool. "The gates in the back fields weren't broken."

"So listen to this, right? Gates are supposed to hold cows in. Those gates? Yeah, no, they were like a suggestion of a barrier, at best. And now they're being replaced, so you're welcome." Cooper takes a long drink and glances toward the door, but Brad's not here yet. Which is too bad 'cause he might've liked to see Whit and him already going a round or two.

Whit pushes his pint glass away so he can lean around Drew. "Being replaced with new gates?"

"With new gate-like equipment." Cooper tips his beer toward Whit. "You're welcome, too, though I know how much you love fencing, sorry for actually finishing a project."

"Almost finishing, apparently," Whit says.

"More done than it was, thank you very much."

"Were you going to tell me?"

"I'm telling you now."

"Guys," Drew says.

Whit opens his mouth like he's got more to say, but the door swings open and Cooper spins away and lifts a hand. "Brad, hey."

Whit lets out a soft scoff. "You invited him?"

"We're just meeting here, it's halfway." Cooper slips down to his feet and calls over, "Got them?"

"They're in my truck." Brad snaps his gum, and Cooper tries not to grimace at the wet smack.

"I can grab them now."

Penny points a finger at Cooper. "Don't you dare take that glass outside."

"Yeah, I'll stay for a drink first," Brad says and smiles at Cooper.

Well, damn. No getting the cattle stops installed tonight if they're going to idle away the evening here. Though Drew's lifting a hand to wave at Brad and that's at least something beyond the thousand-yard stare he's had going on. Maybe Drew will stay out for another bit if all of them are here enjoying themselves. Cooper presses his lips together and sits back on his stool.

Whit leans back to fix Cooper with a look behind Drew. "You bought those cattle guards?"

"Cattle stops, and yep, they're ours now," Cooper says as Brad grabs the stool next to his.

"I got an offer on the land," Brad says and nods when Penny points a glass at the line of beer taps. "The lager, please. They don't want the equipment, so I told Coop he could just have them."

Drew stills with his glass half-raised. "You got an offer?"

"I got an offer and found a new place, a sweet brand-new apartment building, so I might actually stand a chance of being warm next winter without hauling in tractor loads of firewood. Which—the tractor's gotta go too, if you guys want it."

"How much are you selling it for?" Drew asks, then ducks over his beer glass. "No, uh, no thanks."

"An apartment?" Cooper tries not to frown. Brad's knee knocks into his own.

"Get this—modern plumbing." Brad snaps his gum again as he lifts his glass for a drink.

Gum and beer. So gross. Cooper touches his fist to his mouth and clears his throat.

"Do those cattle guards actually work?" Whit asks. "Did you ever use them?"

Brad takes another swallow of beer. "They're a psychological barrier, not a physical one."

Whit lets out a huff. "I get the theory. I'm asking practically."

"The cows don't think they can walk across them, so they don't," Brad says.

"But they can. If they wanted to."

"Which they don't, 'cause get it? They stop?" Cooper points a finger at Whit, though of course he doesn't smile at the joke.

"I get it," Brad says. "Cattle stops, that's funny, Coop."

Cooper sighs and drops his hand. "C'mon, Whit, it's fine, it's a good plan."

"Were you going to ask Drew?" Whit asks.

"Drew's busy," Cooper says.

"Guys, I'm right here," Drew says.

"I think Cooper's plan is great," Brad says, clapping Cooper on the back. It jostles his beer and Cooper sets the glass down on the bar before it can slosh over the rim. Brad leaves his hand there, too heavy and warm for the heat lingering from the afternoon.

Whit stands and pushes his glass away.

"Where're you going?" Cooper asks.

"Out."

Cooper looks around at the bar. "You are out."

"Out, out."

"Oh, out, out, of course," Cooper says. "Who's the lucky guy?"

Whit shoves his barstool in harder than the poor thing probably deserves. "Good night."

It's quiet for a long minute after the door bangs shut, Penny staring after Whit before she slowly turns to Cooper.

"What?" Cooper asks.

Penny says, "Eres igual de tonto que carita."[1]

"Wait, say that slower. I'll get it this time."

Drew turns his glass in a slow circle. "What're you doing these days for work, Brad?"

"Moving on up the supply chain." Brad finally takes his hand off Cooper's shoulder, and Cooper picks at his shirt over his chest. He's already gross with a day's sweat and dirt, and Brad's hand on him doesn't make that layer of grime feel any better. "That market down by the highway? You're looking at their new farmer liaison and purchaser."

Cooper eyes Brad. "Is that even a thing?"

"Sure is." Brad snaps his gum again. In a clear, delightful image, Cooper pictures himself smacking Brad on the back until the wad flies out of his mouth.

"You enjoying it?" Drew asks.

"I'm enjoying paying my bills on time."

"Travis helped you sell your place?"

Across the bar, Penny catches Cooper's eye and grimaces. Yeah, bad. Real bad direction of conversation.

Cooper pushes his stool back and drains the last of his beer. "Brad, let me grab those stops from your truck."

"We can hang out for a minute, yeah?" Brad taps Cooper's stool. "Sit."

Shut up, he wants to say, because Drew's looking thoughtful, spinning his glass of beer in that slow circle, a crease between his eyebrows.

"Nah, I gotta grab them now and get back to the farm before Whit goes filling in all my carefully dug ditches. Drew, you want to come with?"

"Take him home," Penny says. "Drew, go home with Cooper and get some rest. I'll bring your Jeep back to the farm and deal with my bike later."

"Okay." Drew slips slowly off his stool.

Outside, Brad smacks a hand to the stack of grates lying in the back of his truck. "Nice, huh?"

What they are is heavy, and Cooper's shoulders strain as he and Brad slide them from the bed of Brad's truck and into Cooper's. The grates are loud too, as they drop the last one on top of the stack with a clang. Cooper rubs at his shoulders and neck, stretching his head to the side.

"Sure you don't want to stay for another drink?" Brad asks as Cooper grabs the cooler he'd packed full of cheese earlier.

"Gotta start burning the midnight oil, now that spring's here." Cooper pushes a wheel of Brie and some cheddar into Brad's hands. "Thanks, man."

"You know what, I don't think I miss working all day, every day," Brad says. "Hey, Coop, so good to see you, yeah?"

"Talk about separating the wheat from the chaff," Cooper mutters as he and Drew climb into the truck. Cooper puts on a smile and waves to Brad. "A little hard work never killed anyone."

"He really just gave you those cattle stops?" Drew asks.

"For some cheese." *That's piling up with no farmers' markets*, Cooper doesn't add. He slaps his hand over his stomach before he shifts into reverse. "I'll eat less of it this week, make up for it. Gotta stay in fighting shape, anyway."

"Is there a lucky guy you've got your eye on?"

"No, I just have an ongoing competition to have better abs than Whit." Cooper peels up his shirt and looks down at his stomach, mostly to see if Drew will grin. "Someday."

Drew does smile, but it's a weak effort, a shadow of the way he normally does. Cooper slaps Drew's stomach too, poking at his ribs until he gets an exhausted laugh and a halfhearted bat at his hand.

At the house, Drew idly scratches Sadie's head as he makes his way inside. *Don't*, Cooper thinks as Drew glances at the clock over the stove, like he's really considering working on the attic tonight.

Which he might, if Cooper heads back out to keep working himself.

"I wouldn't mind hitting the sack early," Cooper says and ushers Drew toward the stairs. "Get some rest, like Penny said?"

Especially if Whit's really gone tonight. *Finding some guy to fuck*, Cooper can't help but think. Maybe he'll come back in the early hours of the morning and silently slip into the shower. It's bound to happen one of these nights. And it'll be a relief when it does, Cooper wants to believe. Whit gone off with some equally hot, annoying, and pedantic asshole, probably complaining about Cooper the entire time. Better than lying there in the dark silence, listening to Whit's breathing only a handful of feet away as Cooper tosses and turns and tries to sleep.

Cooper points Drew toward his bedroom, pressing a palm to the attic door when Drew glances toward it. "If you start in on a night of carpentry, I'll tell Penny, and then you'll really be in the shitter. Farm reg forty-three point six: not listening to the wonderful roommate who constantly hooks us up with free beer."

A ghost of a smile crosses Drew's face. "That's forty-three point five. Forty-three point six is picking up said wonderful roommate from the bar when it unexpectedly rains and she's ridden her motorcycle there."

"See? You know the rules. Bedtime, Andrew, and don't think I won't send a squirrel to check that your lights are off in ten minutes and no playing on your phone," Cooper says and waits until Drew's door closes before he heads down the hall.

Cooper kicks the bedroom door shut and shucks off his shirt. His fucking shoulder hurts again. Well, a hot shower can help fix that, and maybe no Whit tonight will do even more to ease that building, chronic tension.

Cooper starts on his belt and the bathroom door suddenly swings open. He jumps, belt buckle jangling. "Dammit, Whit, I thought you were out."

Whit crosses his arms. "I'm not."

"What happened to out, out?"

It's only Whit, he tells himself and yanks his belt out of his belt loops. If Whit wanted to watch Cooper strip his clothes off, he's had ample opportunity, and he never apparently does.

"Were you going to bother to tell me you were getting those cattle guards from Brad?"

"You came back to keep yelling at me?" Cooper dumps his belt on his bed and tosses his phone next to it. "Did you park behind the barn, just to be really sneaky? What the hell?"

Cooper's phone chimes. *That cheese is some good stuff,* the text reads.

"Is that the farm in Oregon?"

"Why, you counting down the days until they give me a start date? Nope, still haven't heard from them, which I'm sure you already know, but thanks for your ongoing support. Feels great, bud."

"Is it Brad?"

"What the hell is your problem with him?" Cooper starts to flick the message away, but Whit's still looking at him, so he takes the time to type back, *There's plenty more where that came from.*

"He wants to keep helping you," Whit says.

"And that's an issue for you? That he doesn't want to see another farm go belly-up?" Cooper yanks off a sock. "God forbid he be generous."

"You think that's what he cares about?" Whit puts his hands on his hips. He looks bigger like that, his shoulders filling out his shirt.

Cooper hops on his other foot to get that sock off too. Then he just drops to sit on the edge of his mattress, his elbows on his knees and his feet braced on the cold floor. With both hands, he digs his fingers into his hair. He's tired. His back is sore. He probably should scrounge up some dinner. And he needs his own damn room where he can shove the door shut and not deal with Whit in his face.

"I don't want to fight with you." Cooper takes a deep breath and lets it out again, trying to calm the heat burning through his chest. He really doesn't want to fight. Or he does, just not like this, incessant and unending, and with Drew and the farm at stake, not their normal half-amusing, mostly petty disagreements about which type of grain scoops are the best and how to coil a hose.

"Okay."

"I mean it." Cooper tightens his fingers in his hair, the

strands long enough to brush the backs of his hands. "I think we're driving Drew nuts."

"Then stop."

"You stop," Cooper mumbles. It's driving him nuts, too. He drags his hands down his face, scrubbing at his eyes. His skin feels gritty with the salt of the day's sweat. He really does need to shower. And put on a clean change of clothes. Cool off, get away from Whit, get some food, and let this latest argument blow over.

To his surprise, Whit sits on the edge of his own mattress. It's more obvious how close their beds are like this, the narrow lane between them only the nightstand's width apart. If Cooper wanted to, he could nearly knock his knee into Whit's.

The shirt Cooper dropped sits right in the middle of that cramped space. It's probably driving Whit nuts, just lying there. He sighs, leans over to grab the shirt, and tosses it toward the pile of dirty laundry he's amassed. Right beside it is his duffle bag, which is more a yawning pile of mostly clean clothing that they both have to step over to reach the bathroom. This room is too damn small, and as Whit's eyes track Cooper rubbing at his forehead, Cooper's entirely sure that they're both thinking that same thing.

"I know that Drew values your...innovation," Whit says slowly. Cooper snorts. That must be a much nicer word than Whit probably wanted to use. "But I'm not sure this is the year to be coming up with all sorts of new ideas."

"It's not new," Cooper says. "Farms all over the place use cattle stops to—"

"The farm needs to be making more money, not just reinventing the wheel."

"There's nothing wrong with cattle stops." Cooper rubs his hands down his thighs and forces in a slow, deep breath. "Whit. You—you get freaked out and then you get paralyzed and you don't do anything. Someone around here has to, or that's going to be Drew next spring with a new job and a new apartment, and you and I both know what that would do to him. He got handed his family's farm, and now he thinks he's going to blow his shot running it."

A frown pinches Whit's mouth. "I don't do that."

"You don't?" Cooper waves a hand toward the window and the barn beyond it. "How many times have you taken down those gates, fixed them, and put them back up? And the milking lines? You know that pump is bad and other dairies aren't even using that model anymore. Aren't you supposed to be taking some of this stuff off Drew's plate this summer? Didn't he put you in charge around here this year? He's up to his elbows in Camembert, and if you're not keeping an eye on these things, who is? Penny? Sadie?"

"The pump works fine."

"The pump works fine when it works," Cooper says. "Are you just going to sit by while the farm falls apart the rest of the way?"

"Apparently, you didn't need me to tell you the farm isn't doing well financially, if you know so much."

Cooper spreads his hands out. "Calling it as I see it."

"And you really think that changing those gates for cattle guards will make the difference?"

"I think changing them for cattle stops will. And I think it's a start, and I'll figure out the rest of it, because apparently your plan is to keep your head down and just do what you've always done, year after year. I think it's pretty clear how far that's getting you." Cooper pushes up to his feet, and dammit, his pants leave behind bits of hay all over his quilt.

He shuts his eyes for a long moment. He's tired and cranky, and he really does need dinner. And now Whit's still sitting there, probably pissed off all over again at the dirt

Cooper's tracked in here. Cooper can nearly feel his eyes on his bare chest. He clears his throat and yanks his towel off the footboard of his bed. "I'm going to shower."

"Cooper..."

"I told you, I don't want to argue."

"I wasn't going to." Whit's voice sounds softer than Cooper might've expected, or maybe that's just the door closing between them and the drum of the shower as he turns it on.

CHAPTER SIX

Cooper's boots are wet. And his pants. He stamps his feet at the door of the barn like it'll make a lick of difference. All it does is stick the canvas of his work pants to his legs. He wiggles his toes, and yep, the mud he just walked through has soaked clear through to his socks.

"You're a ray of sunshine this afternoon," Penny says from her perch on top of the cows' fence. In front of her, a calf stands braced on all four legs, its head tipped up and its throat working as it drinks from the bottle in her hands. "Did you sneak in those cattle stops that you're pretending to hide in the back of your truck?"

"Nah, I'm saving that for the crowning glory of the week, and I'm gonna make Whit help me install them as a special present." Cooper bends down and smacks at the cuffs of his pants. That doesn't make a difference either, just gets his hands wet. "I need more socks. Or for the damn farm to dry out."

Penny tips the bottle up higher. "Ah, the joys of spring. Bugs, mud, and more bugs. Come feed a calf, it does wonders for the mood."

"Does that one actually need a bottle or is Drew just

doing you a favor?" Cooper leans across the fence and lifts the calf's ear, checking its tag number. "Knew it."

"Buttercup and I are best bros, so get out of here with that attitude, mister. Drew—the walking, talking grump— just came through, and we're trying to recover."

"Buttercup's a boy."

Penny rolls her eyes. "Which is why I said bros."

The calf sucks the bottle dry and finally releases it. Cooper gives him a scratch under the chin. "Drew's around?"

"He's in with his cheese. But I'd give him a minute."

"It's not going well in there?" Cooper leans against the fence, his shoulder even with Penny's hip. It's cooler in the barn than outside, the sun already shining a sharp blaze into his eyes. "I wanted to let him know that the grass is up enough in the back field to let the cows start grazing."

"That'll make him happier than the ricotta."

"Oh, is he making that?" Cooper looks up at her. She's got her hair in a knot at the back of her head and is wearing an old T-shirt with a couple drops of milk staining the hem. "Pizza night soon? Yes?"

"Clean the grill? Yes?" Penny parrots back. "It's gross as anything, Coop."

She pats the top of Cooper's head, and Cooper pushes into her hand. "That feels good. Buttercup, clean the grill."

"Buttercup thinks that those who let the cheese from burgers they cooked last fall drip all over the grill should clean it themselves."

Cooper leans farther into her and she sighs, petting at his hair. It does feel good, her fingers scratching against his scalp like that. Penny's got a nice touch. Drew isn't crazy to be more than halfway in love with her.

"It burns off," he says.

"Gross."

She lightly runs her nails against the back of his head, and he lets his eyes shut.

"I like your hair long like this. It looks good."

"I need a haircut."

"Don't," Penny says. "Grow it out and I'll braid it."

"Only if you do Buttercup's too." Cooper rolls his head to the side, butting his forehead against her leg. "What's wrong with the ricotta?"

"There's too much of it to sell before it goes bad. And I quote, 'Fucking fresh cheese something, something, fuck, fuck, fuck.'"

"Oof."

"Yeah."

His shoulder hurts like this, leaning up against the fence. It hurt all morning bumping along on the tractor too. He lets out a sigh as Penny scratches down his neck. He's got to go check over the hay equipment, what with the growth the grass has been putting on. *Add it to the list*, he thinks, but lets himself stay right where he is for another moment. It's been entirely too long since anyone's touched him with anything nicer than Drew and one of his crushing hugs.

Maybe he should ask Whit what the hookup scene around here looks like these days. Give his body a change from hefting hay bales and pushing cows this way and that. It sounds nice as anything. Of course, that would involve admitting Whit knows something Cooper doesn't, so no, getting laid may not actually be worth that.

Or we could just fuck each other. He frowns at the thought. Unhelpful, that little part of himself that always crops up when he spends too much time around Whit. He's a jerk and an asshole, and if Cooper's going to actually know anything about a guy he jumps in bed with, he'd like the facts to not add up to *insufferable, fussy, and an utter bonehead.*

"I'm worried about Drew," Penny says softly.

"Do we need to eat all that ricotta? I'm up for it. I'll take one for the team."

"I'm serious."

"Good news, I am too."

"Well, you could use some meat on your bones." Penny pokes a finger into his ribs and he flinches away.

"Maybe I'll have Drew give me some. I still owe Brad a bit for those stops."

She grabs a lock of his hair and tugs gently. "You going to just deliver him a truckload of ricotta that's got to be eaten within the week?"

"Oh, if it goes bad, he won't notice over all that damn gum. Did he always do that?"

"Annoying as all hell, isn't it?"

"Right?" Cooper sighs. "No wonder Whit hates him."

Penny snorts softly and jostles Cooper's head side to side with her grip on his hair. "That's not why."

"Get off," Cooper says, batting halfheartedly at her hand.

"And Whit doesn't hate Brad." Penny jumps down from the fence, landing lightly on her feet.

"Wait, no, go back to rubbing my head."

She walks backward toward the milk room and points a finger toward the house and says, "Clean the grill."

"What's the deal, then?" Cooper calls after her. "With Brad and Whit? Did they hook up? Is Whit super into gum chewers?"

"The two of them?" Penny lets out a laugh. "God, no."

"Then what?"

But she just shakes her head and pushes into the

milking room, and the door that falls shut doesn't give him any answers.

In the kitchen, Cooper wipes Drew's name from the whiteboard and scribbles in his own for who's cooking dinner. He hums to himself, shredding a ball of mozzarella onto a plate, dough rising in a bowl next to him, and Sadie snuffling around the kitchen floor at his feet, licking up bits of cheese that fall. He looks down at her for a moment, and then not-so-accidentally brushes another piece off the counter.

"That's not good for her."

"Jesus, Whit, I'm gonna have to put a fucking bell on you."

Whit pushes the door shut behind him, his cheeks flushed and his hair damp with sweat. Cooper turns back around and sorts through the refrigerator, staring at a hapless bottle of ketchup.

"Ready to eat soon?" Cooper asks.

"I just got back from running."

Cooper pulls out a bundle of asparagus and turns only far enough to point it at Whit. "Obviously." Whit picks at his T-shirt where it clings to his chest, and Cooper goes back to rooting through the fridge. "I'm making pizza."

"Obviously."

"You around tonight, or are you going to your parents'?"

"My parents'?"

"I'm trying to encourage you to disappear." Cooper pokes his head back into the refrigerator, like he really needs the Parmesan right this second and isn't fighting a battle against ogling the drip of sweat rolling down Whit's temple. "The nights you're gone are my favorite if you're looking for scheduling feedback."

"Sorry to disappoint."

"Well, what else is new?" Cooper finds the block of

Parmesan and peels back the plastic wrap. Drew probably made it last summer if it's in the fridge now. And any that he makes this summer...who'll even be around to eat it if he sells the farm? Will Drew just have to toss out all the wheels that haven't finished aging, give the pigs a heyday of cheesy joy and shut the door on the cheese room, to never open it again?

Fuck. What an awful thought.

Cooper gently closes the fridge. "Never mind. There's plenty for all four of us, anyway."

Whit nods and when he goes upstairs, Cooper lets out a breath. Right. Look at them, they can get along. And maybe Cooper can find a chance to have some good old quality time with his right hand soon. He can work on forgetting about how Whit looks when he gets back from a run, which is only moderately more tormenting than how he looks when he gets out of the shower, and is only topped by the sight of him slipping into bed in just his boxers. Whit Morales, Cooper's personal torturer.

The stairs creak once more and Cooper turns back to the mozzarella, because there's Whit all over again, and this time walking toward Cooper, close enough to smell clean sweat and the dampness of fresh spring air still clinging to him.

"Your phone."

"Just leave it."

"It rang twice."

"S'fine." Cooper grates the cheese hard enough his knuckles are at risk of becoming a pizza ingredient. But Whit just keeps holding it out, like not answering a call is a greater affront than even replacing the damn gates, and Cooper sighs and grabs it from him.

"Is this Cooper Langston?"

"Yeah," he says, turning his shoulder to Whit. Cooper

can still smell him. That should be illegal, to come in after a run and stand so damn close. Farm reg eighty-three point what-fucking-ever, no tormenting Cooper.

"This is Cheryl. Cheryl Frederick from Frederick Dale Farms?"

Cooper brushes his hands clean on his pants. "Oh. Hi, yeah."

"So great to catch you. How've you been?"

"Good, yeah, so glad you called." Cooper turns farther away from Whit. The last time he'd talked to Cheryl, he'd been at his winter job up in Maine, sitting in his truck with the heater blowing and looking through the fogged windshield at the dreary gray and brown forest. Anywhere warmer in winter had been at the top of his list for his next job, as he'd watched ice crystals form on his window and held his reddened fingers in front of the air vent as Cheryl went on about her goats.

"Well, I have the very happy news that we'd love to check your references if you're still interested in a job here."

Thousands of miles from Whit? Fuck yeah. "Awesome, yes. References, I can get you some names."

"I don't tell most applicants this, but we'd really love to have you here, Cooper. I'm sorry for the delay in getting back to you over the last couple weeks, but I mean it, so the sooner you can send some names the better."

"Yeah, soon, that's no problem," Cooper repeats. He should stop doing that, echoing her words. But it's hard to focus with Whit's attention on him, quite obviously listening and probably silently grading Cooper's performance on this call.

And now he's got his hand held out too. *The phone,* Whit mouths.

Cooper draws back and shakes his head. *I'm talking on it,* he mouths back.

Whit wags his fingers, like Cooper's Sadie, and if he says "drop it," Cooper will. And then Whit just steps forward and takes the phone from him, too quick to stop.

"I can be a reference," he says into Cooper's phone.

"No," Cooper hisses.

"Whit Morales. I'm his supervisor."

Cooper grabs for the phone, though Whit just turns slightly, and fucking hell, Cooper can't reach around him, not with the handful of inches Whit has on him.

"Oh, he's worked for me for—what is it?—nine or ten years now, off and on."

"Whit," Cooper whispers loudly. "Fucking stop."

"Yep, Two Pines, a dairy farm in upstate New York. He's been a real help totally reconfiguring our fencing system."

Reconfiguring. Fucking shit, this is a nightmare. Cooper tries to grab for his phone again.

"Real good with animals," Whit says and just steps away from Cooper. His shirt's damp when Cooper grabs a handful of it, and he lets go quickly. "Punctual? Hmm."

Whit looks like he's about to start laughing. Which, oh great, the one time Whit decides to have some fun, it's to agonize Cooper. Of fucking course.

"Yeah, he knows how to be on time."

Knows how to be on time isn't at all the same as actually being on time. Which, fuck. Which Whit's right about, but he doesn't need to actually say that.

Drew should be talking to Cheryl. Or Cooper's boss from this winter up in Maine, or any of the last dozen jobs he's had. Not fucking Whit. Cooper reaches for the phone again, but Whit just puts a hand in the middle of his chest and easily, casually, holds Cooper at bay.

Which...yeah, that feels good. Really good.

"Well, he's always full of new ideas," Whit says and

Cooper groans, his eyes closing. That's a deep, coursing note of sarcasm in Whit's voice. Maybe Cheryl can't hear it, but Cooper sure as shit can. Dammit, he's apparently wrong about Whit being able to have a good time, and this is how he fucking finds out.

"Very handy, real good with a wrench."

Fuck you, Cooper mouths, leaning into Whit's hand, though it doesn't budge.

"Hard worker? Well, he was out working most of yesterday evening, after we all quit for the day," Whit says and throws Cooper a look. Ah, still pissed about the cattle stops. Well, at least that hasn't changed. "Sure. Let me know if you have questions, yep, goodbye."

When Whit hangs up, he sets Cooper's phone next to the cheese grater and finally drops his hand.

"Whit."

"You're welcome."

"Fucking hell."

"She seems nice."

"*Whit.*" Cooper groans, digging his fingers into his eyes.

"Say 'Thank you, Whit.'"

"Fuck you, Whit." Cooper drags his hands down his face. "You are not my supervisor."

"Oh, good to know. I'll call her back and tell her to ignore all that."

"I can't tell if that's the nicest you've ever been to me, or if you just lost me any chance at that job."

"I should've told her about the spigot. You're so close to fixing it by just swearing at it every morning."

"Is this revenge for getting the damn gates finished?" Cooper jams his phone into his pocket and grabs for the ball of mozzarella, though there's so little left, he just tosses it to Sadie. "Why didn't you just tell her what you told me last night? That no matter what I do around here, it's not going to make a lick of difference?"

"I didn't say that."

"You did, you said that—"

"And I think you were right," Whit says.

Cooper freezes. Slowly, he turns around to look at Whit. "I'm sorry. I don't think I heard you correctly."

Whit blows out a breath and runs a hand through his hair. It strains his damp shirt along the lines of his body, the flat plane of his stomach and the bulge of muscles in his arm. Cooper frowns at the sight, annoyed all over again.

"Drew asked me to keep the farm running this season while he works on the house and does his cheese, and yeah, I've just been going about things the same way we always do." He looks at Cooper and then away, out the windows where the grass is dancing in the breeze and the lupins are starting to bud. "I, yeah, I do that a lot. Just keep on going with what I've been doing. So."

Cooper wants to jam his finger into his ear and work it around until he can hear Whit right. "So?"

"So okay, the farm needs to make more money and spend less. And that means things have to change."

Cooper squints at him. "So you don't hate the cattle stops?"

"Hate the cattle—no, Cooper, this isn't about that."

"Is it about the gates, then?"

"No, it's—I do hate the cattle—but it's not—look, we gotta help Drew, right? So how're we going to do that? You said you'd figure it out, so what've you got?"

"Um." Cooper leans back against the counter. Sadie presses forward, tongue swiping like if she just stretches enough, she'll reach the entire pile of grated cheese.

"You do have ideas, right?"

"Oh, absolutely." Cooper pulls open the refrigerator

again. Think, think, think. Though the only thing filling his brain is Whit still standing there, handsomely sweaty and so fucking distracting.

"Cooper?"

"Just, you know, turning all my plans over in my head."

Fix this whole place. Combine every working, profitable idea he's seen in his years bouncing from farm to farm, implement them here, and pat himself on the back when he's done.

His stomach grumbles. Fucking hell, Whit's probably delighted Cooper doesn't have a spreadsheet and presentation ready to go, complete with handouts and a diagram on a whiteboard. He doesn't even know what he's putting on the pizza tonight, let alone any type of actual, solid plan. *Winging it*, he'd say if it weren't Whit standing there, Cooper's neck burning.

Asparagus.

Right, he can do this. He already got asparagus out. There's some sausage in the fridge, too. And early spring onions. That and the cheese. He'll just drown the pizza with way too much cheese and that'll solve all their problems. Deliciously gooey and perfect.

Which...huh.

"Pizza," he says.

"What?"

"Artisan pizza shop. Perfect outlet for cheese, yes or yes?"

"Pizza?" Whit says slowly. "Your plan is to help the farm by starting a restaurant?"

"C'mon, it's great." Cooper leans toward the open window above the sink and calls, "Drew! I fixed it!"

"One low-profit, high-capital enterprise with a second one attached to it?" Whit asks.

"Never mind, you're not invited to dinner," Cooper

says. "Sadie's getting your pizza."

"I'd tell you it's the worst idea you've had, but frankly, it's a competition at this point."

"Drew!" Cooper yells again, and ah, that worked, because Drew pushes the kitchen door open, stamping his feet and looking between them. "See, Drew heard me."

Whit huffs a breath out his nose. "Well, when you shout like that."

"Drew, pizza shop," Cooper says.

"Have you two seen my tape measure?" Drew asks.

"Just sell the cheese to a pizza shop," Whit says. "It'd make more sense."

"I thought I had it, but I must've put it down somewhere," Drew says, turning in a slow circle. "I was going to get some more work done in the attic before dinner."

Cooper taps a stalk of asparagus against his chin and pushes another piece of cheese toward Sadie. "Huh."

"Sadie shouldn't be eating all that cheese," Whit says.

"Sadie, don't." Drew pats at his pockets and turns around again. "Did I leave it in the attic?"

"No, wait." Cooper points the asparagus at Whit. "That's...that'd work."

"What would work?" Whit asks.

Drew looks over too, his hands still pressed to his jeans.

But Cooper doesn't answer, just digs his phone out of his pocket and flicks to his texts. What had Brad said? Moving up the supply chain? Cooper quickly types out, *Any interest in selling some of our cheese at the market? I've got some ricotta I can get you at a good price.*

"Totally going to work," Cooper mumbles. *We got mozzarella too*, he adds.

"Coop?" Drew asks.

Cooper's phone lights up immediately. *Enough for wholesale?* Brad asks.

Definitely, Cooper writes.

He catches the corner of his lip in his teeth. Kind of definitely. Almost definitely. Whatever, Drew can make more, and hell if Brad isn't apparently by his phone right this minute ready for an answer. All the cows are coming into their milk now, and if this works out, then why couldn't they just empty out the stock room, pack it up for Brad, and get started making more? So, yes, definitely. They have enough. Or they will have enough, at least.

I'd love to talk about it more, Brad writes. *You around sometime?*

Absolutely. He grins at Drew and waggles his eyebrows. "Problem solved."

Whit tips his chin toward the counter. "Sadie's eating our dinner."

Cooper's phone buzzes again. *Tomorrow? Want to grab a bite to eat?*

Sure, he replies and then sticks the phone into his pocket. "Wholesale. We're doing it. Nobody has to drive to farmers' markets, we'll have more time to increase milk production with all those extra hours each week, and we'll ramp up the entire farm. Brad, a wholesale account, the ricotta. Done and done."

"What?" Drew asks. "Sadie, no."

Cooper catches her by the collar just as her tongue takes another swipe at the pile of mozzarella on the cutting board. "This is genius. I'm a genius. You're welcome."

"Ramping up production?" Whit asks. "With what cows?"

"Cows make more cows," Cooper says. "A bull, plus a lady cow, 'cause see, Whit, when two cows love each other special, etcetera, etcetera."

Whit rubs at the bridge of his nose. "I'm sorry, what?"

"This is—Drew, this is what we need. A big wholesale

account, right? Scale up from selling to local folks and hit the major leagues. We've got the herd size for it, you've got the cheese skill, so what we do is increase production and sell to Brad. Hell, beyond Brad." Cooper pats his hands at the air in front of him, his smile growing as his words speed up. Drew's never tried this, not once, Cooper knows. Of course he hasn't, if Whit's had anything to say about it. *Too risky*, he can already hear in Whit's voice, shooting down the idea before it can get any traction, digging his heels in like he always does whenever there's the slightest possibility he might fail.

"How many grocery stores are there around here? Or in Albany? Hell, down in New York City? Other farms make this jump to a wider market. Why can't we?"

"Coop..." Drew says slowly.

"You need a ton more income for the size of this farm, right? Which worked fine back in your uncle's day when milk prices were higher, but times change and we gotta change with them."

"We," Whit murmurs.

"I can't hire anyone else," Drew says. "C'mon, Coop, more cows would mean more staff and—"

"No, you're not hiring anyone, we just need to change a couple things around. More efficient systems, smoother operations all over. The cattle stops are just the start. Dependable wholesale accounts, higher production, more money." Cooper smacks his palm down on the counter. "Bam. Solved."

"Bam," Drew repeats, far softer. "Wholesale is an entirely different game than what we're doing."

"It's not. I mean, it is, but it's not. It's just cheese, right? And Drew, you make the best damn cheese. Sure, the scale is different, but you can do it, and you and Whit can still manage this whole place. Maybe if it works out, one other person to help Whit out, eventually. That's it. That's all you'd need."

The stairs creak and Penny pokes her head into the kitchen. "What the hell is all the noise?"

"Cooper thinks he has a good idea," Whit says.

"I have a *great* idea." Cooper taps the counter twice and then points at Whit. "His idea, actually. I'm just here to improve on it."

"I," Whit says, "did not suggest working with Brad."

"Brad?" Penny asks. "Oh, Sadie, sweetie, don't eat that."

Cooper drags Sadie back from the counter again. She's got bits of mozzarella stuck to her nose and swipes her long tongue to catch them, her tail wagging.

"Brad and I are going to talk tomorrow," Cooper says. "Get a bite to eat and go over this. Drew, price list? Yes? Send it to me?"

"You're getting dinner." Whit's voice is flat. Pissed that Cooper's stepping all over his toes, Cooper's sure, but hell if someone around here needs to fucking do something. Isn't this what they talked about? Working together to help Drew?

"I don't know. Yes? That's what he said." Cooper ruffles Sadie's ears. This is it. It's big. He can feel the promise of this plan thrumming through him.

"Dinner, dinner?" Penny asks.

"Dinner," Cooper says.

Whit's shoulders rise on a long breath.

"What?" Cooper asks.

"I'm going running." Whit yanks the door open.

"Whit," Penny says.

"This is going to be great." Cooper nudges Sadie's nose away from the cheese again and squints at Whit. He just went running, didn't he? "Fix everything."

Behind Whit, the door bangs shut.

CHAPTER SEVEN

Whit props his hands on his hips, his muscles bulging under the thin cotton of his T-shirt. "The cows are going to walk right over it."

Cooper lifts his hat by the brim and wipes sweat off his forehead. "They are not."

"Farmers use gates for a reason."

"Other farmers use cattle stops for a reason." With the sun pounding down on them, Cooper's head is starting to ache. Or maybe it's the storm clouds lingering on the horizon that haven't moved toward them, breaking the afternoon's humidity and bringing in some fresh air. Forgetting his water bottle back at the house hasn't helped, though he's not quite at the point he's going to cave and ask Whit for a drink from his.

Hell, he'll share the cows' water if it comes to that. They haven't even touched it yet they're so excited to be out of the barn and on pasture, running and playing like they're calves again, kicking their hind legs and jumping through the tall grass.

"Explain again how, exactly, this is going to make such a big difference to the farm?"

"I'm trying to save you time, you genius. You can say thank you, you know, because if you're not running around, messing with opening and shutting gates whenever you want to hay a field or move the herd, you can fit more work into the day. Or quit early once in a while. Like today, for instance. A beautiful Saturday." Cooper presses the heel of his hand to his forehead. It pulls at the muscle in his back, still sore and now all the more painful from a day of dragging the cattle stops around. "Can we be done for the afternoon? Please?"

Works hard, Whit had said to Cheryl on the phone yesterday. Maybe Whit'll call her back and let her know he's revising his esteemed opinion.

"I've got that thing with Brad tonight," he calls after Whit, who heads toward the truck. But Whit just walks faster and Cooper groans and jogs after him. "Weren't you being nice to me for like thirty seconds yesterday?"

Whit unlatches the back of the truck and hops up onto the tailgate.

"C'mon, don't you have some hot date to be getting to tonight?" Cooper asks. "Is putting up fencing really your plan for your Saturday? Or is someone special heading over to spend a romantic evening setting up a cow pasture with you?"

Whit reaches into the bed of the truck and picks up a spool of fencing.

"Lucky guy," Cooper mutters and follows behind Whit with an armful of fence posts.

By the time they finally finish, Drew must've already showered, because the water runs cold before Cooper's even rinsed his hair. He shuts the water off as quickly as he can, shivering and reaching for his towel.

"The water's fucking freezing," he announces as he elbows open the bathroom door, toweling off his face. Then he jumps back a foot and jerks the towel down in front of his crotch. "Jesus. Sorry."

"No, I'm—" Penny holds up both hands, her eyes snapping up to the ceiling. It looks like she'd had a hand resting on Whit's knee, where they're sitting cross-legged on his bed. Quickly, she stands up. "Sorry, Coop."

"No, no, I'm sorry, shit." He carefully holds his towel in front of himself and grabs a pair of boxers out of his duffle bag. Well, this is cool. Now at least Penny has some context for more of Whit's complaints about him, beyond what Whit probably already listed while Cooper shivered in the shower. Leaves clothes everywhere, uses the last of the hot water, and for all Cooper knows, talks in his sleep, too. Whit can top the list off with "walks around naked," which Whit clearly hates because it makes the corner of his jaw flex each and every time.

Cooper ducks back into the bathroom to pull on his boxers, toweling off his hair and settling it into some semblance of tidiness. Probably, he should shave. He rubs his palm over his rough chin, and then shrugs and lays his towel over his shoulder. It's just Brad. Plus, he'll have to then scrub the sink clean or hear it from Whit if he leaves even a speck of hair behind.

"Say something," Penny says softly as Cooper opens the bathroom door again.

"Say what?" Cooper tosses his towel over the doorknob.

There's exactly one hook in the bathroom, and he hasn't bothered to ask Whit if he'd actually share it. They could take turns, maybe. Come up with a schedule where Cooper could use the hook on Tuesdays, Thursdays, Saturdays, and alternating Sundays. Though if they're going to do that, they should just paint a line down the middle of the room, too, so Whit's not toeing at clothes that migrate too close to his bed.

"Nothing. She's leaving," Whit says.

"Pen, you working tonight?" Cooper steps into a pair of jeans and hitches them up to his waist.

"Drew's burning one of the brush piles in the west fields. I'm going to give him a hand. My big Saturday night off."

"You're doing it for the s'mores?" Cooper asks.

"Yep, I'm doing it for the s'mores." She grabs Whit's elbow and jostles it, giving Whit a hard look. "I'm serious. Dile cómo te sientes[1]."

Cooper pulls on a gray T-shirt. "If you guys are still burning it when I'm back, I'll come out."

"We will be, I'm sure." Penny doesn't take her hand off Whit, though she does give Cooper a once-over. "You're wearing that?"

"Yes?" Cooper looks down at himself and plucks at the hem of his shirt where it falls past his stomach.

"Really?"

"I think so?" Cooper holds his arms out and examines his shirt. It's from his clean pile of clothes, as opposed to his somewhat clean pile, somewhat dirty, and definitely dirty. "Am I not?"

"You're going out to dinner," Penny says.

"Yeah, with Brad."

"Cooper..."

"What? I'm clean, I'm dressed."

Penny touches two fingers to her forehead. "You know what, I don't want to get in the middle of this."

"What's wrong with my shirt?" Cooper kicks at his duffle, but there's not anything else in there that isn't just more of the same. "Do I need a different shirt? Whit, can I borrow a shirt?"

"No."

"Whit." Penny lets out a breath. "Whit, go take a shower."

"The water's cold," Cooper says. "What's wrong with wearing this to eat with Brad?"

"Whit, eres igual de tonto que él[2]," Penny says.

Whit heads for the bathroom, pushing past Cooper so quickly that Cooper has to step aside.

"I like this shirt," Cooper says. It's plain. And comfortable. And up until now, he'd assumed it was completely practical, acceptable, and unoffensive.

Penny sits on the edge of Whit's bed again, one leg crossed under herself and her other foot on the floor. "Where're you two going?"

"Just to get a burger. How is this not a cheeseburger sort of shirt?"

"Cooper." Penny touches her forehead again. "You're going to dinner. On a Saturday. With Brad."

"I know. Wearing clothes, even. And I cleaned the cow shit off myself, too. I swear I'm presentable."

The shower starts running, and Penny's eyes dart toward the bathroom door.

"Brad likes you," she says softly.

"Brad? C'mon, no he doesn't."

"Cooper, he asked you out."

Cooper laughs. He needs socks. And a belt too, or his pants are going to be falling down all night. Wallet, phone, keys, and then he can get going so he can get back to the farm and the bonfire all the sooner. "We're just grabbing a bite to eat." He should maybe bring his sunglasses too. He'd wear his hat against the glare of the sun, but even he knows that his ball cap is too gross after days of sweating in it.

"He's taking you to dinner."

"No, he's not. I'm meeting him there."

"Oh, Coop." Penny stands and reaches up to set her

hands on his shoulders. "You are so good at farming and so very pretty and yet so incredibly clueless."

"I am not." He catches the door before she can shut it and pokes his head into the hallway after her. "Brad doesn't like me."

"Let me know who pays," she calls back.

Cooper rolls his eyes and sits on Whit's bed to pull his socks on. When the bathroom door opens, Cooper asks, "Am I clueless?"

"Where's Penny?"

"Am I?" Cooper stands quickly. "Sorry. I know, I know, no touching your stuff, let alone your bed. Do I look that bad?"

Whit has his towel around his waist, and maybe the shower wasn't that cold after all, because his ears are a little red. He glances at Cooper, then turns away, sorting through the top drawer of his dresser.

"You don't," he says finally.

"Thank you." Cooper throws his hands up in the air. "Tell Penny that."

"I'm not going to." Whit pulls out a pair of jeans, rather than his sweatpants, and Cooper cranes his head, trying to see the shirt he chooses from the closet.

"You going out tonight? Got a big hot date?"

"Can you stop asking me that?"

"I don't care." Cooper holds up both hands. Doesn't want to care, is more like. Fucking jealous at the thought and annoyed at that reaction even more. *No*, he tells himself as sternly as he knows how. Too much time around Whit, and this is where it leads: mooning over his body and imagining an alternative reality where Whit's not an asshole, they're friends, and then they're more.

Not going to happen. Really, really not going to fucking happen, so Cooper needs to not linger on the idle delight of *what if.* Because there's no *if.* There's just Cooper stepping into the hall and Whit shoving the door firmly shut.

Besides, Whit's probably getting all dressed up just to enjoy a night without Cooper in his room. Making an occasion of it. That'd figure, a private party for one, as Whit celebrates the fact Cooper's out with Brad, the two people Whit finds most annoying sharing their Saturday night.

The parking lot of the restaurant is already crowded when Cooper pulls in, and by the time he's circled it twice and finally edged in between the dumpster and a sedan, Brad's waiting at the front door. His phone's in his hand and a smile's on his face. No gum, though, thank God.

"Hey, you." Brad pulls Cooper in for a hug. Cooper gives him a slap on the back. *Total dudebro hug,* he'd text Penny if he could, though Brad's already opening the door for them and ushering Cooper through.

"Table or a seat at the bar?" the host asks them, picking up two menus. The place isn't packed, but there's only a few spots left open at the bar, where most everyone's turned toward the Red Sox pitcher on the TV.

"The bar's fine." Cooper looks around again. They've redone this place since the last time he was in here, all exposed brick and blond wood. It's brighter now. Nicer.

"A table," Brad says and turns toward him. "Yeah, that okay?"

"Oh, sure." Cooper tucks his hands into his pockets. It pulls at the ache in his shoulder. "Whatever."

Their table's in the back, beyond the booths full of couples and a group of women laughing, empty drinks and a demolished plate of nachos in front of them. Cooper slides into his chair, and Brad sits across from him, already smiling again. His new job must be treating him all right, for him to be looking so damn happy all the time. Maybe Brad should try out a Saturday being dragged around by Whit until all hours of the evening, it might bring him down a notch or two.

"So the cheese," Cooper says as Brad puts his napkin on his lap. "I think this could be great."

"Oh, yeah, we'll buy some." Brad lays his hand on the table, palm down. His nails are clean. Cooper tucks his own hands into his lap. He's got diesel and engine oil staining his fingers, worn in enough that no matter how he scrubs, it doesn't ever seem to budge. "How's the season going?"

"Yeah, fine. I'm thinking that if it works for you, we could commit to a weekly sort of delivery schedule? We've got plenty of milk this spring, so Drew'll be able to churn out more pretty regularly."

"Sure," Brad says. "All this sun we've been having, you've gotten enough rain?"

"Pretty much." Cooper leans back as the waiter fills their water glasses. "What would you be interested in? Like I said, we've got a lot of ricotta right now, and we can sell it pretty cheap." He should've grabbed that clipboard Drew keeps in the cheese room with his schedule on it. Whit would've remembered it, though fuck it, Cooper's going to nail this sales thing.

"That'd be fine. Didn't realize you'd be sticking around so long this spring. It's great to have you back."

"Drinks?" the waiter asks, his pitcher in one hand.

"Um, the pale ale," Cooper says, nodding toward the bar and the rows of taps. He can barely see the game from here. This place doesn't have Murry's excellent selection of beers, nor nearly as many TVs.

"I'll have the same. You were in Maine all winter, right? How was it?"

"Fine," Cooper says. Brad seems to be waiting for more, though, eyes expectant, and even when a cheer goes up from the bar at what must've been a hell of a hit, his attention doesn't waver. Cooper clears his throat. "Cold. Snowy. Ate some lobster."

Brad leans his forearms on the edge of the table. "Drew must be happy to have you back."

"Well, uh, it's good to be here." That sounded awkward. Quickly, he takes a sip of water. It's not...this is not what he was expecting, Brad leaning across the table like he is. Penny threw him off, and now this just feels weird. Kind of too quiet, back in the corner of the restaurant like this, and all the more so with Brad looking like he'd lean even farther across the table, given the chance.

"You gonna stick around this summer?"

"Just helping out for a bit."

"Oh, bummer, heading out soon?"

Cooper lifts one shoulder in a shrug. "Yeah, I imagine so."

"Nice, just taking it as it comes." Brad grins again.

Cooper gives him a weak smile. He should've dragged Drew along tonight. Had him here while Cooper set up this sales thing. Hell, he might even take Whit and his hard silences over Brad's overeager interest, the halting awkwardness, and Brad gazing at him like he's waiting for something.

Cooper lets out a breath when the waiter comes back with their beers. He leans away from the table so the guy has room to set them down, though Brad doesn't similarly retreat.

"You two know what you want to eat?" the waiter asks.

"Yeah," Cooper says and flips open his menu.

"I probably need another minute," Brad says.

Cooper glances up. The menu's not that big, it's not like there's that much to choose from. And Drew's probably gotten that burn pile going by now. It'd be nice to be back at the farm in time to enjoy the rest of the evening.

He opens his mouth to say that, then shuts it again. He's

not entirely sure he wants Brad to know they're all hanging out later. Which is a real asshole thing to do but...no, it's better that he keeps quiet, rather than have Brad show up and give Drew a look at farm-free life. And besides, Whit's already in a pissy mood, and as fun as it is to annoy him, Cooper gets plenty of Whit's special brand of irritation sharing a room with him.

If Whit's even there. If he's not out with some guy at a restaurant like this one, a conversation sparking up between him and his handsome date who smiles right back at him. Cooper blinks, that image suddenly too sharp.

"Ever think about getting out of farming?"

"Oh. No." Cooper shakes his head quickly enough a lock of hair slips forward from behind his ear, and he has to tuck it back again.

"Think you'll end up owning a place of your own?"

"Seems like a headache of a commitment." He's hungry. He wants to eat and then get going, not do whatever the hell this is. Small talk, in a too-quiet corner of a too-nice restaurant.

"Well, maybe Drew'll end up using you more around the farm. That Whit guy? He found something else, right? Other than being a farmhand? Bartending?"

"Bartending?" Cooper takes a sip of his beer, eyeing the TV over Brad's shoulder. "I mean, he works with Penny over the winter sometimes, when the farm slows down."

"Oh, I thought I saw him at Murry's the other night." Brad shrugs and takes hold of his own beer, though he doesn't drink. Brad's hands look odd, Cooper decides. He's too used to the stain of dirt worked in around nail beds and the odd scratch and scrape from a long, hard day's work. Even Whit, who manages to remember his work gloves most of the time, ends up with banged and bruised knuckles.

"Well, he might've been keeping Penny company. So,

Drew, he's got some cheddar too. I gave you some of it? Good stuff."

"No, I think he was working." Brad shrugs and there's his grin again. His cheeks must get tired, constantly smiling like that. Cooper takes another sip and glances at the TV. He's not going to argue. No, that'd be too much like having Whit with him. Though that might be more fun than slogging through what's apparently an evening of unending questions.

The cheddar, Cooper wants to start again, but Brad leans farther over the table.

"So wait, Whit's still just working for Drew, then?"

"It's Whit. He's allergic to change."

"That's a lot of years to just be a farmhand."

"Whit? He's not a farmhand."

"Oh," Brad says. "Okay."

"He's managing the entire farm side of the operation this year, while Drew does the cheese. He's like single-handedly running the place." *Straight into the ground,* Cooper could add just to be a jerk about it, but it's not as fun without Whit here to aim that jab at.

"I didn't think he was, I don't know, that into it?"

Cooper sets his beer down. "What?"

"Just, that Drew seems to always be cutting his hours. Seems like Whit's hard to work with, maybe?" Brad holds his hands up. "I don't know, don't listen to me, it's just the impression I got."

"Whit's running half that farm. Yeah, maybe he was helping Penny out if you saw him at the bar. He works hard. He's that type of guy."

You're zero fun, Cooper's said to Whit more than once. Meant it too, and he knows full well if Whit's not out on a date or with his parents, that means he's helping Drew out burning the brush pile. He might be there right now, throwing all the heavier branches on himself so Drew doesn't have to do it.

"Plus," Cooper says, "we've got our herd of pigs and all the laying hens. Drew's been talking about getting sheep for ages, and the way things are going, Whit'd be in charge of them, too, if that ever happens."

Which it won't if the farm doesn't make it. Cooper frowns down into his beer.

Though if they produced cheese on a bigger scale, they'd have that much more whey, and they could feed it to the pigs. That'd help cut costs and keep their grain bill down. Or, given Whit's passion for spending all damn day fencing, they could start grazing the pigs on pasture. With what the pigs root up in the fields, the whey, and any extra milk, they wouldn't need much grain at all. "Huh."

"Yeah?"

"Nothing, sorry." Cooper clears his throat.

They could follow up the pigs with the laying hens, let them scratch through the turned-up pastures, then run over it with the plow, reseed it, and have a healthier stand of grass for the next time the cows grazed, and get all that effort back in even more milk. Which plenty of other farms do, but it'd be a big change for Drew's place. Possible, though. And the farm would be so much better for it.

He looks up and Brad's watching him.

"Um, what're you thinking to eat?" Cooper asks, picking up his menu again and studying it even as his mind keeps churning.

Later, Cooper drums his fingers on the table as he figures out his half of the bill. See, he should text Penny, maybe take a picture for her of the two piles of cash.

Though, then Brad puts another one of his smiles on and taps his fingers close to Cooper's. "There's that new brewery. We should go sometime."

"Brewery?" Cooper wants to pull his hand back, but it seems too abrupt. Brad's just being friendly. There's no need for Cooper to be as twitchy as he's feeling. It's just Penny and her teasing getting to him, he doesn't need to actually let it bother him.

"Could be fun."

It won't be, Cooper's sure, though he's hardly about to say it out loud. "Yeah, I bet Drew would like it, too. I'll mention it to him."

"Oh." Brad sits back in his chair and his hand slips away. "Yeah, if you want him to come too."

In his truck, Cooper fiddles with his phone. *You were as wrong as Whit usually is,* he starts to type to Penny, only to delete it and drop his phone into the cupholder. This dinner being just a casual bite to eat doesn't explain the uncomfortable itch between Cooper's shoulder blades. He'll tell her about it in person. Or just ignore the whole thing altogether. Whit'll just be pissy as all hell again if Cooper brings up Brad.

Which...which he doesn't really want to do in the first place. The evening's over and Cooper's ready enough to put it behind him. Through the window, Cooper sees the hazards on Brad's car flash as it unlocks. Cooper shifts into reverse and pulls out, his headlights cutting across the hand Brad raises in a wave goodbye.

CHAPTER EIGHT

A PILLAR of smoke rises above the back hedgerow, gray against the darkening blue of the sky and the tower of clouds outlined in gold as the sun slips behind them.

"Coop!" Drew shouts as Cooper ducks through the fence.

In the quickly gathering dusk, Cooper can make out empty beer bottles scattered over the top of a cooler, an open bag of marshmallows, and the detritus of hot dogs and buns. A plate smeared with ketchup catches the light of the fire.

Drew cups the hand not holding a beer bottle around his mouth. "Coop! Tell Penny that hot dogs are better than burgers!"

"Burger lovers for life," Cooper says, and Penny bumps her fist into his. "Sorry, Drew."

"I don't know why you guys are so down on dogs. Whit! Whit, tell them."

Whit just picks up a branch lying at his feet and tosses it on the fire. Ah, so he is here. Cooper keeps his eyes on the fire, not the play of the light across Whit's white shirt.

"Are you sure that branch is big enough?" Cooper asks. "'Cause you could just drag a tree over."

"But like, dogs. Hot dogs." Drew waves his beer around, and it must be mostly empty, or Penny'd be sopping wet with the circle he draws in the air. "Fucking superb."

He's tipsy, clearly. And happier than he's looked in so goddamn long now. Cooper opens a beer and drains half of it in a long swallow. Hanging out together is what he misses about Drew's farm when he's off working somewhere else: Drew laughing, Penny grinning up at him, and even Whit filling out the rest of the scene.

Cooper rolls his sore shoulder and takes another swallow. The storms might still be lingering over the edge of the trees with no break in the day's humidity yet, but the air's sweet with the smell of fresh grass and the promise of rain to come, and the beer's cold and Drew's smiling.

Penny tucks her leg under herself and sets her bottle on her knee. "How was dinner?"

Cooper shrugs and takes another sip, ignoring the pointedness of how she's looking at him. "Fine."

"Fine?"

Whit adjusts the hem of his T-shirt where it hangs loose over the waist of his jeans. "There's more wood that we should get," he says.

"We can toss it on with the tractor tomorrow," Cooper says. The air smells so good, that snap of woodsmoke in the humid stick of summer, and he just wants to linger here, basking in a truly gorgeous evening. "It'll still be smoldering."

"Not if it finally rains." Whit plucks at his shirt again, his eyes on the hedgerow. Cooper snags another bottle of beer and twists it open.

"Here." When Whit doesn't take it, Cooper pushes it into his hand. "Relax for once. It won't kill you."

114

Hard worker, hadn't he just been telling Brad? He tries not to watch as Whit wipes a drop of water from the bottle onto his pants.

"Dinner was fine." Cooper drops down next to Penny on the cooler. "Drew, that ricotta. Sold and sold."

"My man!" Drew shouts, arms pumping again.

Penny leans her shoulder into Cooper's arm, her weight warm and a little sweaty in the swamp of the evening's air. "Just fine?"

"Fine, full stop." He bounces his shoulder against hers, jostling her lightly.

Whit sets his beer on the cooler on Penny's other side. "I'm going to get some more wood."

"God, Whit, chill." Cooper reaches over Penny's lap and tips Whit's bottle to the side, examining the level of beer in it. "Though I guess that's a start."

"That's his third," Penny whispers loudly.

"No."

"Yes." She bounces their shoulders together again.

"Whit, having fun? Is he okay? Are we learning tonight that drunk Whit hauls wood from hedgerows?" Cooper cups a hand around his mouth and shouts, "Lightweight!"

Above the trees, lightning flashes. Whit pretends not to hear him, just bends down and gathers another armful of wood. It gets his T-shirt dirty, a smudge of wet bark across his stomach and on the inside of his forearm, which he brushes off. The fire sends up a shower of sparks when Whit tosses the wood on the pile and a red and orange glow plays over his arms as he wipes his hands clean on the thighs of his jeans. Cooper sets the rim of the bottle against his lip and swallows hard.

"How was it?" Penny asks. "Really?"

"Oh." Cooper clears his throat. Firelight always does funny things, dancing across Whit like that. Cooper shouldn't be looking to begin with. "Yeah. Cheese. Brad's going to give selling it a try."

"So fucking awesome." Drew tips his bottle up for a long drink. "Thank you, my dude."

"I suffered through a night of hanging out with Brad for you." Cooper lifts his own bottle in a salute. "True friendship. Talk about sacrifice."

Whit scrapes his thumbnail over his palm. Cooper wonders if he's even listening, over there on the edge of the group, probably still pissed that Cooper made a damn sale. Well, whatever. Let him linger just outside the fire's glow if he wants to.

"I still can't believe Brad quit farming," Cooper says. "To just throw in the towel like that and move on."

"Still looking for a farmer boy, Coop?" Drew claps his hand over his chest. "I like to think it's aching, unrequited pining for yours truly."

Cooper throws a marshmallow at him. "You're too fucking goofy, Drew. Nice try."

"Me?" Drew grabs the marshmallow from the ground and pops it into his mouth. "Look at you."

"Did you eat that?" Cooper asks. "You ate that, didn't you?"

"Tastes better off the ground, you weird little—" Drew circles the fire and grabs Cooper in a headlock, scrubbing his fist across Cooper's head to mess up his hair.

"Get off, you giant—"

"Your bony-ass elbow, Coop, you—"

"If you fucking think about spilling that beer on me, Andrew, I swear to—"

"You're going to light yourselves on fire." Whit's voice is as calm and deep as ever. Trapped in Drew's headlock, Cooper can see Whit still working his nail into his palm, but there's a curve to his lips that isn't normally there, like he'd almost smile given another half of a beer.

"Well, Whit, wouldn't you like it if we did?" Cooper asks.

"All that extra work," Whit says, watching Drew. "I don't think so."

Drew wrestles him halfway off the cooler, and Cooper lets him, twisting for another look at Whit. That smile on Whit's face—he seems happy. Huh. Happy that Drew's happy. That's...sweet.

And, that's enough staring at him, cause now Whit's looking back. Catching his eye and Cooper feels his cheeks flush.

Quickly, he shoves Drew. And he might be shorter than Drew, but he's stronger, dammit, and he gets his shoulder against Drew's waist and stands, lifting Drew clear off his feet. "I'm gonna leave you in the hayloft. Make you sleep with Socks."

"Sadie!" Drew hollers toward the house, and he must've had plenty to drink, too, 'cause the only fight in him is smacking at Cooper's back. "Sadie, come save me!"

"Make me a s'more, Andrew." Cooper dumps Drew in a pile on the ground at Penny's feet. "A good one. No burning the marshmallow."

"You're working for me. I'm your boss these days," Drew says from his back, like a giant, drunk turtle.

Penny leans down and gently pats the top of his head. "And landlord. You're very impressive, and we take you very seriously. I want a s'more too. With extra chocolate, please."

But Drew just sits up enough to slump against the cooler, and Penny keeps running her fingers through his hair. Cooper leans down and snags his beer. He holds out Whit's, too, which Whit only glances at.

"Gonna bring the rest of the forest over here?" Cooper wags the bottle toward him.

"A tree fell last winter. I was just cleaning up the brush along the fence line."

"Oh my God, I wasn't really asking." Cooper walks over to Whit, shoves the beer into his hand, and steers him back around toward the glow of the fire. "Try enjoying yourself. See if having fun really is as bad as you seem to think it is."

Whit's stiff. And his skin's warm. It must be the heat from the fire, though there's a tackiness of sweat, too, the back of his neck dewy, and a shine to his collarbone where his shirt is tugged down a little.

Cooper lets him go and steps back. Whit smells like sweat and woodsmoke, and Cooper wants to press his nose into his neck and inhale.

And Whit's eyes are on him again, the fire reflecting in that steady dark-brown gaze. Another night rises in Cooper's mind, a memory of a fire with the crackle of sparks in the darkness, coolers, and beers, and—

Cooper licks at his lips and backs away from Whit.

"S'gonna rain," Drew mumbles, arching into Penny's fingers running through his hair. "S'gonna rain, and there's a giant hole in my house." Drew tips his head back against the edge of the cooler, his eyes closing. The firelight plays over his cheeks, burnishing his hair and beard copper. Penny rubs her thumb gently over his forehead. Cooper looks away from the sight. She touches Drew differently than she does Cooper or even Whit. There's something intentional about it. Slower and more careful.

Too much beer, he decides, frowning at his bottle, though it hardly seems to blame for how empty he feels, especially after pacing himself at dinner so he could drive home.

"There's a small hole in the attic wall that's covered with a tarp," Whit says. "It'll be fine."

Cooper leans down and pats at Drew's cheek with the flat of his palm, shaking his own head like he can clear it. "Go back to being happy."

"The house is just really well ventilated." Penny scratches her nails over the back of Drew's neck. "Breezy. I like it."

Drew tosses his arm across her thigh and lays his forehead on her knee. "I love you guys," he says.

It's a good thing Cooper didn't invite Brad. The four of them here, an evening in the fields they spend their days working in, the comforting weight of company so well-worn...it fits. Cooper crouches next to the fire, heat blasting over his face, and pushes a marshmallow onto a stick. It's home here, as much as anywhere is.

The rain starts in a gentle patter on Cooper's shoulders before thunder cracks the sky. A fat splash falls on the back of his hand, next to a smear of chocolate. Drops darken Whit's shirt. One lands right on Whit's cheek, glittering against his skin. And then the blowing coolness of fresh air they've been waiting for comes, heralded in on the storm. Above them, thunder claps with a peal that jumps under Cooper's skin and the world flashes white.

"Drew," Penny says. "Let's go."

"Yeah." Drew tips his face up. Another clap. Across the fields, a cow calls out. "Yeah, we should go."

Cooper jogs after Penny with the bag of marshmallows tucked under his arm, juggling a handful of empty bottles. He breaks into a run when the rain really starts pelting. It smacks his back and soaks into his hair, and the thighs of his pants grow stiff with water. Down, across the field, through the barway in the far stone wall, up the road to the barnyard, where puddles are already forming.

Cooper splashes through them, the other three just behind him, and the breaths he pulls in are full of raindrops.

"Shit," Cooper says, fingers slippery wet on the doorknob and clumsy from drinking. Inside the farmhouse, Sadie barks back at the thunder, and with a sing of a lightning bolt and a pop, the power goes out. Cooper blinks in the dark.

Drew pushes the door and it creaks open and there's Sadie, all scratching paws and wet, humid breath as she shakes and shivers against the cluster of their knees, all of them caught together in the doorway. Whit turns on his phone for light. A hand on Cooper's back pushes him forward. He goes, and it was Whit touching him, Whit's hand dropping back to his side.

"Sadie, you're all right." Penny pats at her knees. "C'mere, hon."

Cooper fumbles his way toward the sink, catching the back of a kitchen chair with his thigh. He dumps the bottles down in a clatter of glass.

"It's just a storm," Cooper says as Sadie jogs over to him. "You're okay, it's a storm, it's going to be fine."

Sadie circles, panting, then lopes back to Penny again, tongue hanging nearly to the floor and her nails clicking on the wood.

"Anyone grab the hot dogs?" Drew asks.

"How are you still hungry?" Penny asks.

"Sadie." Cooper whistles and she totters over and noses his hand. "Sadie, you're a good girl. It's just a storm."

"I'll take her. She can sleep with me." Drew hooks a hand under her collar, his cheeks a ruddy red in the white light of Whit's phone.

"I'm going to bed," Whit says.

Cooper follows Whit's light up the creaking stairs and

120

down the hall. Behind him, Penny swears once, then tugs her door closed.

"I don't think sprinting and beer are a match made in heaven." Cooper presses their door shut, touching his fingers to his stomach through his soaked shirt. "That, or I'm getting old."

"Or both," Whit says.

"I'm rolling my eyes at you right now."

"I'm sure you are."

Cooper tosses his shirt onto the floor with a wet smack and feels for the closest piece of furniture. The dresser, it must be, and there's the foot of Whit's bed.

A body bumps into his. Wet and humid and too close, damp cotton against Cooper's bare chest and arm.

"Sorry," Whit says, his footsteps sounding awkward, as if he's stumbling.

"S'fine." Cooper pushes his foot out across the floor, feeling for his bed.

It's farther away than he'd expected, despite how he and Whit trip over each other half the time, stuck too close to each other in this room of theirs.

Cooper sits down on the edge of Whit's bed, and his eyes adjust slowly, until he can see Whit standing by the window. Cooper's cheeks buzz with all that beer he drank and he leans forward, resting his elbows on his knees, but it pulls at the muscle in his back. With a groan, he reaches around to try to rub his shoulder.

"Are you okay?" Whit asks.

He jerks his hand back. "Oh. Yeah. Fine."

"That's my bed."

Cooper just scoots backward, his shoulders against the wall and his feet tossed out in front. He wiggles a little to further muss Whit's quilt. "Do you ever think about the fact that you're a grown-ass adult, sleeping in a twin bed?"

"Takes one to know one."

"Ouch. Hard truth to hear, man."

Whit's still hovering over there across the room, though when he catches Cooper looking, he turns around and tugs at the window, trying to close it. Lightning flashes and lights him up, his arms raised, and the shape of his body is dark against the panes of glass.

"Gotta jiggle it," Cooper says.

"I know. It's my window."

"Just sayin'."

One of these days, Cooper's going to find that Whit's packed his duffle bag and set a route in Cooper's phone that ends at the Pacific Ocean. Well, joke's on Whit, 'cause there's probably no getting all the hay Cooper's tracked into the bedroom out of the floorboard cracks. Cooper'll be a permanent stone in Whit's shoe, no matter when he finally leaves.

Which isn't a bad idea, actually. Tossing a pebble into Whit's work boots and seeing if he even notices, or just works all day with a sore foot, stubbornly powering through.

Probably the latter, just like he's pulling mulishly at the window without the little shimmy it needs to slide closed.

"Give it a shake. I'm serious."

"Are you seeing Brad again?"

"I never *saw* him to begin with," Cooper says. "Penny's got all sorts of ideas in her head."

"She doesn't."

"Does," Cooper says, mostly to see if Whit'll take the bait and throw *doesn't* across the room again.

Though of course, Whit just tugs at the window again. The flash from a lightning bolt falls across the sharp angle of his jaw and the wet curls of his hair.

"You had dinner with him," Whit says.

"I have dinner with you, Penny, and Drew all the damn

time. I know it's your handwriting that added me to the dinner rotation on the whiteboard, and then you go complaining I always make pizza. I hope you know I make it special, just for you, 'cause I love the dulcet tones of your complaints."

"You're not interested in him?"

"What does it even matter?" Cooper tries to reach his sore shoulder again, but the most he can do is poke vaguely near that knot. "Is this revenge for me asking about your booming love life? Nosing into my own?"

"Forget it."

Why'd you ask, then? Cooper nearly starts, but he just keeps rubbing his shoulder instead. Whit can do what he likes. Always does. Hell, Whit's probably enjoying watching the parade of Cooper floundering with his own life like he does year after year, when Whit's got some sort of plan hammered out that he's thought about and thought about again, until it shines perfect and bright, just the way Whit likes it, same old after same old.

"Need some dating advice from yours truly?" Cooper scoots over and sets his shoulder against the footboard, trying to rub at that sore spot. There, that feels better, something firm working into the tightness of his muscles. He's getting Whit's quilt wet, though. Well, Cooper can toss over his own blanket and trade for the night, if it gets Whit all worked up.

"When was the last time you even dated anyone?" Whit asks.

Cooper snorts. "Probably more recently than you, Don Juan."

That'd be a hilarious sight, Whit trying to date someone. He'd have to be nice to them, and Cooper would pay to see that. Though he can't even picture it, someone here hanging out with Whit after work and on the weekends.

The idea turns his stomach. *It'd ruin it*, is the first thing he thinks. Drew, and Penny, and Cooper, and Whit, this *thing* the four of them have going here. A fifth person hanging around...no, Cooper doesn't like that idea at all.

"That's not an answer," Whit says.

"Don't want to make you feel bad. Coworker solidarity. Gotta share a room with you and all."

"Did you leave a trail of broken hearts in Vermont?"

"I told you. I was in Maine all winter."

Whit stares out the window, apparently back to ignoring him. Cooper drops his chin to his chest and keeps working at his shoulder. Whatever, Whit probably knows the truth without Cooper needing to let his cheeks heat and stammer it out, that he hasn't dated anyone, not seriously at least, in...a long time. He refuses to let *ever* rise to his mind. It's too embarrassing to admit. *Pathetic*, he thinks in the privacy of his own thoughts, though he's reminded all over again that one-off nights with men he doesn't know has turned out to be a lonely way to go through life.

Cooper clears his throat. "Just waiting for someone to sweep me off my feet."

That sounds right. Flippant. Casual. Like he doesn't care. And he doesn't—maybe he had once, all those years ago, when he'd spun out those dreams about Whit being the one. Drew's handsome friend who sailed into Cooper's life like a rough-handed, broad-shouldered fantasy. But how dumb to nurse that idea, to give it more than a passing thought. He knew it then and knows it now, that to Whit he's a pest and always will be. Embarrassing, to even entertain the idea.

"What're you doing to my bed?" Whit asks as Cooper shifts farther back against the footboard.

"What's it look like I'm doing?"

"You look ridiculous."

"Don't care." Cooper finally gets the angle of the wood perfectly against that sore spot and groans.

"Stop." It only takes Whit two steps to walk over with those long legs of his. "Seriously."

"I am serious." Cooper lets his eyes close.

Whit grabs him. Steers Cooper right around too, settling next to him on the mattress, a thigh pressed to Cooper's. Whit's thumb digs in under Cooper's shoulder blade.

Cooper groans again, without quite meaning to. "What're you doing?" he asks.

Whit rubs harder, and Cooper tightens his lips over the sound that wants to come out.

"You clearly need a lesson on how to throw hay bales," Whit says, "if this is what you do to yourself."

"Oh, ow, God, don't stop." Cooper tips his head forward. "Do it yourself if you know so much."

"I do. Often. And hardly have these problems."

"Asshole."

"And you want to get even bigger bales."

"Size matters, baby." *Stop*, Cooper should say, but he just presses back into Whit's touch. Hands on him, after what's been a...a really, really long time. Warm and strong, and Whit clearly knows what he's doing. Cooper shifts his hips, wanting to squirm backward into that touch.

Enough, he tries to tell himself. He should stand up, get some distance, get some air. His skin feels too tight. And Whit's far too close to him, the space between their bodies warm and humid. Outside, rain splatters against the windowpane.

When Whit rubs circles into the knot in his back, Cooper's voice comes out low. "The nights you do take off," he asks, "are you really leaving the farm to go see some guy?"

"Actually never."

"Tell the truth."

"I am," Whit says and turns Cooper around and kisses him.

Cooper jerks in surprise, but Whit's hand on his shoulder holds him in place, their lips still pressed together. Whit smells like woodsmoke and rain and the day's sweat. Whit's nose brushes Cooper's cheek and his lips tug softly at Cooper's and then press again, firm and slow. Cooper blinks, forgetting to close his eyes. Whit slowly pulls back and Cooper sucks in a breath, too sharp in the quiet of the room.

"Is this okay?" Whit's murmur rings loud in Cooper's ears, a deep rumble to the words like the peal of thunder that rolls through his chest.

No, Cooper should say. Whit's hands fit to his shoulders, his touch heavy, and something about it so certain. Cooper should stand up, find his own bed and lay down, his back to the room and his skin cooling. His head spins and his cheeks prickle. Cooper's sure he's bright red in the dark. He should take his pants off. Slide out of his jeans and let Whit touch him.

"Yeah, it's okay," Cooper says and Whit kisses him again, tips Cooper down onto the mattress and climbs over him, a warm, damp weight. Whit's wet shirt brushes Cooper's bare stomach, and Whit's thighs trap Cooper's hips, his knees pressing tight to the outside of Cooper's waist.

Cooper's thought about hooking up with Whit for years. Imagined it, touched himself thinking of it. And this isn't what he pictured. Not at all. The way Whit is kissing him is far too gentle, too unhurried. Whit's hands are soft, and he's moving slower than he should for a beer-soaked, tipsy mistake. Whit leans over Cooper on his elbows, apparently content to just kiss, lying on top of him, Cooper's head pressed back into Whit's pillow, Whit's lips tugging hot and wet at Cooper's, the slip of a slick tongue into his mouth.

Cooper grabs the back of Whit's neck, fingers digging into corded muscle and soft hair. He kisses Whit back, crosses his ankle over Whit's calf, and arches up against his body. A quicker pace and less thinking sounds better, and already there's heat building between them, the beginning of a spark in how their hips move. But even when Cooper plucks at Whit's T-shirt, Whit still doesn't shift to move things along.

Which is frustrating as all hell. But what was Cooper expecting, that this would be easy? Half-naked when Whit's not, and Cooper's had to look at those damn muscles for weeks—for *years*—and now there's thin, wet cotton between his hands and that skin. Of fucking course.

"C'mon," he says and jerks at Whit's shirt again.

Whit stares down at him with dark eyes, his breath coming fast. "Aren't you going to tell me to stop?"

"Wasn't going to."

"This is a bad idea."

"Damn right it is." Cooper fishes down the back of Whit's jeans, under the elastic of his boxers, and there's smooth, hot skin there, the flex of muscle that Cooper squeezes. It's a tight fit, his knuckles pressed against wet, stiff denim, and there's no give to Whit's belt, the tension cutting over Cooper's wrist. He squeezes again, and his fingers bite into Whit's firm ass. "So let's not, like, fucking talk about it."

Nor take it at a snail's pace. They've got to milk the cows in the morning, and apparently, Whit's turning out to be the type to spend all evening kissing his neck. He tugs at Whit's belt. And finally, Whit reaches between them, his hand bumping Cooper's stomach, then the strain eases with the pop of a button and the jangle of his belt buckle.

Oh, hell yeah.

Years of wanting and waiting and not another minute has to go by. This time when Cooper plucks at wet cotton, Whit sits up to strip his shirt off. He's gorgeous. Cooper touches the ridge of his pec, the bumps of the muscles in his stomach, dimly lit with the shadows that filter through the rain battering the window. Whit's ribs flex on his breath. All that running is clear on his body. And lifting bales of hay, bags of seed, wrestling with the plow—his shoulders are bigger than they look in a shirt, and fuck yeah, this is happening right fucking now.

Blood sings through Cooper's cock. He yanks at his own belt, shimmying out of his pants and kicking them to the floor. He twists onto his side, reaching for Whit's nightstand, though before he can get the drawer open, Whit bats his hand away.

Fine, though that just makes Cooper want to peek in there more. But he can do that later, 'cause Whit's got a bottle of lube out and a condom, and Cooper hurries to kick his boxers off and turn onto his stomach.

"What're you doing?" Whit asks.

"Oh, did you—" Cooper looks back over his shoulder. "Dunno, kinda just figured, but you wanna switch?"

Whit just looks down at him. Lightning flashes, shadowing corded muscles over the ladder of his ribs. And he's still wearing his pants? Dammit.

"I'll just suck your dick, if you'd rather," Cooper says.

"No, I—yes, but."

"But what?" Cooper wiggles his ass. Then he sighs. Okay, maybe Whit's not into this. Or he's actually starting to think this through. Or Cooper's doing this wrong, somehow. That'd figure.

Or...

"Have you done this before?" Cooper asks.

Whit flicks open the bottle of lube. "I've done this before."

"Dude, just asking, no judgment."

"Stop talking."

"First time for everything."

"I'm serious."

"If you haven't, you can tell me, 'cause—"

A slick finger touches him. Cooper arches into it, letting out a breath. Oh, fuck yeah, this is what he wants. And Whit's just as slow as he was with the kissing, like no matter how Cooper squirms, he's going to take his damn time.

And he does, kneeling between Cooper's thighs, his finger exploring as Cooper focuses on relaxing. Whit's good at this. Gentle when he needs to be, and then he presses his other hand to the small of Cooper's back, holding him still when he crooks his finger and Cooper jerks.

"Fuck." He bites at the back of his wrist.

"Yeah?"

"Okay, maybe you've done this." Cooper tries to get his knees under him, but Whit's hand on his back is too firm. And it feels pretty good to be held down like this, no matter that he wants to rock back into the finger inside of him.

"Like that?" Whit asks, still moving too damn slow.

"You can put your dick in there, you know."

"I know."

Though Whit's still holding out on him, because he just circles gently with his finger against Cooper's prostate. The pace is too leisurely to do more than bring a harshness to Cooper's breath over the pleasure it sparks and to make him grind his hips down into the mattress, his cock hard.

When Whit finally stops, Cooper whimpers into Whit's quilt. There's the rustle of pants being stripped off and the crinkle of the condom wrapper. Cooper scrambles to his knees, and the bed squeaks as Whit kneels behind him.

"Do you want to turn over?" Whit asks.

Cooper braces a hand on the wall above the headboard, his other fisted in the quilt beneath him. "I want you to fucking fuck me."

Whit sighs, loud enough to hear it. And Cooper waits for the argument, but instead there's the touch of Whit's fingers again, slick and a little cold, and then a bigger, blunter pressure.

Cooper reaches for his own cock, but the headboard smacks into the wall as Whit pushes into him.

"Put your hand back," Whit says.

"No." Cooper wants to touch himself. He flexes back on Whit, his big hands framing Cooper's waist and the pressure almost deep enough, almost as hard as Cooper wants it. "C'mon, would you?"

Whit grabs Cooper's wrist and sets his palm flat against the wall, above the headboard where it was. He thrusts and Cooper grunts. Whit's hand slides firmly down Cooper's forearm, tracing over the flex of muscle there as Cooper tries to dig his fingers into the wall, straining with the push of Whit into him. Whit's hand slips away, and then there it is, wrapped around Cooper's cock with a squeeze, and oh fuck *yeah*, Whit's done this before.

Cooper's breath catches. It's a relief. It's torture. It's horribly wonderful. That sure, firm grip on his cock, the twist of Whit's hand, the way his fingers tighten with each slow tug. The circle of Whit's grip draws down and back up, and pleasure sings through Cooper's gut. Another firm, unhurried thrust into him, Whit's thighs pressed to the back of his own, Whit's hips flush with Cooper's ass. Cooper lets his head bow down, his mouth open, and his arm flexing to take the slow momentum of the way they move together.

Whit's knee shifts forward and he thrusts, and Cooper's head jerks up, a hot spike stabbing the base of his spine.

That's it, that's the right angle. And Whit apparently knows it, 'cause he does it again. Fuck yeah, that's good. So goddamn fucking good. A hand closes over Cooper's shoulder, yanking him back onto Whit's hard cock.

More, he wants to say, but his cheeks burn at the thought. He wriggles instead, trying to shift Whit's cock inside of himself.

"Stop." Whit's hips flex slowly.

Cooper's toes curl. "You," Cooper gets out. He's panting. "Are so annoying."

Whit's fingers wrap into Cooper's hair, press him face-down into the pillow, and Whit starts up a short, hard rhythm. Heat flares through Cooper's stomach. It should hurt, that grip Whit has on him, but instead he likes it. He really, really likes it. The sensation lights up his thighs until they shake and centers on Whit's hand tugging on his cock, the spot he hits with each firm thrust. Pleasure hooks deep in Cooper's gut, and maybe Whit had a point about going slow, because now Cooper doesn't want this to end, wants to live his life right here, Whit's cock inside of him.

No, not yet, Cooper thinks, but that hot, deep pleasure flashes outward in a sharp rush, and Cooper's fingers scrabble against the quilt as he comes. He bites at his lip and groans as his blood hums and his pulse pounds. Cooper puffs into the pillow, his eyes screwed shut. His skin's tingling. Whit's fingers dig into his hair, and then Whit grunts once, softly, his hips shoving fast and hard into Cooper, and then stilling as Whit lets out a slow, long breath and his body relaxes.

Get up, Cooper tells himself. But he just slips down onto his stomach, his knees giving out when Whit shifts back. Cooper licks at his lips. Slowly, Whit pulls out of him. Cooper's fingers cramp, knotted too tightly in the quilt.

This bed is too small for both of them, no matter how

Whit nestles between Cooper's back and the wall. A breeze shifts through the window, tickling over Cooper's slick skin, the freshness cooling him. His breath slowly evens. Whit's warm, pressed up behind Cooper, breathing hard but otherwise silent.

A floorboard creaks in the hallway. Cooper jerks, tensing.

"Goddammit," Drew mutters, his voice pitched low enough he's got to be talking to himself. Cooper squeezes his eyes shut, and behind him, that looseness is gone from the press of Whit's body.

The door to Cooper's old room creaks open. *The rain,* he thinks. It's still battering wet slaps against the windowpane and probably dampening the wall his bed used to be set against.

Cooper clears his throat, sounding loud enough to him that Drew can certainly hear it. All of it. What he and Whit just did. *He can't hear,* Cooper tells himself. Not over the pounding rain. Still, he gets a knee under himself and then a foot on the floor, peeling himself upright. There's his wet shirt, and beyond it, the edge of his mattress, his blankets still a mess from when he kicked them off that morning. How goddamn long ago that seems now, waking up at Whit's alarm to drag himself up for a day of fencing.

Cooper wants to run the sink in the bathroom to clean himself off. Or shower. Wash away the churn of uncertainty, and the deeper, surer guilt of a bad mistake with steaming hot water. Though the idea of Drew sticking his head in here, asking what's up at this hour...and he can't shower, anyway, not with the power off and the well pump therefore not working. Cooper wipes himself off with his shirt the best he can and tosses it into the corner.

Whit's bed shifts, the blankets rustling. Cooper swallows. He should say something. Or Whit should. Instead,

Cooper lays down on his mattress and rests his arm across his eyes. It's enough to block out the flash of lightning, though it hardly does anything at all to drown out the sound of Whit breathing just there across the room, and Cooper's own racing pulse, only beginning to slow.

CHAPTER NINE

Morning dawns with the glare of the summer sun, and it shines straight into Cooper's headache. The room's empty. And Whit's bed is neatly made. Cooper shoves his hand into his hair, his head throbbing. He feels gross, all sticky and tacky and sweaty after a night of tossing and turning.

And he feels good. Amazingly, bone-deep good.

Well, that happened. Years of imagining, wishing, wondering and...yeah. He and Whit fucked.

And it was *awesome*.

It's even better that Whit's cleared the hell out of here so Cooper can sprawl on his tiny bed and spend a long, happy moment basking with no Whit staring at him.

Though fucking hell. He's going to have to see Whit today...and Penny and Drew—with the knowledge that he so recently, so deliciously had Whit buried deep inside him. *Awkward*, he thinks and kicks at the blankets twisted over his feet. *Let's do it again*, crosses his mind next, immediately on the heels of the deep churn of reservation in his stomach. But, no. Once was a bad idea. Twice is real fucking stupid.

Cooper tests the lights and with the power apparently back on, he showers slowly, touching his waist where Whit had gripped. But there's no mark to trace over, no sign at all beyond the deep looseness in his muscles and the zip in his stomach. Which is good. One drunk tumble and back to normal.

When he turns off the shower, he listens for any sounds above the drip of water down the drain, straining to hear a shuffle from their room that would mean he's not alone. *Very normal*, he tries to think and makes his way downstairs carefully, like the steps will creak any less if he moves slowly. In the kitchen, the screen door rattles and his heart jumps. But it's just the wind banging the frame against the wood.

Cooper rubs his palm over his face. What the fuck did he think would happen if he and Whit ever finally fell into bed together? That Whit would just magically disappear into the ether, and they wouldn't have to dance through an uncomfortable morning shuffle? Maybe Cooper can just slip away and live in the woods for the next forever, and he'll never have to see Whit again. Or deal with every memory that flashes through his mind, of soft lips and a wet mouth and the strong touch of long fingers.

"Coop!" someone shouts from the barn. Cooper jumps.

Though it's just Drew's voice, thank God.

But still, even the sound of his own name makes Cooper want to duck behind the counter, where Sadie's sprawled in a beam of sunshine. Maybe he can hide out with her for the day and not have to actually see Whit, let alone talk to him. Drew and Penny won't mind stepping over a Cooper lump as he holes up next to the fridge, his face buried in Sadie's fur, daydreaming over memories that by all rights he shouldn't have.

Cause he...he regrets what they did. Or it was the best idea ever. He rubs at his forehead, where that twinge of too much beer is sitting like a dull, pulsing reminder that without that last drink and the blunders it brought, this morning might be like any other.

"Cooper!" Drew shouts again.

Cooper winces and opens the door to call back, "Yeah?"

"Where are the fucking cows?"

"The what?" Cooper shouts. God, his head hurts.

"The cows! Where are they?" Drew yells from the open door of the barn.

"In their pasture where we put them yesterday?" Cooper squints against the sunlight. "The barn? I don't fucking know."

Drew jogs toward him, his boots splashing through the puddles dotting the barnyard and his eyes too wide. "They're not there."

"They're not where?" Cooper presses his palm to his forehead. "How the hell are you so goddamn chipper? You drank more than I did."

"They got out. All of them, the calves too." Drew sounds out of breath. Looks it too, skidding to a stop in front of Cooper. His cheeks are flushed and his hair's a mess from the wind kicking off the fields. "They're not in the back field. They must've got out."

"Okay."

"Cooper." Drew grabs his shoulders. "Where the fuck are they?"

"We'll...we'll find them." Cooper nods once, to prove his point. He's a little nauseous. And he still feels good. Heavy with the release of a really good fuck. If he focuses, he can remember the feel of Whit inside of him.

"The storm spooked them, fuck, this is so much worse than just the heifers going for a damn stroll," Drew says, holding Cooper way too tight. "Where's Whit? We need Whit."

Cooper jerks backward. "I don't know. Why would I know?"

"Running, he's probably out running." Drew turns in a circle like the cows might be just behind him. "We're—I'm going to take the truck. No, you should, or I can drive to the—"

"Drew." Cooper closes the door and steers Drew back around again. "Go get a bucket of grain. And take a deep breath. They probably just went down the road again."

"Grain," Drew says, nodding quickly. He grabs Cooper's arm again and shouts, "Whit!"

"Ow, fuck." Cooper rubs at his ear with the heel of his hand.

He has to shield his eyes against the sun to see Whit. His stomach turns over. He needs another couple minutes to figure out this new dynamic between them. Or a day. A day would be good. A week, even. Maybe he'll just jump in his truck, drive to Oregon, and come back in half a dozen years, and by then, he'll know how to handle the fact that he finally, wonderfully, deliciously fucked Whit.

But Drew drags him forward. "Whit! The cows are out."

Whit slows from his run into a walk. "I know."

"Hey," Cooper says. His face feels too warm. The sun, he wants to believe.

"You know?" Drew jerks Cooper another step toward Whit. "Did you see them?"

"Their tracks." Whit wipes his palm over his forehead. His shirt is already clinging to his arms and shoulders, and the day hasn't really started to heat up yet. Those shorts on him look...they look good. Even the mud splattered up his muscled, tanned calves catches Cooper's eye.

Cooper turns and frowns at the fields, where the cows

should be. He's not going to stare at Whit. He's going to be utterly, perfectly normal.

"I'll get the truck." Drew finally lets go of Cooper's arm. "No, I'll get the grain. You guys get the truck. Whit, take Coop."

"No," Cooper says.

"No?" Drew asks.

Cooper wipes his hands on his thighs. "I'm driving, I meant."

"You're not," Whit says.

Cooper's closer to the farm truck, and it's only a handful of steps to beat Whit there. *Go with Drew*, he silently pleads, though Whit's footsteps follow him.

"They went into the woods past Caroline's fields." Whit slips into the passenger seat and Cooper can smell his skin, the sweat from his run. It takes Cooper two tries to fit the key in the ignition.

He looks over his shoulder to back the truck up, even though he hardly needs to. He's been reversing this truck out of this barnyard since before he was old enough to legally drive, but it keeps him from staring at that bead of sweat rolling down Whit's neck.

"You forget to shut their damn gate?" Cooper asks.

Is this what he's going to be like anytime he's around Whit from now on? Trying not to stare at Whit's hands out of the corners of his eyes, strong and broad, with veins running down the back and his skin the deep brown of summer? Anyone else and it'd be just another morning. Hell, anyone else, and Cooper would reach right over there and lay his hand on the muscles cording Whit's thigh, feeling up sweaty shorts and warm skin.

"You were there yesterday, it was shut," Whit says.

"I just know what a fan you are of gates."

"And this isn't possibly because of your cattle guards?"

Cattle stops, Cooper thinks a beat too late. He presses his lips tight. *You were there too*, he could snap back. Or something better, more heated. And witty. Though, there's just the headache and now the heat of embarrassment flushing through him where those words should be. Of course, Whit can be as normal as he ever is. It was just a quick fuck for him. It's Cooper who fell into an awful crush all those years ago, and here it is, rearing its ugly head and rising through him again today, fumbling his words and setting his heart pounding.

Whit clears his throat. "Sorry."

"Huh?"

"I'm sure it was the storm." Whit stares out the window, his cheek turned so that Cooper can't see more of his face.

"Oh." He'd kissed Whit, right on that mouth of his. "Okay."

Whit points toward the side of the road, and sure enough, muddy hoofprints line the way down to Caroline's land. Cooper parks the truck and follows Whit until the tracks duck into the woods. Cooper breaks into a slow jog, pushing aside tree branches and wading into the trees.

"C'mon, girls," he shouts. But it never does work to call for the herd, unless he's got a bucket of grain to shake and rattle, enticing them away from their adventure and the snacks they've found for themselves.

Behind him, Whit's not even out of breath, though where mud falls in clumps from Cooper's boots, it works into the mesh of Whit's running shoes. Whit must be cold, with sweat dampening his shirt and now the coolness of the forest, all bare legs and arms.

No, Cooper can't even begin to handle that sight. Of all times, now is when he most needs to be irritated with Whit, not mooning over his pecs. He needs that old, familiar barrier of annoyance between them, built of all the reasons Cooper shouldn't ever really, actually like him.

"Any other sign of them?" Cooper walks quickly to try to leave Whit behind him. "For fuck's sake, where the hell are they?"

"They're cows, they can't have gone far."

Argumentative, Cooper thinks. That's reason one.

"All it takes is one hungry coyote," Cooper says.

"Well, we'll make sure to tell them that next time."

That acerbic dryness to Whit's tone. How quickly he dismisses Cooper. *Be more of a dick, help me out here*, he thinks.

"Why don't you just ask them to stay put, if you're going to go talking to them?" Cooper asks, squinting into the forest so he doesn't have to look over at Whit. "I'll check over there."

"Come with me," Whit says.

Bossy as fuck, Cooper adds to his list. "I'm sorry, what?"

"Come with me, let's go together. It'll be easier if we do find them."

Cooper can't stop staring at Whit's mouth. It was so soft last night. And he knows how to use it too. Cooper turns back to the patch of woods in front of him and stares at it as hard as he can. "Is that a good idea?"

"I wouldn't have suggested it if it wasn't."

Too sure of himself. Can't take input. Hates all of my plans. Cooper presses his lips together. Some time apart might settle the blush he's sure is still sitting on his cheeks. Though dammit, Whit's not wrong. One of them versus a herd of cows isn't exactly a recipe for success.

Fuck him. Treating this morning like any other, when Cooper's falling all over himself after a single drunk fumble.

He draws his shoulders up. "Got an idea of where to start?"

Sticks snap under Whit's running shoes as he heads into the woods. He probably doesn't even really know where he's going. Still, Cooper follows him, pushing branches away from his face and sidestepping a puddle when Whit does. *Like a fucking magnet*, Cooper thinks as he trails after that broad back, as if he were in high school all over again, drawn toward Whit and fighting that damn pull every step of the way.

The only difference is that back then, he wasn't old enough to drink himself into a mistake, so chasing cows wasn't this nauseous, hungover drudgery, singed through with too many memories.

So much simpler back then, all of it. *Before that kiss*, he thinks, and his cheeks flush hot. But no, the farm really was more manageable. A smaller herd, when they made their escape and led everyone on a merry chase. And this patch of woods was thinner when Cooper started spending summers here, less overgrown. In the years since, the understory has filled in, and soon enough, it'll be an impenetrable tangle of saplings and fallen logs that Whit and Cooper can't move through at all.

If...if there're even cows around here to chase when that happens.

Cooper rubs his fingers over his mouth. His throat hurts. He clears it, though the sound makes Whit turn around.

"Do you see them?"

"Oh," Cooper says. "Oh, no, I just..."

"Their tracks?"

"I can't imagine Drew really selling this place."

"What?"

"Never mind." That wasn't what he'd meant to say. He didn't mean to say anything at all. Silence was working so well for them, and now Whit's staring as Cooper starts toward another patch of woods.

"Did Drew say something?" Whit asks.

"No, you were the one who told me—I have no idea, why would I know?"

"Because you have this whole plan."

"The cheese? And Brad, I'm trying, but—"

"Oh God, Brad." Whit touches his forehead. "Right. Brad."

"What the hell do you not like about Brad?"

"I thought you said you were going to fix the farm."

"I'm trying, I just—" *Can't hold a real conversation,* Cooper adds to his list. Ass. "I was just thinking about it. And Drew. But whatever, forget it."

Though Cooper can't. He chews over the thought like a cow with a mouthful of cud, his headache churning it back around again as he tries to brush it away.

"Are you nervous?" Cooper finally asks.

"That we're never going to find the cows?"

"That Drew really will sell the farm?"

Whit runs his fingers into his hair and stares off towards the woods as if the stand of trees will cough up a wayward cow. "It's fucking terrifying. I'd have to find something new. And it'd suck. I'm not, whatever, like you. I'd be awful at it."

You absolutely would be, Cooper nearly says. He can't even imagine it, Whit stumbling through job applications and trying to fit his life into a new shape. A new place to live, new roommates, unless wherever he ends up, he and Penny keep living together.

Which hurts to think about, Drew off on his own, if he didn't follow the two of them. Drew and Sadie in some sort of sad, gray apartment, only a tiny square of grass for Sadie to laze around on, and the fridge full of pre-sliced cheese from the grocery store.

Awful. All of it.

"We'll find the cows. They're probably already on their way back," Cooper says. "And you'd be fine. You have your parents nearby, it's not like it'd even be that far to move."

But Whit just squints past Cooper's shoulder, his eyes fixed on the forest.

Cooper turns to look, but there's no herd of cows staring back at them, just the trees, leaves, and roots.

"They're moving," Whit says, his voice flat.

"The...cows?"

"My folks. Don't tell Drew."

"Don't tell Drew what?"

"Travis, Caroline's son, helped sell their house back in March. They're closing soon and are moving to an apartment in Albany. And Drew doesn't...I haven't told him."

"Okay." Cooper lifts his hat off his head and scratches his hair. Already, it's damp with sweat. "Are they okay?"

"They're old."

"Most parents are."

"They're older than—they had me when they were already old." Whit pulls in a breath. "And this winter was a lot for them."

"Why haven't you told Drew?"

"He'd..." Whit shakes his head. "You're right, the cows probably circled back at some point. We should check the south fields."

"He'd what?"

"I just—I don't want him to worry."

"Why would he worry?"

Whit pushes on into the woods. "He won't. Never mind."

Cooper catches a branch that snaps backward with his forearm and chases after Whit. "You're a real shitty liar."

"I really think we should check the fields."

"How about you tell me, and then I won't have to get it out of Penny?" Cooper pushes through a shrubby bush and then pauses, his head cocked. "Are you—are you moving, too?"

"It's none of your business," Whit says, his voice hard, a coolness to it that replaces whatever soft trace of vulnerability had crept in.

"You are? You're moving to Albany too? Even if the farm's okay, you're—"

"No."

"But you're thinking about it?"

"I told you I'm not."

"But—"

"Stop," Whit says.

Stop, Whit had said last night and crossed to the bed.

"Fine." Cooper hops over a log and keeps his head down, fighting the blood that rushes to his face. Rushes other places too, though at least he's in jeans, not running shorts like Whit is.

This'll pass. Cooper's anxiety, stirred up on a morning hangover, a search for the cows, and played out in spiraling ideas of the farm's murky future. Whit's peevishness will blow over, too. Eventually. They'll go back to some sort of normal, all of this forgotten. They did once, tacit in their silent agreement to never mention kissing all those years ago. Cooper blows out a long sigh.

A snort echoes it. A tree branch waves slowly, stirred by the wind. Leaves rustle too, and there's the wet huff of another puff of breath.

A calf emerges from the woods, legs stained with mud, head held up, nose outstretched.

"Buttercup," Cooper says. "Hey there, buddy."

Whit points. "There's the rest of them too."

"You weren't in the fields, were you?" Cooper gives

Buttercup's neck a scratch. "You're right here, we found you. No, I don't have a bottle for you. You gotta wait till you're back at the barn, after staging your jailbreak."

Buttercup still nuzzles all over the pockets of Cooper's pants, leaving wet marks from his nose and a swipe of saliva across his thigh when he licks him.

"Gross." Cooper shoves at Buttercup's head, though it's far more of a pat than any real attempt to push him away. He taps out a text to Drew on his phone with his other hand, scratching behind Buttercup's ears. "Keep your tongue to yourself, my man."

It's a quiet wait. And a long one. More cows gather around, one rubbing her back against a sapling until it threatens to bend under her enthusiasm, and two others gently sniffing Whit as if wondering what he's doing out here, too, and how he happened across their patch of woods. The entire herd finally wanders into sight, chewing their cud and unconcerned with the wrench they've thrown in the farm's morning. They blink sleepy brown eyes and shuffle to let the sun filtering through the trees warm their backs.

"I asked Drew for some extra hours," Whit says.

Cooper turns, his hand hovering above Buttercup's nose. "You did?"

"My folks sold their house for less than they wanted to and—and my dad had skin cancer. Last year."

"Holy shit, is he okay?"

"He's fine now, but the cost of the medical bills—"

"Drew said no? To you working more?"

Whit's eyes cut toward him. "He didn't have the money. He was already paying you."

"Oh." Cooper shifts his weight to his other foot. "I'm sorry."

Whit pushes his mouth to the side. "It's not your fault."

"Still, I—" *Don't think of you as a person who might ever actually care about something* was probably going to be the end of that sentence. "Um, that sucks, though."

"I don't want to bring it up with Drew again, he's got enough on his plate. I'll figure out how to help my parents at the end of the season."

Buttercup nudges his nose into Cooper's hand for another pat.

Slowly, Cooper scratches beneath his chin, still staring at Whit. "You've been working with Penny. Picking up shifts at Murry's."

"She told you?"

"Brad said—um, I heard, is all."

"Right." There's that curtness again.

Cooper licks at his lips. "You don't like Brad."

"No, I don't."

"Well, at least it's never a mystery with you," Cooper says to lighten the heaviness on Whit's face. Whit's expression stays stony, though, and the joke falls flat. Still, Cooper tries again. "I always know exactly what you think of me too, that's for sure."

Whit huffs out a breath, the corners of his eyes creasing as he stares off toward the road. His mouth works once, a flex at the corner of his jaw, though he doesn't say anything, and eventually the rumble of Drew's Jeep cuts through the woods.

The cows' ears prick at the rattle of grain in a bucket as Drew shakes it on the other side of the tree line. With a slow lope that turns into a jog, they're off, the entire herd crashing through the underbrush and weaving through trees to try to get a nibble of that grain.

"Stampede," Cooper mutters, following after the stragglers.

The more dominant cows in the herd, the ladies who

are the oldest and Drew's worked with the longest, will make it to Drew first to get their handful of grain, and that'll be enough to lead them back to the barn with a promise of more where that came from.

Sure enough, Drew's Jeep sits empty, idling at the edge of the road when Cooper and Whit reach it. The driver's door hangs open and hoof tracks lead down the road that curves eventually into the barnyard. Drew'll be jogging ahead of them now, calling to the girls to follow him. Cooper lifts himself into the driver's seat as Whit pops open the passenger door and climbs in after him.

Halfway back, Cooper pulls to the side of the road and parks in the same spot where they'd parked the truck yesterday. "It wasn't the cattle stop," Cooper says as he jumps out of the Jeep.

There's a tree down, the fence snapped under it, and perfect impressions of hooves in the mud on either side. It'll be good firewood at least, a huge oak that apparently couldn't stand up to last night's storm. Cooper pushes at the strands of the barbed wire fence with the toe of his boot and sighs. One more thing to fix. Don't tell Drew indeed, or hell if they ever get him back to that loose, good mood he was in last night.

"We can get this restrung," Whit says, pulling at a length of wire like he can just brush the branches and shattered trunk aside.

"We've got to get the tree cleaned up first," Cooper says.

Whit's arm flexes as he tugs and Cooper tries to ignore the heat that immediately builds under his skin. He needs to find some chill. Just like Whit, who's breezily moving on as if last night wasn't a big deal at all.

It was just sex.

With Whit.

Holy hell, Cooper thinks, his memories of warm, smooth

skin mixing with the thread of disbelief still coursing through him.

"We can string the fence over it." Whit sets his foot on top of the trunk, his running shoes still coated with mud. Trust Whit to want to work on this, rather than return to the house to change first, or even get the farm truck back from Caroline's. "It's low enough, it'll work, and we can leave the chainsawing until the winter."

"Yeah, that'll be great until a cow decides to just walk up the trunk, step over your brilliant fencing plan, and stage an escape, round two."

"They're not acrobats." Whit kneels to pick up the line of broken fence.

"Oh, right, they're cows." Cooper lifts his eyes to the sky. He hates how Whit's shirt stretches over his back and hates all the more that he wants to stare at it, those dips of muscle the damp fabric clings to. "You know so much about farming, it's incredible."

Whit doesn't bother to say anything, which is typical, his ping-ponging between acerbic cuts and steely silence. Whit stares at the fence, not even looking at Cooper, just studying his lap. Of course he is, 'cause he's not spending all morning mooning over Cooper, because he's able to keep his head on straight, which is only more irritating.

"Any other stupendous insights to share with the group?" Cooper asks.

"My, ah, hand."

Cooper jogs over to him. Whit cups his right hand in the palm of his left, holding both away from his body. There's blood on the grass. And a drop of it on Whit's shorts, right in the middle of his thigh. It coats his fingers too, shiny and pulsing slowly from a gash across the base of his thumb.

"Whit," Cooper breathes.

"I'm fine." Whit presses with his other thumb, but the blood just seeps around the pressure, the cut too wide.

"You're not." Cooper tugs at his arm. There's the shine of blood on a rough, sharp spur of barbed wire next to Whit's knee. "C'mon."

Cooper grabs a wad of napkins in a cupholder in the Jeep. They're none too clean, but neither is the hand Whit's still pressing to the cut. Cooper cups Whit's wrist and nudges his thumb to the side, pressing hard. "Hurts?" Cooper asks.

"I'm fine."

"Yeah, you look fine." Cooper shouldn't be holding him like that. He steps backward, and slowly, Whit curls his own fingers over the wad of napkin. "Try to keep your blood inside you, where it belongs."

"If only you'd told me earlier." Whit wipes his other palm on his shorts, then reaches for the tangle of fencing.

"What the hell?" Cooper grabs his wrist again. Whit's so strong, tugging back against Cooper's grip. Cooper learned that well enough last night, didn't he? His cheeks flush hot. "Are you trying to cut both hands, you genius?"

"How are we going to put the cows back out if this isn't fixed?"

"The only thing you're doing is going to the hospital."

"I'm fixing the fence, my hand is fine."

"We have, I don't know, dozens of other acres of pastures the cows can eat."

"We're about to cut it for hay."

"You need stitches. A lot of them. And a workers comp form and a little thing called a tetanus booster. Get in the Jeep."

Whit inhales through his nose. "I'm fine."

"Oh Lord, I'm not going to argue with you."

Whit's eyebrow arches. "That would certainly be a first."

"Funny." Cooper gives Whit a push away from the fence.

Cooper parks next to the barn and a cow pokes her head out like she's been there the whole time. Drew touches her nose as he waves, then stops short at the sight of Whit's bloody hands held out the window of the Jeep.

"Is this what happens when I leave you two alone for too long?" Drew asks.

No, what happens is the clusterfuck of last night, Cooper doesn't say. He jumps down from the driver's seat. "Whit was just being a dummy. I'm surprised he even has any fingers left. I gotta grab my wallet, I'll take him to the hospital."

"I don't need to go to the hospital," Whit says.

"Just gonna wipe it off on Drew's seats?" Cooper asks.

"Oh wow," Drew says, leaning through the open driver's door to get a look at Whit's hand. "Now, that's a cut. Coop, I'll take him."

"I got it, you have all that cheese."

"It's no problem." Drew glances over his shoulder and catches Cooper's eye with a smile and a lift of his eyebrows. *You don't want to be stuck with Whit all day,* Drew might as well say out loud.

Right. Of course. It'd be a disaster, sitting with Whit in a hospital waiting room for hours on end.

The Jeep rattles off down the driveway in a crunch of gravel. Already, Drew and Whit are talking, silhouetted against the day's sunshine. Drew laughs and the Jeep turns a corner, and Cooper works his finger into a hole at the bottom of his pocket. From her spot in front of the barn, Sadie yawns and stretches all four legs, then slumps back onto her side. *The cows,* he reminds himself, and he doesn't watch the last glimpse of the Jeep or the billow of dust kicked up behind it.

I wanted to go with him. Cooper sucks in a breath as he spins the handle of the spigot, like it'll force the water to flow any faster. The thought is as crystal clear as the sun streaming in the barn, dust motes playing in the beams like flecks of gold. He wants to spend today with Whit. All that time to hang out together, to chat and squabble, and drink in the lines of Whit's profile. To hear more about Whit's parents and chase after that soft note in his voice. That tenderness, that sweetness Whit normally holds at bay around Cooper. It's always been there, just reserved for Penny and Drew, but now that Cooper's gotten a taste—

Fuck. Fuck, fuck, fuck. He stares at the bright square of barnyard through the barn door and pulls a breath in, a burn of want rushing up his throat. Idle hours with nothing much to talk about, no distractions, no work, no Penny and Drew. Just him and Whit and hours to while away—no. No, no, no.

Fucking absurd. It would be a drag to be stuck with Whit today, not any sort of fun. *Absolutely awful to spend time with,* he should add as the final point to his list, but he feels for that edge of irritation and all that sits there is the soft ache he knew so well in high school. It comes crashing through him now, a soft, delicate part of himself echoing that fragile tenor in Whit's voice.

Oh *no*. He doesn't want to fucking *care*.

Water dribbles over his boots. From the trough. The cows' trough is overflowing right onto his feet. He pulls the hose back and fumbles to turn it off.

In the kitchen, he scalds his tongue on too-hot coffee.

"You okay?" Penny asks, tying her hair up in a bun as she comes in. "What was all the shouting?"

"Cows got out."

"Again?" Penny pours herself a cup of coffee, picks up Cooper's toast, and bites off the corner.

He shoves the plate toward her. "You can have it."

"I was just messing with you."

"I'm not hungry."

You okay with the farm? Drew texts as Cooper sips at his coffee. *Seems like this'll take a while.*

Cooper could text back that he's leaving. That it's suddenly, unexpectedly time for him to clear out for Oregon. Be gone by the time Drew and Whit get back. Or at least have his truck packed and go through a quick, cursory round of goodbyes. Except he doesn't really want to leave. Not with that aching pull Whit yields over him.

He tips his head back and blows out a breath. His crush on Whit sits at the edges of his thoughts, all consuming.

"Coop?" Penny asks.

"Yeah, I'm good."

I'm on it, he texts back to Drew.

He's got to get his shit together. And then he'll leave. *See?* he would ask if Whit were there. He can make a goddamn plan. One that doesn't involve hanging out with Whit all day and giving into that infatuation that's plagued him for so long.

Fuck, he thinks again. He swallows another drink of coffee, like the heat will help cauterize the soreness of the scab that gets picked away every time he spends too long with Whit, when he shouldn't have messed with that old wound in the first place.

CHAPTER TEN

As the sun peaks overhead, Cooper sets the gate against the fence post and closes it behind the last of the cows. "It's always greener, isn't it, ladies?" There's no Whit there to roll his eyes. *Good*, Cooper makes himself think. "At least you all appreciate my jokes."

Something hits his arm. A nose. A cow's nose. Buttercup butts him again, and finding Cooper lacking a bottle, prances away, tail swishing and head tossed up in the sunshine. Ah, the carefree life of a calf on a sunny summer day. Maybe Cooper should sprawl out on a pillow of grass and spend the rest of his early afternoon lolling in the sunshine, blowing on puffy dandelions, and braiding a flower crown of clover for Sadie.

Though, no, because Whit's got this place set up like he's determined to drive Cooper nuts, even when he's off getting his hand stitched up. It took the entire damn morning and now into what should be lunch to feed the herd, get them milked, and send them back out on pasture. That's just like Whit, to struggle through chores every day instead of ever looking around at the farm and having the bright idea that what he's been doing all these years isn't actually working. Cooper squeezes his eyes shut and tries to focus on that old, well-worn annoyance. He's still got the pigs to feed. *Scoops and buckets*, he hears in Whit's voice, and he grinds the heels of his hands into his eyes, groaning out loud at how his stomach pitches at the memory of Whit's low, deep voice.

And fuck. There's the man himself, standing across the field. And probably sure as shit examining the cattle stop that's replaced the gate. Working up an argument too, 'cause that'd be just like Whit.

Yet more reasons for Cooper to not cartwheel down the waiting chasm of his embarrassing crush.

"Thought you were at the hospital," Cooper calls when he's close enough.

The bandage on the hand Whit holds up is a bright white, wrapped from his knuckles down to his wrist. "Just got back."

"Too bad, guess they didn't get my request in time to suture up your mouth too."

"Shame."

Cooper's struck by the sudden urge to laugh. He presses his jaw tight, because then, where would he be, but stupidly grinning in the middle of the damn field?

"I moved the hens," Cooper says, "so don't go sounding the alarm if you spot them in a different field."

There, that's better. Business as usual, his voice cool, like he doesn't want to rest his hand on Whit's arm and bat his fucking eyelashes at him.

"You didn't need to do that."

"Yeah, but you were gone, so who was going to stop me? Next up, I'm finally fixing that damn spigot."

"You've been here weeks. I can't believe it's taken you so long to begin with."

"Just working up to the good stuff."

"Why are you always trying to change things?" Whit asks.

You were the one who went and changed everything, Cooper wants to blurt out. How fucking embarrassing, when Whit's talking about the farm, and Cooper wants to hold hands and stroll on a goddamn beach together.

Cooper lifts his hat and rifles his fingers through his sweaty hair. Focus. Farming. Whit's an asshole. Cooper got over him once and he can do it again.

"There's a lot of good ideas out there," he says. "I know this will shock you, but other farms do things differently."

"Obviously."

"No, not obviously. I mean, yes but—you should see some of the places I've worked. Drew would have to hire five people to do the amount of work one person could finish in a day. Automatic waterers, fencing systems that don't have you trekking all over the farm, the pigs out in the pastures, and the chickens after them, and with all that manure, the grass regrows so quick that the cows can be back on it much sooner."

Whit sniffs. "I know what rotational grazing is."

"Then give it a try. It's absurd that I only just got the cows back onto pasture, and it's almost midafternoon. And I know, I know, I show up here and want everything to be different, I have stupid ideas, I don't know anything, etcetera, etcetera, but really, Whit."

"I wasn't going to say that."

"Yeah, sure you weren't. But we should try it, okay? Drew's farm—it should be the best one there is, you know?"

"We," Whit echoes. He kicks at the cattle stop. When grass starts to grow over the edges of the grate, it won't look as out of place as now, newly installed and too obvious with shiny metal that'll be dinged and scratched soon enough.

Argue with me, Cooper wants to snap, but Whit stares

off across the field without levying at Cooper the heated, exhaustive list of how and why everything he's said is wrong.

Whit nudges the cattle stop again, like he's decided it's crooked, that Cooper fucked up installing it, along with everything else he's ever failed at, and that tiny kick is enough to shift it into a neater position.

"It's a couple weeks until I can get my stitches out," Whit says.

"So?"

"So, I guess I gotta ask Penny to help out with chores and all, 'cause I'm not sure how much I'll be able to get done."

"I'm literally standing right in front of you."

"You'd stick around that long?"

"If I can change everything that you've set up over the past couple years and make you watch me do it, then hell yeah."

"You sound delighted."

"You have no idea."

"What about seeing your parents?" Whit asks.

"They can come visit," Cooper says. *They won't*, he thinks before he can begin to imagine it, all the excitement of a trip that's never happened and never will. "And I'm serious. What the hell is your plan, Whit, if Drew needs to make more money around here? Clone yourself so if the herd grows, there'll be two of you to slog around this place with double the cows?"

"Apparently I don't need a plan with all your great ideas," Whit says.

There it is, that perfect coolness to Whit's tone. Though it's not nearly as fun when Whit looks as tired as he does now, like Drew's defeat wore off on him, too.

Cooper wants to fucking hug Whit. Walk forward, wrap him up in his arms, and promise it'll all be okay.

Wow, he needs to get his head on straight. Or maybe he needs a time machine, needs to go back and warn himself that this is where he'll end up if he gives in to the searching softness of Whit's kisses. A rewind button for his entire fucking life.

"Look, I was thinking about this the other night," Cooper says. *Thinking about it while at dinner with Brad,* he doesn't say, just points across the pasture so he's not looking at Whit any longer. Cooper wonders if Whit can see the mark he left on his throat, the one Cooper had touched a finger to as he'd brushed his teeth that morning. "Let's leave that fence up so we can move the pigs onto this field."

"The pigs are in the woods," Whit says.

"Right, which is why I said move them. As in, relocate. Point A to point B."

Whit's lips purse. Cooper hates that he knows how soft they are. "They'll make a mess of the pasture."

"Well, that's just rude. Don't let them hear you say that."

"They're pigs."

"They'll kick up the grass a bit, but if we move them quick behind the cows, it won't be that bad." *Focus,* he tells himself. Talking about farming is good. Easy. He can do this. "It's going to cut down on how long fencing takes each day."

"It doesn't take that long."

"Whit, it'd be a better use of your time to watch paint dry. Or actually try training the squirrel army."

Whit squints across the field. "You really want to put the pigs out on this? To graze?"

"No, to play croquet." *Keep it normal,* Cooper thinks.

"Yes, to graze, you goddamn genius. It's gonna cut down on the grain bill. And I want to figure out how to give the pigs whey to eat out here in the field, too. A whey way, if you will. More milk, more pork, more money, less work."

"A whey way," Whit murmurs, his mouth pursing.

It's too much to look at Whit, at the shadows of his cheekbones in the brightness of the afternoon light, the cast of stubble on his face. He didn't shave this morning, Cooper's suddenly sure. That must be a first for Whit. Cooper points at the corner of the field, trying to keep himself staring at the stone wall that leads along the edge of the forest and not at Whit, who's close enough to touch.

"We can put a water tank up at the top of the hill," Cooper says. "We'll lay out a couple hundred feet of piping and set out a bigger trough, save all that time schlepping water around. We also need to get a lane set up."

"Now you're building roads?"

"Just a path for the cows to use to get back to the barn for milking so you don't have to chase them across the fields."

"They know the way," Whit says.

"Well, if you set it up right and put the gate on a timer, you could have the herd walk themselves to the barn every morning and evening without you needing to go out there. They can even put themselves back out on pasture. You could be getting something else done in the meantime. May I suggest the spigot?"

"What about when it rains? They won't want to leave the barn."

"Cow umbrellas. And galoshes."

"Cooper."

"Okay, okay, inclement weather, and sure, they need some encouragement, but just 'cause it doesn't work perfectly doesn't mean it's not worth it."

Whit blinks once, slowly, those long lashes fanning over his cheek. "The farm is huge. Setting up a fence along all of the pastures will take a good while."

"Well, invest the time now, and get it back tenfold once you're done."

"If it doesn't work?"

Cooper shrugs. "It will."

Whit's shoulders draw up. "Do you ever worry about anything?"

Yes, that I'm going to embarrass myself confessing my love the next time you glare at one of my wayward socks on your damn floor. "Nah, seems like a waste of time."

Whit holds up his bandaged hand. "I really can't do much to help."

"Look, I know this will surprise you, but I do actually know how to farm."

Whit puts his other hand on his hip. He's going to argue. Insist they go find Drew and get permission. Dig his heels in and simply refuse. Though, instead, he nudges the cattle stop again with his toe and says, "I'll go get the trailer to bring the pigs over."

"Yeah? Really?"

"And I think we have some pipe lying around that we can use for the water, but I'd have to look for it."

"So you think this is a good idea?"

"I didn't say that."

"C'mon, throw me a bone."

"Or, if you want to hunt down the pipe, I can get evening milking set up. I was going to head out to give Penny a hand after that."

Work a shift, Whit doesn't say, though Cooper hears it all the same. Right, because if Cooper's here, Drew certainly can't pay Whit any more. Whit kicks a tuft of grass toward him, one Cooper tore up with the tractor just the other day.

"Now's where you say I'm never that helpful anyway," Whit says.

"What? Oh, yeah, that. Right, get the hell out of here and quit bothering me."

"There you go, what's wrong with you?"

You, Cooper could answer. *Sorry*, sits on his tongue. For taking Whit's extra pay here, for coming in and turning both of their lives upside down. For saying *yes* to the insistence of Whit's hands and mouth, when one of them should've been thinking straight.

"I can't believe you're going to set up milking and then go work at a bar the same day you end up in the hospital," Cooper says instead. "All with stitches in your damn hand. Though maybe you're just staying on brand, mister brainiac over here."

"Glad to hear you think I'm so smart."

"Well, we'll see if you can figure out whether you can get over that cattle stop, or if you're more on Buttercup's intelligence level."

"Are you coming by tonight?" Whit asks, the words quick and his voice quiet.

"What, to Murry's?" Of course Murry's. What else could Whit mean than stopping by the bar? Cooper works his finger into the hole at the bottom of his pocket. "Maybe, just for the fun of messing with you. Order some complicated-as-hell drink and put you to the test."

"You only drink beer."

"With a perfect quarter inch of foam, thank you."

Fencing, setting up those water lines, hell, just dealing with moving the pigs could take all day, and evening too, if Cooper let it. He could. The work would be enough to lose himself in, and Whit wouldn't question it. It's summer. It's what they're all used to, burning the candle at both ends, not carving out evenings to relax with each other. With *Whit*.

"Yeah, sure, I could swing by," Cooper says.

Get yourself together, he tells himself as Whit heads off toward the barn. Cooper leans against the fence post, arms folded. He shakes himself when he realizes he's just been staring at the far stone wall across the field, lichen-covered and so old the stones are weathered and dull against the brightness of the grass.

Later, Cooper stands in front of his gaping duffle bag. *It's Whit*, he tells himself and pulls on a T-shirt, like he even has anything nicer stashed in there. Cooper's been through this, and he isn't going to walk backward into his teenage self and become a blushing, tongue-tied mess.

Whit just wants some company tonight. That's the only reason he asked if Cooper'd be coming by. And Drew's in Albany picking up more rennet, and Penny's at Murry's too, so what the hell else is Cooper going to do? Hang out with the squirrels? Cooper meeting Whit isn't a *thing*. He's just going to the bar, their bar, their very normal bar that all of them always go to.

There's a spot of engine grease on Cooper's T-shirt that long since stained the hem a darker blue. He rubs his thumb over it like it'll budge now, when dozens of washings haven't cleaned the grease from the fabric. Cooper's stomach jumps and he frowns. *Hungry*, he figures, as if he didn't just wolf down a sandwich.

It's a slow evening at Murry's, and Cooper gets his favorite parking spot, though not his favorite barstool. Where he and Drew normally sit, a man and a woman are perched, their fingers entwined and knees knocking together.

Sure enough, there's Whit behind the bar, wiping a pint

glass. He fills it as Cooper walks over, one hand on the tap, veins running down the smooth skin on the inside of his forearm. Whit's pouring brown ale, Cooper's long-standing favorite. Cooper slides onto a stool and takes the glass.

"Did you finish reinventing farming?" Whit bends down to grab the rack of dishes from the dishwasher, his shirt tight enough across his back that Cooper can see the ridges and dips of muscle in his shoulders.

"I gave up when the rooster protested." Cooper holds up his hand. Whit barely glances at the mark there. "C'mon, feel bad for me, I'm injured."

"Get a handful of stitches, and I'll think about it."

"Oh, you barely have a scratch, Mr. I'm-fine-let-me-just-keep-working-all-day." Cooper spins his stool to the side and back again, his forearms on the bar. It's weird to watch Whit put away cocktail glasses, one hand covered in a latex glove over the bulk of the bandage. "Besides, after I'm done with my grand plan, the farm's going to be so laden with Drew's cheese that it'll be pizza night every night, and all my dreams will have come true."

"Good to know you have such lofty goals."

"Saving my favorite farm and eating my weight in cheese, all in a day's work." Cooper lifts his glass toward Whit. Absolutely perfect, really, that image he holds of Drew's farm. His favorite by far, of all the different farms he's ever seen, with its barn and fields and cows, and the house vibrantly full of Whit, Drew, and Penny, and Sadie tottering after them on her old, arthritic legs.

Something sharp pangs through his chest at the thought. *Happy*, he wants to think, but the image he has of them is more like watching through a window, caught outside of that cheerful tableau.

A hand touches Cooper's shoulder and he turns. "Yeah?"

The woman on Drew's favorite stool asks, "You make cheese?"

"Uh, no?"

"Oh." Her head tips, straight brown hair falling over her forehead. "Sorry, I must've misheard."

"The farm I work at makes cheese," he says slowly.

She raises a finger. "Knew it. Brad? He was talking about ordering from you."

Whit half turns from the computer screen he's tapping at, looking over his shoulder at them.

"Brad?" Cooper asks. "Yeah, I was talking to him about selling some."

"I'm Elaina, Brad's boss at the market, and we definitely want to place an order. I was going to tell Brad to give you a call, but you're here now."

"That's great," Cooper says. Behind Elaina, her date counts out money onto the receipt Whit just handed him. "Um, I can—what in particular were you thinking?"

Whit picks up the handful of bills, then tosses a pen and a pad of paper to Cooper.

"Mozzarella, for sure," Elaina says.

"Yeah, absolutely, and we'll have even more soon." Cooper writes *mozzarella*, then pauses, his pen hovering over the paper.

"The end of the week," Whit says.

"Yeah, the end of the week. You want to just try some? A couple pounds?" Or no, Cooper should suggest a bigger order. Oh hell, this is not his strength. Fencing. He's good at fencing, not actually selling cheese.

"We can get you a full batch of it," Whit says, rubbing the cloth along the counter beneath the beer taps.

Cooper nods quickly. "Right, and we can get some ricotta to you quick."

"And some cheddar," Whit says.

"And the cheddar." Cooper nods again. "The next round of Brie is nearly ready too, and the Camembert is, um—"

"Ready next week," Whit says.

"Ready next week," Cooper echoes.

"What's your discount for wholesale orders look like? Any room to maneuver in there?" Elaina asks.

"Yeah, uh." Cooper holds the pen just poised above the paper, like it'll let him know what numbers to write down. He sucks his cheek between his molars. Wholesale discounts. Right. He can...he can figure that out. Quickly. Now. He can figure it out now. *Math*, he thinks desperately and touches the pen to the paper.

"In general," Whit says, "we do fifteen percent, though we could do eighteen if you can commit for the rest of the season." Whit's just pulling that out of his ass, Cooper knows, though hell, if he doesn't sound downright confident. "Twenty, if you pick it up from the farm."

Elaina looks over at Whit, brushing her hair back from her shoulder. "And you are?"

"He's my coworker," Cooper says.

Whit holds out his good hand to shake hers. "I'm the farm manager."

"Co-farm manager," Cooper says.

"Cooper's my assistant," Whit says.

"Well now, that's just a lie." Cooper holds out his own hand too for a handshake. "He works for me, actually."

"Call me." Elaina looks between them. "Somebody, call me."

"I will," Cooper says.

"Tomorrow morning," Whit says. "I'll be in touch."

"Absolutely," Cooper says, and when she leaves, her date in tow, Cooper throws the pen at Whit, smacking him square in the chest. "Asshole."

Whit neatly catches the pen on the rebound. "How're the notes you took?" he asks.

"How clean is that counter? You gonna keep wiping it until you've rubbed a hole straight through to your feet?"

"Buttercup can be your assistant. I think that would work out great," Whit says.

"M'gonna tell Buttercup to escape again just for you."

"It won't be too hard, since he'll be able to just walk over one of your cattle guards."

"Buttercup would never."

Fresh air blows in and Penny steps through the door, smiling and waving to them both. Cooper waves back and says, "Brad's boss was here, I singlehandedly secured a giant sale of cheese."

"Wow, really? Awesome, Coop."

"One part of what he said is actually true," Whit says.

Penny rolls her eyes. "The two of you."

She slips into the kitchen while Whit counts out his tips, turning each bill to face the same way. He probably puts them in order in his wallet, too. Cooper takes the last drink of his beer.

"Have you talked to him today?" Whit asks suddenly.

"Who?"

"Brad."

"Brad?" Cooper shakes his head. "No."

Whit's eyes are on him. Cooper's stomach shivers.

"Good."

"Yeah."

"I'm done here, if you want to head out."

"Right." Cooper sets down his glass. He would've had a second beer, if offered, still well within his ability to drive. But Whit's still looking at him, and heat builds beneath Cooper's skin.

That's...that's a hint. Cooper's not so dense as to miss

the look in Whit's eyes or the tension that sings between them.

They should be arguing about the pig fence, by all rights. Poking at each other over wholesale percentages and who could sell more wheels of Brie. He shouldn't be here at the bar on Whit's invitation, returning the look in Whit's eyes, and certainly not agreeing to leave together. *No*, he should say. He should stay and have a drink as Penny starts her shift, order a plate of greasy fries, and wander back to the farm late enough that the excuse of the hour and early milking can easily staunch the suggestion hanging in the air between them.

Or, he could get laid. With Whit. Again. Oh hell *yeah*.

He jumps off his stool. "Let's go."

In the parking lot, Cooper slips Whit's keys out of his hand. "You're not really driving with a palmful of stitches."

"Got here, didn't I?"

But Whit doesn't argue when Cooper opens the driver's door to Whit's truck and climbs in. He'll have to come back for his own. Drew might ask. Might notice tonight, when he's back from Albany. And if not then, tomorrow morning, he'll see Penny's motorcycle and Whit's truck are parked in the barnyard, but that Cooper's is conspicuously gone.

Drank too much to drive, flat tire, Whit's stubborn refusal to admit his hand is injured—Cooper pokes his tongue into his cheek and lines up his excuses as Whit fumbles with his seatbelt.

Cooper leans across the cab, adjusting the strap so it lies flat against the strong lines of Whit's chest. He can smell his skin, can feel Whit's breath on his cheek. "There." Cooper clicks the buckle closed.

Whit's good hand covers Cooper's over his breastbone. Readjusting what Cooper just arranged.

No, drawing his thumb over the back of Cooper's

fingers, light enough to raise goosebumps on Cooper's skin. Slowly, Cooper pulls his hand away, feeling for the gearshift. He finds cold metal instead and a curl of rough sisal twine. The wrenches, still tied together, set in Whit's cupholder.

"That way I'll know if you steal them again," Whit says.

Cooper grabs the bundle, sticks them beneath his thigh, and turns the key. Whit fishes for them, like he's going to snatch the wrenches back, then just rests his hand on Cooper's leg and keeps it there as they drive back home.

CHAPTER ELEVEN

THE TRUCK FALLS silent as Cooper shuts off the engine. Outside, the air's filled with the chirp of crickets and croaking frogs. The gravel crunches beneath their boots as Cooper and Whit walk toward the house. The hinges squeak on the kitchen door, and Sadie's slow, rhythmic snores come from where she's sprawled on her dog bed, one ear inside out.

Drew's still out for the evening, his Jeep missing from the driveway and his shoes gone from next to the door. Cooper carefully turns Sadie's ear over, gentle so as not to wake her.

It's just him and Whit, then. Nobody else to bear witness to the creak of the stairs as they climb nor the soft snick of their bedroom door as Whit presses it closed behind them.

Whit kisses him open-mouthed and eager, drawing Cooper close, crowding against him in the narrow space between the dresser and door. Cooper presses into him, the pull of Whit's mouth better without the sludge of too much beer dampening his senses. There's just the clear crispness of the spark of Whit's lips tugging at his, how his arm wraps low around Cooper's waist, and his good hand cups Cooper's ribs.

What a delightful mistake to be making. An absolutely wonderfully terrible idea. Whit's fucking gorgeous and Cooper's got the stillness of their room, the emptiness of the house, and the evening ahead to make damn well sure he enjoys it.

And then his phone buzzes in his pocket. It's the longer vibration of a phone call, not the quick hum of a text. Cooper fishes into his pocket, slips his phone out, and tosses it onto the dresser.

"Your phone's ringing," Whit says, hot breath against Cooper's ear.

Cooper tilts his head so Whit can kiss his neck and slips his hands higher under Whit's shirt, tracing over warm, strong muscles. "Ignore it."

But Whit's Whit, so what he ignores is Cooper and reaches for Cooper's phone, tipping it so he can see the screen.

"Oregon's calling." Whit steps back, his lips shiny and wet.

"Oh goddammit." Cooper rubs his face, straightens his shirt, plucks at his pants. He doesn't give a flying fuck about anything other than the bulge against Whit's zipper and the handful of steps to Whit's mattress. Hell, his own mattress, too. He'll sacrifice his sheets to get fucked again, hard and firm, and probably better this time without the tipsiness and the shocked horror of what they're doing.

Cooper slides his hands over the swell of Whit's ass. "I'll call them back."

Whit just waits, holding out the phone.

Cooper sighs. Knowing Whit, what's coming is probably a lecture on professional responsibility. It'd probably get Whit all hot and bothered, too. Cooper takes the phone and slides his thumb across the screen. "Hello?"

"Cooper? This is Cheryl, so glad I caught you. I wanted to talk to you about offering you a position. Is this a good time?"

Cooper shoves his hair back and smooths his shirt. "A great time."

Lying to a new employer, really starting this off right. Cooper slips into the hallway before Whit can levy one of his cool, assessing looks.

"Listen, we'd love to have you. I just have a couple questions first. Well, mostly just one question, about your previous employment."

"Is there a problem with it?"

"It's...thorough."

Cooper edges a couple steps farther down the hallway. "Thorough?"

"You've got a lot of experience, I mean, a lot of jobs over the years. It seems like all of these places you've worked, it's six months at most and nothing even lasting a year, unless I'm reading your résumé wrong."

"No." Cooper glances back at the bedroom door and slips down the hall to Drew's room, empty and the lights off. He presses the door closed and sits on the edge of Drew's bed. "No, that's right."

"Well, clearly, you'd be a great fit here, and we'd love to have someone with so much experience, but come September, would you be off somewhere else, and we'd just be rehiring for your position?"

Cooper's cheeks heat. "No, no," he says, "I really liked the look of your farm and our interview, I—it'd be a good fit, yeah, like you said."

"Well, we'd really be looking for that commitment into the fall, at the very least."

"Fall, right, that makes sense."

"And it's already getting close to summer, so we're aiming to have someone in this position quite soon."

"Soon, yeah." Fuck. He shoves his hair back. "No, yeah, I—actually, speaking of commitment, I'm working at a dairy in New York right now, and so—"

He can hear his own breathing, interrupted finally by Cheryl asking, "So?"

"I think I'd have to let you know about when I could start."

She sighs in a rush of static. "Then I'm not entirely sure I can hold a position for you."

"Yeah. No, of course. But, uh, commitment-wise, well, it's really the exact opposite of just cutting and running from a job—the, well he's sort of the manager here, Whit just got hurt, and it'd be pretty awful to split right now. He can't really work. I wouldn't want to leave them in a tough spot, you know?"

"Well, why don't you give me a call back when you're the one who knows. Bye, Cooper."

"Bye," he murmurs and his phone beeps as she ends the call.

Well, fuck. That was less than ideal. *Commitment*, he hears in Cheryl's voice. He'll...figure something out. Try to hammer out a timeline for the work he wants to get done. Maybe talk to Drew. Though, as soon as he thinks it, he knows he won't.

So there goes his Oregon plan, in all probability. He'll find something else. He always does. *Lots of experience*, he thinks and tries to grin.

"That the boss?" Whit asks when Cooper pushes their door open.

"What the hell are you doing to your bandage?"

"It's annoying."

"Then stop picking at it."

"Thank you for the reference, you mean."

Call her back and tell her I can commit to things, Cooper wants to ask of Whit, but it'd just earn him a cool look. Whit would only too happily call Cheryl back and tell her what he really thinks, thinly veiled hints at Cooper who "knows how to be on time." Fuck. He tosses his phone onto the nightstand.

"She's indescribably happy to have me," he says instead.

"You leaving?"

Yes, he could so easily say. Dial Cheryl's number, apologize, and promise to be out there as quick as could be. "Nah, she gave me a while. I think the universe wants me to enact my grand plans around here." *I think I just lost a job,* more like. He puts on a smile.

"Is that what's going on?"

"Obviously."

Whit lifts his eyes to the ceiling, still adjusting his bandage, and says, "Yeah, obviously."

"What're you doing to that? Stop it."

"It's sore."

"Yeah, 'cause you sliced it open," Cooper says. "That's what happens. Stop messing with it."

"It's nice that you're staying." Whit edges the bandage down a half an inch and flexes his hand. "I mean, for Drew."

"Well, I said I would." Cooper winces as Whit works a finger at the gauze. Fucking *commitment.* "If you're going to pick at it—Jesus, Whit, stop, or I'll send you back to the hospital to get them to do your good hand, too."

"Rewrap it?" Whit grabs a roll of bandage from the top of the dresser. "Not as tight."

"The doctor didn't do it to your specifications? I'm shocked. Absolutely shocked, I tell you."

"Tell it to the cows."

"Sit," Cooper says. "Or I really am going to send you back to the hospital for stitches for your mouth."

And fucking hell, Whit sits. Perches on the edge of Cooper's mattress with his knees far enough apart that Cooper can step between them. Oh shit, that's a nice sight. *Sorry, Cheryl,* he thinks, letting his eyes trace over the shape of muscle in Whit's thighs.

"Did you get this wet?" Whit's wrist is warm, the skin soft as Cooper tips Whit's injured hand side to side.

"I had to shower before I went to the bar."

"Did you even try to hold your hand out of the water? Make any effort at all? Ever heard of a plastic bag and some rubber bands?"

Cooper's mouth is too dry. *Exhaustion,* he'd say if Whit asked, from slogging through Whit's awful farm work all day. Cooper braces for the question like it really might come, a quick draw of an answer so he doesn't have to stumble over words. But Whit's quiet and when Cooper darts a glance at him, Whit's just watching him, his chest rising softly on his breath. His thighs look so nice in his jeans. Strong, with all the slimness and power of his daily runs.

"I had to open the shampoo."

"Oh, of course, your gorgeous curls." Cooper presses his mouth shut and quickly unwraps the bandage, revealing a smaller square of gauze sitting against the heel of Whit's hand. He didn't mean to say that.

"And then it turned out the bottle left in the shower was empty," Whit says.

"I don't know anything about that."

"When there was a new one beneath the sink."

"I think I saw a squirrel in there, must've been them."

It's quiet in here. Whit's voice sounds too loud. Though

Cooper's does too. As quickly as he can, he rewraps Whit's hand, careful over the taped piece of gauze and fumbling to press the adhesive smooth.

"Cooper," Whit says. He sounds too serious. "You're doing a good job."

"What?"

"Your ideas for the farm. I could see it making a big difference around here."

"You're making fun of me," Cooper says.

"I'm not."

"You are, you're not serious."

"Maybe I am," Whit says.

"Oh, stop, now you're just being an ass about it," Cooper says, though he knows there's no heat in his voice. "Is this just Drew telling you to be nice to me?"

"No," Whit says, and that sounds more like him, the curt answer and look he gives Cooper all disgruntled exasperation. "Though trust you to argue about it."

"Me, arguing? Look in a mirror."

"Pot, kettle," Whit says.

And then he reaches up, a finger hooking into the waistband of Cooper's pants. His eyes on Cooper's, he leans forward, brushing Cooper's shirt up and kissing once, softly, at his stomach just above his belt.

"Okay?" Whit asks.

"Yeah." Cooper's voice sounds too low.

Whit looks up at him through the dark fan of his eyelashes, his mouth parted and level with Cooper's zipper. Cooper shifts slightly and Whit's hand tightens on his hip.

Cooper helps with the buckle on his belt, the metal jangling loudly in their quiet room. Oh, that is a fucking sight, Whit tugging at the elastic of Cooper's boxers with his good hand, pulling them down to Cooper's knees.

Whit leans forward and kisses just below Cooper's belly button.

Cooper's stomach jumps. For a moment, he feels too naked. Standing here, with Whit staring. Probably appraising him, though Cooper can't get a good look at his face to tell. The thought is unnerving, imagining being compared to whatever's going through Whit's head.

But then Whit wraps long fingers around his cock, and Cooper jerks at the wet, warm lick of his tongue.

"Fuck," he breathes at the wet slip of the inside of Whit's cheek, the bump of the roof of his mouth. Whit's tongue works, and Cooper bites at his lip, catching a groan and holding it in, until he can't anymore.

Oh God, Whit's good at this. He tugs at Cooper's balls with his good hand and licks at the head of his cock. It's too fucking good. Didn't Cooper used to think about this all the goddamn time, years ago, when he'd been strung up on the thought of Whit and that mouth of his? This is even better, Whit's deft tongue and how fucking into it he looks, his eyes dropping closed. Carefully, Cooper touches his fingers to the top of Whit's head. His dick is in Whit's mouth. *Whit's* mouth. And it's so, so good.

When Whit pulls off of him, cool air hits Cooper's wet skin.

"C'mon," Cooper groans.

The front of Whit's jeans are tented. Whit covers the bulge with his palm and squeezes. Cooper licks at chapped lips.

"Yeah," Cooper says and jerks open the drawer on the nightstand. There's that bottle of lube and a couple condoms. Fucking perfect. He fumbles for them, clumsy with the urgency singing through his blood.

Whit slips out of his clothes and grabs Cooper when Cooper tries to get on his knees again. Even with one hand,

Whit's strong, wrestling Cooper's shirt off and pushing him down on his back. Quickly, Whit kneels over him, spreading Cooper's legs and smoothing his hand up Cooper's thigh, his stomach, and back down to his cock until Cooper's hips jerk.

Cooper wants to look at Whit. He didn't get the chance the other night, and now Whit's kneeling between Cooper's thighs, cock hard against his stomach and the dim light playing over the shape of his muscles. Whit's big. The size of him, his body rising up like that. His cock, too, though that Cooper remembers, buried deep in him and the strain of how it filled him. Cooper lets his knees fall open wider and tears at the condom wrapper.

He has to sit up to put it on Whit, and the angle's awkward, his heels propped against the mattress for balance. Whit helps him roll down the condom, his hand warm and strong over Cooper's. *Hurry up*, Cooper wants to whine. Would, too, if morning wasn't coming for them, and all the harsh brightness of another day working together.

Cooper closes his eyes as Whit's fingers gently probe him, Whit's bandaged hand by Cooper's head, and his weight braced on his elbow. A breath eases over Cooper's cheek, and he turns his face to the side, surprised to find Whit so close. All the more so when Whit kisses him, a finger pressing up and into Cooper, and Whit's tongue parting his lips. Cooper breathes sharply, air caught in his throat, and with it the taste and smell of Whit's skin, clean soap and cotton.

"Okay?" Whit asks.

"S'cold," Cooper mumbles.

Whit's weight shifts over him, their stomachs brushing. "Think you'll survive?"

Cooper rolls his eyes. Whit's gentle with him, both his finger exploring, and then the bigger, thicker press of his cock. Cooper can feel Whit's hand against the back of his thighs, his ass, guiding himself in. Cooper bites at his lip.

"Got to," Cooper says. He sounds like a gasping fish. He squeezes his eyes shut and tries to make himself relax. "Someone needs to keep you in check."

Whit's nose presses against Cooper's cheek. His hips rock and Cooper rests his palms on Whit's waist. It feels crowded like this, Whit's weight over him so close, the air of their room pressing warm against his skin, the narrowness of the twin bed. Whit's hips flex again and Cooper takes a breath as Whit pushes into him.

"Is that what you think you're doing?" Whit's voice is even, but underneath there's a breathiness to it.

His bandaged hand lies next to Cooper's head, his weight on his forearm, and gentle fingers shift through Cooper's hair, brushing it back from his face. Whit thrusts shallowly and Cooper winces, biting at the inside of his cheek. It feels so good. Whit inside of him, but that soft twine of long fingers through his hair too.

"Go slow," Cooper says.

He wants to enjoy this. Blood rushes to his face. That's more embarrassing than begging for rough, thoughtless sex. And isn't this slower pace all the worse for the time it gives Cooper's mind to catch up? The dresser Cooper can see over Whit's shoulder with all the familiarity of their room, how the quilt bunches against Cooper's bare back. A quick, hard fuck would be better. Easier, for sure, and especially so come tomorrow.

Whit sets his mouth against Cooper's jaw and nods. His lips drag down Cooper's chin, across his throat. It's as foreign as having Whit's mouth wrapped around his cock, the fact that he's kissing Cooper's neck so gently, not the harsh bite of teeth that Cooper might've expected.

But Whit's body is something solid to hold on to, his

skin soft and his muscles moving with slow, long thrusts. Cooper lets his eyes close, his head tipping to the side. Whit's mouth finds the underside of his jaw, the line of tendon in his neck. That's nice too, the stubble of Whit's chin scratching over Cooper's skin, the nip and swipe of tongue and teeth.

How long has it been since Cooper's slept with someone he actually knows? *A hell of a nice way to end a long day*, Cooper thinks, relaxing into it. This could be all too easy to get used to. *We shouldn't*, is what he should've said, but instead Cooper grips his bottom lip between his teeth and presses at the small of Whit's back, tracing through the beads of sweat there and warm, tacky skin as Cooper urges him on.

"Yeah?" Whit asks. His tongue works behind Cooper's ear. He shifts his weight to his elbows, space opening between the stick of skin on their chests. "Touch yourself."

"Bossy," Cooper says.

"Not that you listen."

"No." Cooper slides his hand down his stomach to grab himself. It's humid between their bodies and he likes the flex of Whit's abs against the back of his hand. "I don't."

Whit's hips snap into him and Cooper hisses through his teeth.

"Sorry," Whit says, his shoulders trembling.

Whit looks down between them, and Cooper's cock pulses in the grip of his own fingers just from Whit watching. Cooper rubs his thumb through the bead of moisture on the tip of his cock, and there's a soft, unfamiliar sound from the back of Whit's throat.

"Don't you dare fucking come," Cooper says into Whit's ear, all hot breath and his teeth scraping over the lobe. Whit's breath hitches and Cooper bites harder.

Whit's sharp inhale catches and he thrusts hard, his

back tightening. Cooper digs his fingers into the dip of Whit's spine and Whit does it again, his pace picking up.

"Good," Cooper grunts.

Whit probably doesn't need the encouragement. Insufferable, the guy is, and that's without Cooper panting under him. But it's good and Whit's making a little, sharp noise with each thrust, his eyes closed now and his mouth lax.

"You better wait," Cooper says. "I'm so fucking serious."

"I'm sure"—Whit's out of breath and he sucks down air —"I'm sure you—*ah*—are."

Cooper lets his hand speed up. Whit's forehead wrinkles and creases line the corner of his eyes. It hurts a little, that punishing pace Whit sets. And then Whit's bending down and kissing him hard, Cooper's lip caught between their teeth, foreheads knocking, and Whit's gasping into his mouth.

"Fuck," Whit groans and the weight of him shoves Cooper into the mattress, Whit's hips pumping until he stills, shaking.

Cooper lets his eyebrows rise, his mouth touching the corner of Whit's lips as he whispers, "It that the first time you ever swore? The second?"

"Shut up." Whit's back heaves as he tries to catch his breath. Cooper squirms under him, his skin flaring hot with Whit's weight and the sweaty stick of him.

"Was that good?" Cooper asks. He squeezes himself. "I'm accepting compliments."

"Of course you are." Whit kisses him once, wet and messy.

Whit drops the condom on the floor before batting Cooper's hand aside and tugging at Cooper's cock. He sits back on his heels, Cooper's legs still draped over his thighs, and oh, that's a damn nice sight, Whit's skin dewy with sweat, and Cooper's cock in his hand, the head swallowed by Whit's broad palm with each stroke.

Cooper licks at his lips, his hips lifting. "That the best you can do?"

Whit just jerks him all the faster, his forearm flexing. Heat builds in Cooper's stomach, rolling over itself with each pass of Whit's thumb over the tip of his cock, each squeeze of his fingers and twist of his wrist.

"Oh," Cooper breathes, his head tipping back. He scrambles for purchase with his feet, but all he gets is Whit's bandaged hand falling to his knee. Cooper presses his palm down on his own stomach. "Fuck, Whit..."

"Yes?" Whit asks, his voice low and deep and his eyes on Cooper. Oh shit, he's going to just keep watching. Cooper scrambles, his fingers scrabbling at the sheets, pleasure pulsing hot in the base of his spine, gathering in his stomach as he squirms and Whit's eyes are on him, heating his skin with each slow look over Cooper's body.

Cooper comes like that, staring up at Whit, coating Whit's fingers and his own stomach, and air caught deep in his lungs, pleasure like a hot knife cutting through him.

"I'm accepting compliments," Whit says when Cooper's eyes slide shut.

"Oh, I think I hate you."

"As much as you hate getting out a new bottle of shampoo?" Whit asks.

Halfheartedly, skin buzzing and his hands heavy, Cooper tries to smack at Whit.

Whit just catches his hand and presses a kiss to his palm. Whit's still kneeling. And Cooper's bed is in a state. Whit's going to stand up, Cooper's sure. He even lifts Cooper's leg and slings it to the side, but then Whit just settles on his hip, stretching out between Cooper and the wall.

It's nice, not that Cooper'll tell Whit that. All that naked skin pressed up against Cooper's, the warmth of another body next to his. Cooper yawns. He's going to fall asleep like this, even all gross and sticky, unless Whit moves. He doesn't, and Cooper doesn't move either, and when the sun rises, Cooper can't pull the pillow over his head like he wants to 'cause Whit's using the other half of it.

Outside, the rooster crows. They're going to be late for milking. Whit's foot lies crossed over Cooper's ankle, his knee crooked over his thigh. He's sleeping still, by the slow pace of his breath against Cooper's shoulder. *Work*, Cooper thinks again. He needs to shower. But he lies there longer anyway, far longer than he should, studying the sunlight that glows over the ceiling and the warm hand lying over his stomach.

PART 3

JUNE

CHAPTER TWELVE

THE BLAZING heat so early in the morning and swarming bugs aren't Cooper's favorite, but Whit working without his shirt certainly is. Smooth brown skin, shifting muscles as Whit picks up the sledgehammer, and the shine of sun across the beads of sweat dotting his spine—

"Cooper," Whit says.

"Huh?"

"Hold it straight."

Cooper tilts the fence post upright. "I wanna do the hammering this time."

"No, you put them in crooked." Whit holds the hammer away, as if Cooper's going to really lunge for it.

Which...he could do. And be pressed up against that torso, shiny with sweat.

Fencing, he tells himself. "I do not."

"You do." Whit points with his bandaged hand back at the line of fence posts behind them, stretching up the hill and off toward the back fields. "You can literally see which ones I did and which ones you did."

"You always hit my fingers, though."

"I've never once hit your fingers."

"And besides, being straight has never been a particular strength of mine."

Whit just grabs Cooper's wrist, sets his hands around the post, and raises the hammer. "Hold it still."

"My fingers!"

"You're fine."

"You're going to be real sad the day you do hit them."

Whit gives the fence post a solid whack and ignores him, his abs flexing above where the waist of his pants sits flat against the V of his hipbones.

"Cooper," Whit says.

"It's straight!"

"I'd send you over to Drew to help him with the clapboards except, oh wait, then the outside of the house'd be crooked too."

"This lane is my genius idea if you'll remember," Cooper says.

"You tell me"—Whit brings the sledgehammer down —"every"—another *whack*—"day."

"'Cause it's great." Cooper lets go of the post, and when it stays where it is, driven far enough into the ground to hold, he steps back. "You know, if we had a hydraulic post pounder, we'd have been done last week."

Though, then he wouldn't have gotten glorious day after glorious day of Whit lifting the sledgehammer, triceps tensing, his back flexing, and his pants slipped low on his hips. But on the other hand, they could still be in bed, naked and sweaty, in the early morning heat. A toss-up.

But as far as having his cake and eating it too...

Cooper slips his hand into Whit's back pocket. T-minus three seconds until Whit sighs, pulls Cooper's hand away, and points to the next fence post, but hey, Cooper can enjoy that firm curve of muscle until then.

Whit kisses him. Softly, once, then pulls back and looks

over his shoulder toward the barnyard. From here, the whine of Drew's saw is barely noticeable, and wherever Penny is, she's not outside where she can see them. Cooper squeezes his delicious handful and Whit kisses him again, walking him backward into the side of the pickup truck, the metal already hot from the sun.

"Here I thought you were our taskmaster for the morning. What happened to your work itinerary?" Cooper bites at Whit's lower lip and squeezes again. "Or is this a yes to getting a post pounder?"

"Is that an attempt at a joke?"

"If you like dirty talk, you can just say so." Cooper kisses Whit again, a pleasant hum beginning to light low in his stomach.

Insatiable, he's thought more than once, and apparently today's only difference is they're not waiting for the privacy of nighttime and their room. Whit licks into his mouth and Cooper spreads his hands over Whit's chest, all firm muscles and soft skin.

Already, Cooper's breath picks up, blood pulsing in his ears over the soft smack of their mouths, and Whit's low grunt as he hooks his hand beneath Cooper's thigh and yanks their hips flush. Somewhere, Sadie barks and the circular saw spins. Cooper tips his head back and winds his arms around Whit's neck, letting Whit hold him off balance, the truck against his back and Whit's body pressed in close.

Sadie barks again.

"S'just Socks messing with her," Cooper murmurs as Whit sucks on his neck.

Whit presses their foreheads together and hikes Cooper's shirt up to his ribs and says, "Good."

"Yeah, good, like that." Cooper pushes into Whit's fingers on his fly.

They're not really going to get each other off in the middle of the pasture, are they? Whit edges Cooper's zipper down. Oh, fuck yeah, they're really going to get each other off in the middle of the pasture. This is a goddamn dream come true.

Good news, fifteen-year-old me, life turns out to be truly excellent, Cooper thinks and shoves both his hands between Whit's ass and his boxers.

Sadie barks again. She follows it with a yip, and then her deeper bellow that isn't her years-long war waged with Socks but an announcement of a car arriving. Cooper peels his eyes open and peers around the back of the tailgate. A truck, actually. And climbing out of the cab—

Cooper jerks his zipper closed. "I didn't invite him."

"What?" Whit wipes the back of his hand across his mouth. He looks dazed, a little dreamy, until he blinks, and there's his normal coolness and a pinch on his forehead as he cranes his neck to look. "Is that Brad?"

"Hey guys!" Brad shouts, waving his arm over his head.

Cooper ducks behind the bed of the pickup, straightening his hair and pulling down his shirt. Brad can't really see them, not with the truck parked how it is, but fucking hell, this is awkward. "I don't know what he's doing here." Cooper grabs his hat where he'd set it on the tailgate, jamming it onto his head like it's any sort of real barrier between him, Whit, and their apparent audience.

It's fine. Brad didn't see anything. And neither did Drew, who walks around the side of the house, lifting a hand in hello, or the other man who gets out of Brad's truck.

Huh.

"Travis?" Cooper asks.

Whit pushes his arms through the sleeves of his T-shirt. He already looks cool as a goddamn cucumber, while Cooper's skin is still buzzing. "Yeah, that's Travis."

"And I thought you were stuffy as all hell. He gives you a real run for your money," Cooper says, squinting at the neat tuck of Travis's crisp button-down into his slacks. Even from here, his shoes look shiny.

Up close, those shiny shoes are even more out of place in the dust and gravel of the barnyard, the toes clean and the laces neat. Cooper shakes Travis's hand and probably leaves a smear of dirt behind, his hands grimy after a morning of milking, chores, and fencing...and Whit's ass that he could still be grabbing right now.

Cooper forces a smile. "So good to see you again."

"Yeah, it's been a while, hasn't it?" Travis rocks back on his heels, looking around the barnyard. "Penny around?"

"No," Drew says.

"What're you two working on over there?" Brad shields his eyes against the sun with a cupped palm, cracking his gum. "New pasture?"

"Just a lane between the pastures and the barn," Cooper says.

"What a great idea, Coop, I should've thought of that. Saves some time, yeah?"

See? Cooper could ask Whit. Dig his elbow into Whit's ribs, toss him a smile and tease, *Brad gets it.*

Instead, he just shrugs. "That's the hope."

Brad claps him on the arm and Cooper shifts away, though his shoulder bumps into Whit's chest. "Sorry," he mumbles.

Didn't know Whit was standing right there and now it's just awkward, crammed between the two of them. Cooper backs up a step and bends to rub Sadie's ears.

Brad snaps his gum again and says, "Thought I'd pick up this week's order for the market, if you've got it ready."

"Brad's politely not mentioning that I dragged him over here, wanted to see if I could get a bit of cheese too." Travis turns in a small circle as he looks around. "And I wanted to see the place. It's looking pretty good, Drew. Things going well?"

Drew shrugs, his hands deep in his pockets. "It's going okay."

"Well, I picked up some of your Camembert from Brad when I was up here the other day, and let me tell you, I think it helped sell a three-bedroom weekend home over near Albany. Real into local food, a lot of these buyers are."

"How is it local if they're only up here for the weekend?" Whit asks.

Stay in the city, Whit probably thinks whenever he comes upon leaf peepers and skiers. Hell, he probably thought that a dozen times at Cooper himself, freed from the city for the summer and heading upstate as soon as he could.

"That's real great to hear," Drew says.

"Thought I'd stock up while I'm visiting my mom," Travis says. "I'd keep buying out the supply at the market, but I think they're down to just some blocks of cheddar."

"Yeah?" Drew asks. "Well, sure, I've got more. How much do you need?"

"How much you got that Brad's not picking up? I'm telling you, an initial meeting with buyers in my office, where I set out a plate of cheese and crackers and tell a story about growing up down the street from here? Hook, line, and sinker, don't tell the competition." Travis lets out a loud laugh.

Cooper scratches beneath Sadie's collar, trying not to grimace. All he can picture is an entire office full of Travises, all of them with too-white teeth, holding out perfect platters and celebrating the chime of dollar signs. Fucking hell, Travis spending his life holed up under fluorescent lights in a stuffy office building when—if he wanted to—he could be working his mom's land, not leaving it for Drew to hay every summer.

Though, maybe someday that house will be Travis's "weekend home." Or, God, he'll sell it to some equally polished city-weekender, who'll complain every time a cow makes a peep, let alone wanders over after staging their latest escape and rooting through the lawn for a snack.

The door to the house squeaks open and Travis grins, his arms spread wide. "There you are!" he says.

"Oh." Penny looks between Travis and the rest of them. "Hi."

"Hi, you."

Travis holds out his arm for a hug, but Penny turns her side to him, letting him only squeeze her shoulders quickly as she cradles her coffee mug in both hands. She steps back as soon as he's done.

"Didn't know you were in town," Penny says.

"I texted you."

"Let me grab that cheese for you," Drew says.

"Yeah," Travis says, still smiling at Penny. "Whatever you've got on hand."

"Why don't you come look?" Drew asks.

"You know, if this works, maybe I could swing by more often, grab more cheese as I need it, yeah?" Travis throws another smile toward Penny. "Be great to see you guys more."

Go away, Cooper thinks. That'd be nice, if he and Brad just disappeared back down the road, some extra cash filling Drew's wallet, and the farm quiet and peaceful again.

"Get cheese from your own damn shop," Cooper whispers to Sadie. Then, he straightens. That's not a half-bad idea. "Hey, Travis, rather than running out of our cheese all the time, is there a place near your office we could set up a wholesale account?"

Travis laughs again. It's really too loud a sound and his mouth opens too wide, like he's practiced in the mirror to figure out the perfect angle for his jaw. "I don't know much about the cheese world, I'm afraid," he says.

"C'mon, there's got to be places near you. You've got your office near Fulton Street, right? What about Annabelle's Market?" Whit glances at him and Cooper shrugs. "My mom works near there."

"Annabelle's buys from a distributor, but you might have luck with Cedar Street Markets," Brad says. "They own our market too."

Cooper turns toward Brad. *Don't start*, he wants to whisper to Whit, 'cause that's some damn helpful information. "They do?" Cooper asks. "You know anyone there?"

"Well"—Brad snaps his gum—"you gonna tell my boss if I say yes?"

"I'm gonna give you a dozen fresh eggs and some of Drew's Parmesan."

"Well, yeah, I might've been chatting with them recently." Brad shrugs. "They've got some job openings and I'm not sure I don't want to move somewhere more exciting, if I'm not going to be farming."

Exciting. Cooper nearly laughs. "I think I call predawn cow escapades as much fun as I need."

"Come down to the city with me, Coop, I'll introduce you," Brad says. "Myra is who you want to talk to."

"No." Whit's arm brushes Cooper's. Again, standing so damn close, like Whit somehow doesn't know it's already a million fucking degrees and the morning's not half-over.

"God forbid we change the plan for the day, you mean." Cooper hitches his thumb over his shoulder toward Whit. "Six fence posts by ten o'clock or Whit's eye starts twitching."

Whit shakes his head. "No, I just meant—the account, if

you're setting something up, Drew should go, or I should, not just Cooper."

"I can do it," Cooper says.

"The discounts," Whit says.

Cooper scoffs. "I can do math."

"Can you?" Whit asks.

Cooper pokes him in the ribs. "Fuck you."

He pulls his hand back quickly. He didn't mean to touch Whit, with everyone standing around. Argue with him, like they're alone in their room. *Flirt*, a small voice whispers to him and he frowns, his cheeks heating. Embarrassing, all of it. *Just sex*, he thinks. Fucking focus.

"We'd love any chance to talk to them. Myra, you said? Is she around today?" Cooper asks.

"Yeah, I can definitely take you down." Brad looks over at Whit. "Though I've just got the truck, so it'd probably be more comfortable if only Cooper and I go."

"I could follow you." Drew casts a look toward the barn. "The milk'll keep."

"I'll go," Whit says.

Cooper blows out a breath. "I can make a damn sale. And I'd like to see my moms if anyone is going down to the city."

"No, I know, I just meant—" Whit licks quickly at his lips. "Coop, we can head down together. No need to interrupt your day, Brad. And, Drew, you can work on the cheese."

"What about the fencing schedule?" Cooper asks. "Kind of a drop-of-the-hat redirect to your day, Mr. Morales."

"Yeah," Brad says. "Wouldn't want to throw you off, Whit, seems like you have plenty to do around here."

"Da pena verlos[1]." Penny claps her hands together. "Whit and Cooper, you two go. I have today off, I'll take

193

care of milking this afternoon, yeah? I wouldn't mind a day on the farm."

"You sure?" Drew asks.

"Well, you're making me dinner as a thank you, and Whit and Cooper are bringing me back some sort of over-priced, delicious treat, so yeah, I'm sure."

"Yeah, I'll make you dinner." Drew's cheeks turn a little pink. "Yeah, cool. And let me just grab that order, Brad, and I can get some cheese for you too, Travis."

"Awesome, so are we doing this?" Cooper asks. "Yes? Getting while the getting's good? Hey, Drew, put some cheese together for us to take down to the city!"

Drew waves a hand to show he heard as he disappears into the barn, Travis and Brad trailing after him.

Whit glances toward the field and the truck still parked there, the bed stacked full of fence posts and the roll of wire glinting in the morning sun. "It'll take all day to get down there and back."

Cooper grabs Whit's arm, steers him after Penny as she walks towards the house, and says, "And yet, opportunity beckons. I swear, if you start in on the schedule for getting the fencing done, I'll remind you, this doesn't have to take as long if we get a post pounder to—"

"Rentals cost money."

Cooper spreads his hands wide, walking backward toward the house. "Which is why I'm bringing home the bacon with cheese sales, babe."

Oh, fuck.

Babe.

Cooper wants to crawl under a rock as he follows Whit up to their room, pretending texting Terry takes more time than it does just to be able to mess with his phone. Just sex, just sex, just sex—Whit has no problem keeping that damn fact straight.

Sorry, he nearly blurts out as Whit shuts the door behind them. But maybe Whit didn't hear what Cooper said. Or maybe he's just politely ignoring that slip of an endearment, his head too full of the work they're not getting finished today and the discomfort of the spontaneity of heading down to the city spur of the moment.

Cooper tosses a clean sock onto his bed and kneels to root through his duffle bag for another. "I really can handle going down to the city," he says, "if you don't want to come. I promise I can even count to ten, and all the way to twenty if I use my toes."

"I was just messing with you about the discounts."

"And I'm not—whatever. Look, I know the farm is really yours and Drew's. I'm not trying to horn in on that."

Since his first summer here, acne all over his chin and punch-drunk in love with Whit, Cooper's known it's Drew and Whit, Whit and Drew, and then Penny, too, when she moved in after Drew's aunt and uncle retired. So no, he doesn't need a reminder.

"Hey," Whit says softly.

"Really, you don't have to come." Cooper jams his arm into the far corner of his bag.

"I want to."

Cooper straightens, his knees digging into the floor-boards. "Don't lie."

"I do." Whit shrugs. "And maybe I want to meet your mom."

Cooper huffs a laugh and tips his bag upside down, shaking it until the sock finally falls out. "Don't hold your breath. We're competing for her time with her sacred meeting schedule."

"Hey," Whit says again and nods toward the bathroom. "Come here, would you? You smell like a cow."

"Cows smell great." Cooper lets himself be tugged up to

his feet. "You're the one who fed the stinky-ass pigs this morning, bucket by agonizingly slow bucket."

Cooper tosses his phone next to the sink and turns the shower up hot, like Whit likes it. The dial's always set to a temperature ready to scald Cooper's skin lobster-red, whenever he showers after Whit. Though he'll take it now as Whit steers him under the spray of water.

Cooper shoves Whit's arm so his bandaged hand sticks out past the shower curtain. God, Whit feels good. All the better with the hot water billowing steam around them, and the slippery flow of Whit slicking soap across Cooper's chest. They should shower together every day, should've been doing this for weeks now. *Saving on hot water*, or some such reasoning, when the truth is Whit's cock is stirring against Cooper's stomach.

Cooper sucks lightly on the ridge of Whit's collarbone, all fresh water and the faint bite of soap. Lower, across the plane of Whit's pecs, Cooper bends to lick the water streaming off the bulges of his abs. A vein runs down the flat of Whit's stomach beneath his navel, and when Whit presses his shoulder, Cooper kneels, tracing the course of water with his tongue.

Whit grabs Cooper's head as Cooper kisses the tip of his cock. Dark eyes, water streaming over his nose and chin, his lips full and parted—damn but Whit's a sight. Cooper leans forward and kisses him again, his tongue just barely darting out.

"C'mon," Whit grunts. His grip tightens.

"C'mon, what?"

Whit inhales, his chest rising. Gently, he presses and Cooper lets himself be pushed forward, taking Whit's cock in his mouth. He tastes so good. He always does, but this is all the more fun with water streaming over Whit's skin, the slipperiness of the shower, and the humid rise of steam.

Cooper grabs the back of Whit's thighs and sucks just how Whit likes it, drawing his tongue up the length slowly and dipping back down quicker. Whit tilts his head back, his hips pushing forward. Yeah, fuck yeah, just like that, Whit's cock bumping the back of Cooper's throat. Cooper could do this all damn day, until his knees go numb and the shower runs cold, Whit clawing at his hair and Cooper catching the rhythm of the tiny flexes of his hips.

Whit's breathing speeds up, like it always does just before he comes. Cooper flicks his tongue faster and looks up the length of Whit's body. He could stop. Pull off Whit, tease him and mess with him, and see if this morning's frolic doesn't involve getting shoved facedown onto his own bed, Whit climbing behind him, just how Cooper likes it.

Though Whit shakes his head, a tiny, short gesture, and Cooper would laugh if his mouth wasn't full of that gorgeous cock, sure that Whit knows what he was thinking. Whit's hand tightens, holds Cooper there, and Whit comes with a hard gasp, fingers flexing on Cooper's head and flooding his mouth.

Cooper pulls off Whit's cock, pokes a finger into his thigh, and says, "You keep your other hand dry?"

"Fuck you."

"Please."

Whit hooks a hand beneath Cooper's arm and hauls him upright. Whit's mouth falls to Cooper's neck and their skin slides together, and Cooper tips his head back and guides Whit's hand to his cock.

"Like that," Cooper says.

"I think I know how to do it."

Cooper tugs Whit into a faster pace. "C'mon."

"Shut up and let me—"

"No, like that, I—"

Whit kisses him. Slows his pace further, elbows away

Cooper's hand, and presses him in to the side of the shower stall. And fucking hell, that's something, to be held so still, water beating at them, and Whit jerking him slowly.

Which works so fucking well. Cooper bites back his whine, and when he starts panting, frustrated and so goddamn turned on he wants to crawl out of his skin, he turns his face away from the curl of Whit's mouth. This shouldn't be so good. It can't be so good, slow and just with Whit's hand, but it is, and Cooper wants to scream or squirm or fuck blindly into Whit's fist, but every time he moves, Whit just holds him tighter.

Cooper comes on a high, keening cry he's going to be embarrassed about later. Oh God. Oh, fucking hell dammit, that was better than any hand job has any right to be, the hot blaze of pleasure, the burst low in his stomach, the chase of his hips in Whit's grip.

Whit kisses Cooper before he's caught his breath, and he smacks at Whit's back, trying to grab purchase on Whit's slippery skin. But Whit just keeps holding Cooper, kissing him even as Cooper's lungs burn, and he comes down off the high of his orgasm, slumping into Whit's body.

Good. So, so good. And he could just stay like this, Whit kissing lazily over his skin, his arms hooked around Whit's neck, and their world shrunk to the flow of the shower and the rise of steam curtaining their bodies.

Above the patter of the shower, Cooper's phone beeps. He blinks water from his eyes.

Right, his phone.

The city.

Cheese, he thinks dimly and nudges the curtain aside to tip his phone so he can read the screen.

Your mom's around if you're here by lunch, Terry texted.

So probably, he still won't see her. But maybe. *Maybe.*

Whit bends and kisses the back of his neck.

Cooper shrugs him off. "We gotta go."

"Right now?"

"I'll give you a shampoo hairdo another time. C'mon, get a move on."

Cooper jumps on one foot to tug his jeans on over skin he dried too hurriedly. Whit fusses with his hair in the bathroom, his eyes drooping with that post-sex haze he gets. Cooper smacks the flat of his palm against the doorjamb and jerks his chin toward the door. They have time later to linger over a longer shower, and he ushers Whit toward the stairs, yanking the keys out of Whit's hand and checking his watch.

CHAPTER THIRTEEN

On the train into the city, Whit stares out the window, his eyes tracking across the landscape and his thumb rubbing against a crease in his jeans.

Cooper leans into him, bumping their shoulders together. "What're we looking at?"

"I can't remember the last time I was down here."

"Ooh, buildings, pretty."

"Did you always take the train?"

"I know you're a glutton for punishment, so I'm sorry I spared you the experience of driving into Manhattan," Cooper says. He's close enough, he could rest his chin on Whit's shoulder, though he draws back an inch before he can give in to the urge to cuddle up to Whit's warm, broad back. "Yeah, Grandpa'd drop me off at the station upstate."

"And your mom would pick you up?"

"Smarty-pants here." Cooper taps a finger against Whit's temple. "But I'd just take the subway back to good old Brooklyn."

Farm boy in the city, Cooper thinks. And maybe in some other life, Cooper would tease Whit, press a kiss to his cheek, and whisper into his ear about being a country bumpkin.

But no. Cooper sits up a bit straighter and says, "Which is the train that goes from Grand Central to where I grew up."

"I thought you said your mom worked near where we're going."

"Yeah, but 'working' is the key word."

Cooper can smell the soap still on Whit's skin. *Not a couple*, he tells himself when he wants to tuck his nose into Whit's neck and breathe. Not a couple, not dating, and not snuggling together, because scratching a mutual itch is real different than a romantic fucking train ride.

Cooper forces a couple more inches between them, though he lets himself reach past Whit to press a finger to the window, his arm brushing Whit's shoulder. "Look," he says, "oh my God."

"What?"

"You see that?"

"See what?"

"Is that—oh shit, hey, Buttercup!" Cooper slaps the flat of his palm against the window, waving excitedly, and Whit bats his hand down. "He must be making his big break into the city life. Look at him keeping pace with us."

"You're ridiculous."

"Think he wants to be an actor? Showbiz, this is where it's at!"

"Absolutely absurd."

"Too bad you're stuck with me anyway."

Whit settles back into his seat. His knee knocks into Cooper's, jostled by the motion of the train. "Too bad," Whit says.

In Grand Central, crowds sweep out onto the platforms. Cooper grabs the bag of cheese, checks the ice packs nestled carefully around the packages Drew selected, and steps into the swirl of pedestrians.

"Where're we going?" Whit asks.

Cooper slips between a trash can and a family with a stroller and shopping bags. "Just follow Buttercup." He turns, ready to catch the roll of Whit's eyes.

Whit isn't behind him.

No, Whit's stymied in the crowd, stutter-stepping when a knot of teenagers passes in front of him, like a calf unsure how to push forward to the hay feeder.

Cooper works his way back and snags Whit's wrist. "We're heading for the four, five, or six."

"The green trains?"

"Please, we don't call the trains by colors, this isn't Boston."

"What?"

Cooper tugs. "C'mon."

Long, warm fingers lace through his. Cooper's stomach leaps and he presses his teeth together. Oh, how easy it would be to pretend. A day trip down to the city with his gorgeous boyfriend, lunch with Mom and Terry, an idle wander down the sidewalk as they sip expensive coffees and window shop, shoulders brushing together.

Cooper pulls Whit forward, unrelenting against the press of the crowd. They're delivering cheese and he's embarrassing himself.

"Would we have to do this every time to make a delivery?"

Business as usual, Cooper thinks and jerks his wallet out of his pocket in front of the turnstiles. He's got an old metro card in here somewhere, creased and bent but a couple dollars on it still, and he swipes it twice, nodding Whit through ahead of him.

"We get this account humming," Cooper says, "and

Drew can probably just hire someone or arrange something with Brad's market."

Whit's hand twitches at his side. Cooper tucks his into his pockets, refusing to reach for that warm palm and those gentle fingers again, and winds his way toward the stairwell, far slower than he would if Whit weren't following him.

A stop before the one he'd take to get to his mom's office, Cooper steers Whit off the train and jogs up the stairs until they emerge into the heat of the midday sun, towering buildings and crowded sidewalks.

The market is all modern glass and polished counters. Cooper wants to check the soles of his shoes for mats of hay and manure, as if a drive and a train ride and the subway isn't enough travel from the farm to wipe him clean.

Hot farmer look, Penny had called it once, when they'd sat on the tailgate of the truck at a farmers' market, swinging their legs and watching the vendors and customers. Canvas work pants, sun-bleached T-shirts, and scuffed leather boots, and yeah, Penny wasn't wrong that it's a damn nice style.

Now, he just feels as out of place as he did when he was a teenager, back in the city again after weeks on the farm, wishing for rolling pastures and the call of birdsong. Though, at least he's not balking like Whit is. Cooper grabs Whit's wrist and drags him to the market that Brad had described—white walls and industrial light fixtures and displays full of cheeses and cured meats and baked goods.

Catching the eye of the woman behind the counter, Cooper puts on a smile and steps forward. "Hi," he says, "can I get one of those cupcakes to go? Boxed up, please, it's gotta survive a train trip. And while I've got you, we're here from Two Pines Farm. We're looking for Myra."

"You found her."

"Well, hi there." Cooper sticks his hand out to shake hers. "Brad sent us down to talk with you."

"Brad?"

"Works for Elaina, at your upstate location? He said he'd been chatting with you about a position as a purchaser here? Great guy, knows his stuff, and look at him already sending folks your way." Cooper slips the bag of cheese out of Whit's hand and sets it on the counter. Maybe Brad really will move to the city, and Cooper won't have to hear the crack of his gum ever again. "I've got some samples here. Pasture-raised, Jersey cow milk, all from our own herd. The farm owner, Andrew Madison, he makes it himself."

Cooper sets out the wheel of Brie, the wedge of Parmesan, and the block of cheddar. The mozzarella, ricotta, and burrata all survived the trip in their plastic containers, and he stacks those, too. Gorgonzola, Gouda—he fishes under the ice packs and draws out the final small box of cheese curds.

"Almost ate those on the way down," Cooper says with a smile and a wink. "They go fast."

Myra turns the Parmesan over in her hand. "Do you do any cultured butters?"

"We certainly could."

"We have a lot of suppliers already," she says. "And I'm not sure I see anything here that we don't already carry."

"But how much of your cheese comes from dairies within the state, like ours?" Cooper asks. "We're making all our products from the milk we produce ourselves. We're farmers you can put a name and a face to, cows that we raise from calves, and an operation we oversee every step of the way."

Myra taps the Parmesan against the counter. "Such a small farm. You could keep up with demand?"

"No problem at all. We'd rather have a great relationship with one or two stores. Get to know what you guys want and need." Cooper elbows Whit a step forward. "And this guy here is super organized. I'm really just a pretty face."

Finally, a smile for that. Myra sets the Parmesan down and picks up the block of cheddar. "You came down all this way?"

"What can I say, the good people of New York City deserve this deliciousness." Cooper points toward the cheddar. "You open that up, eat a slice, and you'll know exactly what I'm talking about."

"Well, I'm not opposed to giving it a try."

"Perfect." Cooper slaps his palm gently on the counter. "This is your card? How about we just give you a call once you've had a chance to enjoy your samples and we can go from there?"

Cooper leaves with his cupcake and an empty bag, Whit trailing behind him, and once he's out of sight of the window, pumps a fist into the air. "And that, my man, is how it's fucking done."

Whit lets out a long breath. "Do we really have enough milk for all this cheese?"

"If we're careful with production, sure. But if this works? Yeah, might need some more."

"Keep back some calves, are you thinking?"

"Probably. It'd be cheaper than trying to buy new cows."

"It'd take some time before we could breed and milk them," Whit says.

"Are you already arguing with this plan, before it's even gotten started?" *Just a pretty face*, Cooper'd said to Myra. "I'm sure you and Drew can figure it out. Aren't you the brains of the whole operation?"

"No, I meant—thank you." Whit's fingers brush Cooper's elbow. "I'd have never done anything like this."

"Yeah, you'd still be asking directions to the green train," Cooper says.

"I'm serious. You—you said I always just do what I've always done, and you're right. When the farmers' market closed, I was trying to think of others we could sign up for, definitely nothing on this scale."

Cooper fishes his phone out of his pocket and checks the time. How odd, to have Whit looking at him like that, all earnest and soft. "You'd have gotten there."

"No, I don't think I would've. So, thank you. Really."

Cooper holds up his phone. "Say that again, let me record it," he says. "C'mon, I'll play it back to you next time I drive you nuts, and then you'll tell me I'm driving *you* nuts, and then I'll just say I'm doing what I do best. Now, let's go, enough chitchat, we gotta boogie."

"I'm really trying to talk to you," Whit says.

"Talk and walk."

Cooper checks the time again as they wait at a pedestrian stoplight. He pushes his phone into his pocket, grabs Whit's forearm, and drags him through a break in the traffic. Two more blocks, then one. Cooper raises a hand to wave at Terry's familiar profile, her blond hair cut short on the sides and back and falling long over her forehead.

But it's Terry and Terry alone who waves back. Cooper slows and Whit nearly bumps into him.

"Where's Mom?" he asks.

"Hey, kiddo."

"She couldn't make it?"

Terry wraps him in a hug, rubbing briskly at his stiff shoulders. "I'm so sorry, sweetie."

"But we're here by lunchtime, so—"

No. Of course. Of fucking course, Mom missing his visit

was always going to happen. How dumb, to imagine otherwise. He closes his eyes and scratches a finger over his eyebrow, his thumb pressed into his temple. If they'd come here before dropping off the cheese, if Whit hadn't taken so damn long to make his way to the subway, if they'd hustled out of the farm rather than lingering in the shower—

Whatever, he tries to think. Mom was probably never really going to find the time, no matter how he hurried.

"This is Whit," Cooper mumbles and shoves his hands in his pockets. "Whit, Terry."

"Cooper," Terry says, her voice soft.

Cooper turns to look at the front of the restaurant. "Food, yeah? I'm hungry, but I know, I know, what else is new?"

He yanks open the door so he doesn't have to see how Whit's looking at him, his head tipped and eyes too intent.

At their table, Terry rifles her fingers through Cooper's hair before she pulls out the chair across from him. "Whit, you know, I've heard a lot about you over the years."

"All of it good," Cooper says. The joke sounds weak. He cracks open his menu but stares at it blindly. He ought to be hungry, but his stomach churns with a slow, hard knot. He should've expected this. Should've known. Shouldn't have even gotten his hopes up that, for the first fucking time ever, Mom would take a goddamn break from her work to see him.

"I doubt that," Whit says. He turns his menu to read the cover, and then flips through the pages that list pizza after pizza. "Cooper, what're the chances you chose this restaurant?"

Terry rips the top inch of wrapper from her straw. "Family favorite," she says.

"Let's spare me the embarrassing childhood stories, please," Cooper says.

Grinning, she tugs the remaining wrapper slightly down and places the straw to her lips.

Cooper holds up a hand to shield himself. "And don't."

But Terry blows the wrapper at him anyway and hits him in the forehead. Cooper balls it up, throws a perfect shot into her water glass, and Terry laughs.

"Cooper has eaten every single one of those pizzas," she says.

"Terry."

"I used to find receipts in his pants pockets whenever I did the laundry."

"Terry, please."

"When he was little, he knew the names of each of the chefs here." Terry nods toward the half wall dividing the seating area from the kitchen. "And he used to be obsessed with watching them throw the dough, like a cat watching the dryer spin."

"This is all a lie," Cooper says.

"There's still a stain on our kitchen ceiling from him chucking dough at it."

Whit sips at his own water, his eyes on Cooper over the rim of the glass. "The grill at the farm has a permanent circle of burnt cheese," Whit says.

"Cooper's calling card." Terry plucks the soggy straw wrapper from the top of the ice in her glass and deposits it neatly into Cooper's cup. "We love you so much, Coop."

Cooper slumps in his seat. "I'm getting mine to go."

"Now," Terry says, "tell me all about your summer so far, and don't leave out any of the good parts."

Cooper flicks the wet straw wrapper at her. "You mean Sadie?"

"I definitely mean Sadie."

After lunch, it's only hotter outside, but Terry still draws Cooper close, cupping his cheeks in her hands, a small, hard smile on her face. "I'm going to have a word with your mother about this."

"Give her hell," Cooper mumbles.

"But I'm so glad I got to see you. You're my favorite stepson, Cooper."

"You're my favorite stepmom," Cooper parrots back, like they always have. *My favorite mom*, he thinks, squeezing his eyes shut.

Terry leans forward and drops her voice to a whisper. "And I like your young gentleman."

"Terry."

"He's cute and he's very sweet."

"C'mon, it's not like that."

"Well, he clearly likes you."

Cooper squirms, but she just chuckles.

"He tolerates me," Cooper says.

"In that case, I hope you two are having a fun summer 'tolerating' each other."

Cooper wiggles again. "Gross, Ter."

"I love you." She kisses his cheek with a loud smack. "Love you, love you, love you, and I'm so happy I got to see you."

Cooper waves until she's disappeared into the crowded sidewalk. Then he turns, looking for the closest subway entrance. Enough of the city for today. Cooper wants the dirt and dust of the barnyard and even the damn broken spigot to groan over.

"I thought that was your mom," Whit says.

"Terry?" Cooper pulls out his metro card. There's probably enough left on it to get them back to Grand Central. There'd better be, because suddenly the idea of having to punch buttons on a screen and get it to accept crumpled old bills exhausts him. "My stepmom."

"She picked you up from the farm once."

"Oh, yeah, I guess. That was ages ago."

"But you took the train the rest of the time?"

Maybe Whit has a crisp five he'd be willing to throw toward today. Cooper rubs his palm over his forehead. "Yeah," Cooper says. "Grandpa would drop me off at the station, but I guess the train wasn't running that day for whatever reason and it was too long a drive for him to make it all the way down here, so Terry had to come up."

Rented a car, 'cause it's not like she owns one, and she'd even let him choose the radio stations the entire way back. Because his mom couldn't pick him up herself. *Wouldn't*, he's thought more than once.

Whit asks, "When you said you took the subway back to your house—"

"Apartment, please, don't be ridiculous—"

"Was your mom supposed to come get you from the train?"

Cooper huffs out a breath. He doesn't want to fucking *talk* about this. Living it was bad enough. He starts down the sidewalk, but Whit just jogs to keep up with him.

"Did she just...not?" Whit asks.

"I grew up in the city, I think I could navigate a subway or two."

"She didn't?"

"Look, my folks are different than yours, okay? Leave it at that."

"I'm sorry."

"Yeah, well, she was too."

Mom had left a note for him and everything before she got up to leave for work the next morning, arriving home again long after he'd jerked his bedroom door shut tight, like it hadn't been all summer since she'd last seen him and another day wouldn't make a damn difference.

Cooper swipes the metro card but the light doesn't

flash. He swipes it again, harder. He has enough on it for at least one damn ride. Whit's hand covers his, warm fingers and that broad, big palm. Gently, he turns the card around.

Right.

Cooper was holding it the wrong damn way. How embarrassing.

He swipes it again and steps back to let Whit walk through ahead of him, and then does it once more for himself. *Plenty left*, he thinks dully as the small screen flashes the remaining balance.

Cooper shoves the card into the back of his wallet. There're pieces of hay caught in there. He touches one, then folds the wallet carefully closed and slips it back in his pocket, before he follows Whit's wide shoulders through the crowd.

CHAPTER FOURTEEN

COOPER'S HEAD pounds and his eyes feel scratchy as Whit steers the truck past Caroline's house and the turn for the farm comes into view.

"I'll go see how Penny's doing with the milking," Whit says as he parks in his usual spot next to Drew's Jeep.

Crazy that they only left that morning, and here they are back again within the same day, afternoon light slanting over the barnyard and Socks strolling by with his typical unconcerned saunter.

"Yeah, I'll be out in a minute," Cooper says.

Though when he gets inside the farmhouse kitchen, he just pulls open the fridge and stares at the carton of eggs and bottles of beers. *Eat something*, he tells himself. His head hurts. Probably not enough water, and really, that was too long a trip to make in one day.

Drew definitely would have to hire someone or see if there's already deliveries traded between the market in Albany and down in the city. But still. That's a problem that can be solved. *Success*, Cooper thinks, though he can't even begin to get excited about it. He should make himself a snack, head out to the barn, and find Drew to smack him on the back. He pulls in a long breath and blows it out again, gently letting the fridge door fall shut.

His phone buzzes in his pocket. Cooper closes his eyes, and the old, well-worn, desperate wish claws up his throat, that he'll pull his phone out and find a text from his mom, *So sorry, I love you, I'm sorry, I'll drive up to the farm and see you tonight, I'm sorry, I'm sorry*. But no, it's Whit.

Penny finished everything and she likes her cupcake, he's written. Cooper drops his phone on the counter. It buzzes again. *Buttercup made it back, he says hi*. Cooper locks the screen and flips the phone over, facedown.

A bird lands on the windowsill with a skitter of wings and a soft chirp against the screen before it flies away again. Outside, gravel crunches under truck tires. Someone's here, but Whit doesn't come inside.

Good, Cooper thinks. He picks up a snap pea from a full bowl on the counter and chews on it slowly. He left his work pants on the floor before leaving for the city, and they're still lying upstairs in a crumpled heap. Cooper really fucking doesn't want to hear about him making a mess in the bedroom from Whit.

Outside, there's laughing, big and loud. That's Drew's laugh. His normal, goofy, too-noisy laugh that he makes when his face turns bright red and rivals his hair. *Like a goose*, Cooper told him once, and Drew had only laughed harder, until he snorted. There're more voices than just Drew, Penny, and Whit now. He can hear the slam of a car door, Sadie's tags jingling as she jogs around, and the rapid patter of Spanish.

Through the window, Cooper sees Drew with his head tipped back, his entire body shaking, lit up by the evening golden glow of summer. Beside him are Penny and Whit, and they're all standing around a small sedan.

"The hell?" Cooper asks.

The screen door bangs open. Whit's dad, Cooper registers, nearly dwarfed by an armful of boxes, though he manages to wave despite them.

"Cooper," Luis says, dropping the boxes on the table as he comes inside and pulling Cooper into a long hug. "Cooper, Cooper, Cooper. We heard you were still in these parts. So good to see you."

Diana, who's walked in right behind, hugs Cooper as soon as Luis lets him go. *Mrs. Whit's Mom*, Cooper had called her once, and she'd laughed like Whit never does, a tinkling chuckle, her smile creasing her eyes that look so much like Whit's.

"You *are* here," Diana says, stepping back to hold Cooper at arm's length as the others file in. "And we've heard so much about all the changes to the farm. Penny just showed us the fence you boys are setting up."

"Mom," Whit says, shutting the door.

"We'd have come by sooner to say hi, but every time we started packing up these albums to bring over"—Diana nods at her husband, who's already opening a box full of old photos—"well, it's a bit distracting."

"Just look at them." Luis turns an album to show around the room. "Whit in that tuxedo. You clean up good."

"I didn't know they were coming," Whit says. "Papá, please."

"Is that prom?" Cooper takes the thick book and tips it toward the light. Whit in a tux, with Penny next to him in a shimmery purple dress, her hair swept up on top of her head, with curled bits hanging near her face.

"And graduation," Luis says, flipping forward a page. "Look at him. Oh, we were so proud."

Whit and Drew, Whit and Penny, Whit and Penny and Drew. Some others too, people Cooper half recognizes. Travis was on their football team, a freshman when Whit was a senior, and some of the girls on Penny's lacrosse team, who used to come by the farm once in a while back when Cooper first started spending time here.

"I've got the box from high school," Drew says, waving a picture toward Cooper. "And by high school, I mean Whit's freshman year, and I'm keeping it."

Penny opens an album as thick as her palm. "Please, that's nothing on baby Whit. I mean—look at those curls. And those cheeks, oh my God, Whit."

Whit touches his fingers to his forehead. "Guys."

"I'll raise you braces." Drew slides a photo across the table toward Cooper. "What a looker, am I right?"

Whit crosses his arms. "Everyone else had them off by ninth grade."

"Coop, tell us honestly, would you or wouldn't you have fallen desperately in love with this handsome gentleman if you'd known him in high school?" Drew holds up a picture of Whit in his baseball uniform, his hair cut too short, and his mouth full of metal.

Cooper did know Whit in high school. He pushes out a laugh. *No*, he wants to say, but it'd probably come out like the lie it is. He shuffles through the photos, plucking one of a school play, Penny on stage in a scarecrow costume, and another of Whit holding a basketball.

Cooper reaches beneath a stack of sports photos to one of Drew and Whit at what must be Whit's house. Cooper never went there, never did more than drive by the outside of Whit's family home, but it looks like the right type of kitchen to fit the space.

Whit's parents don't know about him and Whit, Cooper realizes. No, there's no gentle chiding from Luis and Diana, no significant looks, no sense of a hint hanging in the air that they have any idea that their son and Cooper have spent this spring and early summer...

What? Sharing a room? Messing around? Cooper tosses the photo back into the pile. It skids across the table and pushes another to the side with its momentum. Penny and Drew in this one, their heads close together, Penny's hair braided into pigtails, a hat sideways on her head, and a summer sunburn across Drew's cheeks and nose. Late in high school, it must've been, because Cooper recognizes the T-shirt Drew's wearing from a concert they'd driven all night to go see. And the next photo beneath must've been the same day, and Whit's in it on Penny's other side.

Hell if Cooper's in any of these. Maybe he took this shot and doesn't even remember now. Though no, it was more likely Drew's aunt, and Cooper had probably already headed back to the city, a too-quiet apartment greeting him as he shook out clothes that still smelled like hay and sunshine.

Whit reaches past Cooper, his arm brushing against Cooper's shoulder. "Pen, you were cute as a button."

Penny grabs the photo from him. "C'mon, tease Mr. Lobsterman Drew here. Could you even fit more freckles on your face?"

Cooper tries for a smile, poking a finger into Drew's cheek. "The beard only does so much, my dude."

Drew bats him away. "It intimidates the squirrels and that's all I need."

"You kids," Diana says, her voice fond.

Cooper bends down and rubs behind Sadie's ears. *The three of them*, Diana might as well say.

"Barely kids anymore, you all are old." Luis curves his arm around Whit's shoulder and jostles him, pressing a kiss to the side of his head. "Speaking of, we gotta go, 'cause we got the rest of the garage waiting for us."

"The garage?" Drew asks. "You're welcome here for dinner, if you want."

"Cooper's making pizza," Whit says.

Cooper huffs a soft laugh, scratching up under Sadie's collar.

"Thanks, but we still have some more organizing to do," Diana says. "All the fun of years of stuff to finish going through."

Drew nods toward the door. "At least let me get you some cheese before you go."

"Pizza?" Penny asks as the door creaks shut behind them. "Again?"

Whit's eyes follow Drew as he leads his parents across the barnyard to the cheese room and the cooler.

"Yeah," Whit says, "we had pizza for lunch, so Cooper's internal clock is already ticking down until he desperately needs another slice."

Cooper cups Sadie's chin in his hand. "Sadie, you'd never treat me like this, now would you?"

"Farm reg sixteen point four," Penny says. "Household members can only cook repeats of meals three times before we're all allowed to put squirrels in their bed."

Cooper rests his cheek on top of Sadie's head. "Farm reg sixteen point five states that it's actually illegal to put a squirrel in my bed and I'll call in Constable Buttercup."

Drew pushes the door open. "Whit?"

"Sorry, Coop, sixteen point six invalidates Buttercup's authority in this situation," Whit says.

Cooper stands and elbows Whit in the ribs. "You're just making that up."

"Oh, as opposed to you and Penny, who are actually—"

"Whit?" Drew asks again.

"Yeah?" Whit asks but instead of turning toward Drew, he elbows Cooper right back.

"You know what," Cooper says, "I'm probably your best

bet against the squirrels. They know they have the three of you wrapped around their tiny, creepy fingers."

"Whit, did your parents sell their house?" Drew asks.

Whit freezes. "Uh, yeah."

"And they're moving?"

"I mean..." Whit shrugs. "Yeah."

"To?"

"Albany."

"Why didn't you say anything?"

"It wasn't a big deal."

"They're moving to a—a, like, apartment place, they said?"

"That's right," Whit says.

"So they can—your dad had fucking cancer?"

Silence. Whit and Penny glance at each other. Drew's face reddens, his mouth open.

"He's fine," Whit finally says.

Drew points a finger at Whit. "This spring, when you asked—"

"Drew, forget it."

"Is this why you wanted—I told you I couldn't pay you more and—"

"C'mon, it's fine."

"It doesn't sound like it's fine."

"I said it's fine and it's fine."

"Are your folks okay?"

"My dad's great. And their house was...well, it was a lot for them to handle over the winter. You know how much snow and ice we got. So, it was either an apartment, or I could've moved back in with them. Win, win."

"You were going to move in with them?"

"No."

"But—"

"Drew."

"But if I can't pay you more, are you going to?"

"Well, they sold their house. It's kind of a moot point."

"Yeah, but they said they sold it in March, and you asked in April and—"

"What're you going to do, Drew, if I say yes?" Whit asks.

Penny purses her lips. Drew inhales sharply, his shoulders rising.

"You had some of your own shit going on," Whit says.

"But that's—we're supposed to be—you didn't even say anything." Drew touches his forehead. "This is so like you! You just clam up and say nothing. Your dad had fucking cancer!"

"C'mon, Drew—"

"And then I just have to assume that when you say it's fine, that it's really fine and it's clearly not fine. Fuck, Whit!"

"Oh, he's actually mad," Cooper whispers and Penny grimaces and nods.

Madder than Cooper's seen him, that's for sure. Drew, who was laughing a minute ago, and who couldn't even muster more than an anxious irritation when his house fell apart and his farm took a nosedive. Now, the door slams behind him.

"Fuck," Whit says softly. He jogs across the kitchen, and in his socks, pushes out the door. "Drew!"

But the engine in Drew's Jeep turns over, gravel crunching beneath the tires.

Cooper edges toward the window. Outside, Whit turns in a sharp circle, his hands in his hair. Penny bumps her shoulder into Cooper's and they watch Whit pace one way and then back again.

"Well, shit," she murmurs.

"Whit miscalculated that one," Cooper says.

"To be fair, I told him that."

"To be fairer, I'd have nearly enjoyed Whit being so wrong if Drew didn't look so butthurt." Cooper blows out a breath. "I think Drew might be under just a touch of stress."

"Just a tiny bit."

"Just the smallest, life-shattering crises of his family farm on the brink of going out of business, falling behind on his bills, and swamping his entire future."

"No biggie."

"Not at all."

"He'll be back in a bit," Penny says and Cooper nods. "You gonna go talk to Whit?"

She's looking at him steadily, her head tipped.

Yeah, Cooper nearly says but chokes on the word before he can let it out.

Talk to Whit and say what? Cooper straightens from his lean against the windowsill. He can't touch what Whit and Penny have. What Whit and Penny and Drew all have— *he'll be back in a bit.*

This isn't the first tiff in the roommates-coworkers-friends thing they've had going on for so long now. It probably plays out like this more than Cooper knows, feathers getting ruffled and the proverbial pot boiling over, a hint of awkwardness and irritation staining the air until it clears out again.

Cooper tries for a smile. "Nah, go work your cousin magic. I'm gonna call that cheese shop and follow up with Myra."

He goes upstairs to their bedroom to make the call, though he just gets Myra's voicemail, and after he leaves a message, he kicks off his jeans and slowly lowers himself to the edge of his bed.

Years of stuff, Cooper thinks, imagining Whit's parents and their garage. In his mind, it's full to bursting with

Whit's childhood, the detritus of a happy family and proud parents who carefully collected any and every keepsake. What had Whit said once? That they'd wanted a full house of kids, but only Whit had come along, and he'd gotten the full force of their excitement and delight?

Cooper's own pictures from high school, his diploma, his shin guards, cleats, and old soccer jersey are...somewhere.

Though no, Mom probably got rid of them.

He rolls onto his back. Not *probably*. Definitely. His old bedroom is an office now, and last time he stayed over, Terry put sheets on the couch for him. He had laughed and made some joke over the knot of hurt and laid awake all damn night, picturing himself anywhere else but there.

Cooper glances over at his duffle bag—it's still upside down where he left it, and all the clothes he's got in the world fit inside. Enough for ten days, two weeks if he's careful. His heavy insulated boots are jammed behind the passenger seat in his truck, along with his winter jacket, and his hat and gloves that he hasn't needed in weeks now. And that's it, isn't it? The sum of his entire damn life.

By the time he hears the Jeep again, it's dark enough that the headlights cut across the walls of the room. Cooper listens as Drew's familiar steps creak down the hall. He knocks gently at the door and Cooper calls out, "Yeah?"

Drew pokes just his head through. "Is Whit around?"

"He and Penny went for a walk, I think."

"Okay."

"You all right?"

"Yeah." Drew lifts a shoulder. "No. I don't know."

"You wanna talk about it?"

"Just tired. I'll be okay."

Drew shuts the door softly. Footsteps down the hall, the squeak of Drew's bedroom door, and then the snick of it closing again. Cooper lets his head fall back against his pillow. That's better than Drew retreating to the attic and his hammer and his ongoing revenge against the squirrels. Quieter at least, if it isn't a bit depressing how silent the house is.

Maybe Cooper should get up and pull a conversation out of Drew. Though he'd say what, exactly? Sorry he showed up here in the first place? Walked right into the perfect balance of the three of them and upended it all?

Cooper can hear Sadie shuffle across the floor downstairs when Whit and Penny come back, their voices low. Cooper turns on his side and presses his face into his pillow as Whit pushes open their door.

"Drew was looking for you," Cooper says.

"His light's off."

"Hmm." Cooper peels an eye open. Whit looks tired, his hair rumpled like he's been running his fingers through it, and the skin around his eyes is drawn. "Long day, huh?"

"Long day," Whit says.

"D'you eat dinner?"

"No."

Cooper nestles his cheek into his pillow. "Me neither."

"Wanna order a pizza?"

"Funny."

"Scooch."

"What?"

But Whit just crawls over Cooper instead of answering, settling on his side between Cooper's back and the wall and wiggling until there's room for both of them.

Cooper kicks at Whit's shins. "This is my bed," he says.

"Technically, it's my second bed."

"Technically, I think you're getting hay on my sheets."

"Maybe you'll finally wash them."

"Please, I'm practically pristine."

Whit pushes his nose into the back of Cooper's neck, a heavy hand falling to his waist. "M'gonna get you a dictionary, if that's what you think that word means."

Cooper waits for that hand to wander down the front of his boxers, pluck at the cotton and pull at the waistband, but Whit just leaves it where it is, his thumb stroking over Cooper's ribs through his T-shirt.

Okay, so they're just lying here, not fucking. How weird. Nice, though, too. Cooper shifts and Whit tugs him backward into the warm line of his body.

"Are you going to go talk to Drew?" Cooper asks.

"I'm not going to wake him up." Whit's hand slips around to press to the flat of Cooper's stomach, holding him close. "Should I leave?"

"I mean, it's your room, so—"

"The farm?" Whit asks.

Cooper twists to look at him, though with Whit's strong grip, the most he can see are Whit's messy curls.

"What the hell?" he asks.

"I'm clearly not doing much to help Drew."

"Um, you're not—I'm sorry, what?"

"I've been here every step of the way with him. And the finances of the farm just aren't working, and I'm as much at fault for that, especially this summer since Drew asked me to step up and help out. You've been here for a couple weeks and we're selling more cheese than ever, the fencing is so much better, and what's it going to be next, Coop? It seems like you're just getting started."

"Better?" Cooper asks. "Say that again, I kinda like the ring it has."

"I'm not kidding."

Cooper blows out a breath. Fuck, he's not good at this kind of thing. He wants to make a joke, strip both their clothes off, and ignore any type of actual conversation for the allure of bare skin.

But, no. This is Drew. And the farm. *Try again*, he tells himself, but it might as well be, *try for real.*

"You're not going to leave," Cooper says. "You love this place as much as Drew does, and when his uncle left it to him, you were right here to help him take over the business."

"And look at the shitty job we've done."

"So? Turn it around."

"You say it like it's that easy."

"Well, when you don't spend years overthinking stupidly simple things, it kind of is. Maybe instead of beating yourself up, how about you take these challenges as a wakeup call? What worked for Drew's uncle doesn't fit here anymore. You two can make this farm your own."

"He needs someone other than me to make that happen," Whit says.

"Nah, he needs you to get your head out of your butt."

"I'm not good at big changes."

"Well, no. And Drew's right that you're not good at talking about stuff, either. Though, to be fair, it's not like he's a model example of examining his feelings."

"It's hard."

"So? Things are hard. Farming's hard. Life's hard. Working with you every damn day is hard and you don't hear me complaining."

"I do. All the time."

"You and Drew get so stuck in your damn ruts around here is all I'm saying. Yeah, you need some inertia to break free of that. It's probably difficult, but whatever, man. Live your life."

Like Cooper should go off and do, rather than let the lull of time here continue to grow. So easy to let one day fade into the next. Nice, too, in a simple, comfortable routine. Maybe he can see the appeal of tying himself down to one place, but...what the hell kind of future is that?

A farm that can't really afford to pay him, the gray area of hooking up with Whit endlessly, until what? They get tired of it? One of them meets someone else? The newness and excitement of sex frays and leaves them stilted and awkward? And Cooper goes back to chewing over his crush while Whit continues on with his life?

I want you to like me, he wants to blurt out. Seal this moment with a long and sweet kiss.

No, he tells himself. Stop fucking wishing. Cooper pushes his face into the pillow. Enough idle daydreaming. Talk about being stuck in a damn rut—how long is he really going to do this to himself?

"I'm sorry about your mom," Whit says softly.

Cooper pulls Whit's hand up to examine the bandage. "How's this feeling?"

"I'm getting the stitches out tomorrow."

"Really?" Cooper asks. Though of course, it's Whit's day off. Another week gone by, time ticking on toward the height of midsummer.

"It really sucks your mom didn't come to lunch."

Cooper drops Whit's hand. "We're not talking about it."

"When was the last time you saw her?"

Cooper kicks Whit square in the shin, though lighter than he sort of wishes. "Let's go back to the delightful image of you with braces."

"Has she ever come up here?"

"Or take your pants off. Let's put this secondary bed of yours to good use."

"Cooper."

"No, she hasn't fucking ever been up here. She couldn't even visit her own dad, my grandpa. Now shut up so I can make fun of the fact that you were literally the chubbiest baby to ever exist."

Whit tightens his arm over Cooper's waist. "I'm being serious."

"Well, stop it, it's weird."

"Penny said I wasn't good at talking. Well, she said I fucking suck at it, along with some other choice phrases. And that I should have told Drew about my dad, like she told me to." Whit pokes Cooper's stomach gently. "Why don't you ever see your mom?"

"'Cause we don't all have parents who carefully curate years of photo albums." Cooper tries to squirm away, but Whit just tightens his arm. "She just works a lot, okay? It's not a big deal."

"What does she do?"

"Shouts into her phone and sends emails."

"No, really."

"Yes, really. Sometimes she takes a break to ask when I'm going to quit bumming around and get a real job, but then her phone rings, so it's not like I ever have to answer."

"She doesn't like that you farm?"

Cooper pushes out a hard laugh. "I'm not sure she likes anything about me."

"But she's your mom."

"I'm a mistake she made with a guy before she settled in for a life with the ladies."

"She told you that?"

"She didn't have to."

Don't assume, Terry had said once, smoothing Cooper's hair back as she sat on the edge of his bed. Cooper wiggles again, trying to put a couple inches between himself and Whit. Well, Mom's had a lifetime to tell her side of the story, but hell if she'd ever take the damn time.

"Do you know your dad?" Whit asks.

226

Cooper shoves at Whit's arm. "We're not doing this."

"Do you?"

"Yes, okay, I have met the walking, talking cloud of cigarette smoke that contributed half of my genetic makeup, and no, we didn't go play catch in the park, also fuck you, I don't want to talk about it."

"How long has Terry been around?"

"You want a goddamn report in a three-ring binder? Laminated, too?"

"You never talk about any of this."

"Listen, mister, today is all about you failing to communicate with our buddy Drew at every turn. Don't drag me into this."

"I was always so confused why you were around all summer. I had no idea."

"What, that I got shipped off upstate?" Cooper tries to free himself again, but Whit won't budge. "It was visiting my grandparents and getting dropped off here at the farm most days, or an empty apartment. My mom might not give a shit about where I am or where I go, but she definitely read at least one parenting blog when I was a teen that told her I'd end up a degenerate if I was unsupervised for too long. Joke's on her, 'cause look at me anyway."

"C'mon, you don't really think that."

"Hello, you're the one who likes to remind me I barely ever have steady employment." *You and good old Cheryl*, he thinks.

"Coop..."

"You know, Mom would really appreciate your opinion of me: useless, flaky, and unreliable. It'd confirm everything she's ever suspected."

Whit lets out a soft breath, warm against the back of Cooper's neck. "I'm sorry."

"You already said that."

"I just meant—" Whit shakes his head, his nose tickling through Cooper's hair.

Cooper shifts, trying to stretch out his legs, but Whit's knees are tucked behind his own. This bed isn't big enough for both of them. Though maybe he's finally getting used to it, because he finds an empty spot for his foot, draping his ankle over Whit's and wiggling the pillow a couple inches closer.

"Meant what?" Cooper finally asks, watching the shadows lengthen, the sharp relief of the shape of leaves shifting against the walls in the moonlight.

Whit jerks a little, like he was sleeping. "Just that you deserve better."

Cooper huffs out a breath. There's a retort to be had if he can just find it. Something about his mom, or maybe a steady job for himself, or maybe about Whit and this summer of eager, secret fucking. But it's slow to come, and by the time he's dredged up words to shoot back, Whit's breath has evened out again. There've been enough nights to know the rhythm of that puff of air against his shoulder when Whit sleeps, the laxness of his hand against Cooper's stomach and the heaviness of his arm.

Cooper has half a mind to kick Whit in the shin again. *We didn't even fuck*, he could say, *so what the hell is this, spooned up together with our clothes still on?* Whit murmurs something and tightens his hold on Cooper's waist before he relaxes again.

It's like something out of his high school fantasies, to be held all night by Whit. And fucking hell, it feels so good it hurts.

Be happy for what you do get, Cooper tells himself and presses back into the warm, strong line of Whit's body. Hasn't he told himself that for years now? Yeah, for far too long, ever since he was a kid and waited, held his breath, hoped and hoped that the clatter of typing would stop long enough for blankets to be pulled up to his chin, a soft kiss pressed to his forehead.

Fuck, he thinks and turns in the circle of Whit's arm, presses his face into that broad, strong chest, and curls up there, his eyes too hot and his throat sore.

CHAPTER FIFTEEN

THE SUN SHINES TOO bright into Cooper's eyes and he squints, tucking his face into Whit's neck. Whit slowly stirs, his palm pressing to the small of Cooper's back, brushing his shirt up and aside to touch Cooper's skin.

Milking, Cooper thinks, but he stays right where he is, nudging his knee between Whit's legs and snuggling a little further into his body. He could just stay like this, ignore everything outside of this too-small twin bed, and doze like they have all morning to wallow in the warm sunshine.

Apparently, Whit could too, his arm tightening around Cooper. Oh, this is so nice. So, so fucking nice. Waking up like this, to warm skin and Whit's hands on him, his arm still across Cooper's waist, like he held him there all night. *Perfect*, Cooper thinks and nestles into Whit's neck.

A knock sounds at the door.

Whit jerks and sits up so quickly that it pushes Cooper nearly off the narrow mattress. He scrambles, floundering at the empty air behind him, trying to find his feet before Whit can finish shoving him away.

The door creaks open and Drew calls, "Whit?"

Cooper gets a foot on the floor before he ends up on his ass, yanking his shirt down, shoving his hair off of his face, and jerking his boxers up.

"Hey, you awake?" Drew asks.

Whit pulls Cooper's sheets over his lap. "Yeah, guess I am."

"Sorry, your day off, I forgot." Drew crosses his arms over his chest, already dressed for work in his jeans and T-shirt. He glances at Cooper as if surprised to find him there.

Right. The cows. Farming. Not lying in bed, cuddled up and drowsy.

Well, another way of things between Cooper and Whit, and Cooper would be shoving Drew back into the hall, ready to give him hell about interrupting what would've otherwise been quite an enjoyable morning. Instead, Whit's clearly mortified to have been nearly caught curled up with Cooper like that, carefully not meeting his eyes. And it's fucking embarrassing for Cooper too, bodily shoved out of bed. He shuffles through his pile of clothes, trying to ignore the blush sitting on his face and the small, sick slick of hurt at how quickly Whit's smoothing out the bedsheets.

Drew coughs into his fist. "Just wanted to talk."

"Yeah." Whit gets to his feet and reaches for his jeans. He must've kicked them off sometime in the night, and Cooper pushes them closer with the side of his foot. "Yeah, no, I'm sorry. I should've told you about my parents, you were right."

"Yeah, you should've," Drew says and casts another look at Cooper.

Cooper busies himself sorting through his pairs of pants. There's a reason to keep clothes in a dresser and not on the floor, though it's not like Cooper even has an option.

"Your folks okay?" Drew asks. "Your dad?"

Whit shrugs, pulling his pants up to his waist and zipping his fly. "They're doing fine, Dad's healthy, and a smaller place is working out for them. Besides, now they don't have to deal with another winter in their own house."

Drew puts on a small smile. "Yeah, otherwise face the wrath of squirrels."

Whit smiles back, just as small and tentative. "Exactly. Drew—" Whit smooths his shirt and takes a deep breath. "I tell you everything important, I promise."

"Yeah." Drew tucks his chin down toward his chest and nods at his feet. His expression is still a little too tight, shoulders too tense. Though when he looks up again, his smile is bigger. This'll blow over, clearly. It apparently nearly already has. "Which bed is yours, anyway?"

Cooper's stomach turns. Tells Drew everything. Of course. Everything except this, Whit cuddling Cooper close a minute ago and then a mad scramble to pretend they weren't doing exactly that. *Ouch*, he thinks and tries to find the humor in it but feels only a dull ache.

"The one that doesn't have an entire bale of hay in it," Whit says. "Listen, Drew, we're in this together, okay? You and me. You're not on your own here. I want you to know that."

Drew nods and that tight smile loosens a little bit, reaches his eyes even as he holds his arms out for Whit. They hug, clapping each other on the back. Cooper sniffs at a stray sock. He should do laundry. He should get the hell out of here, leave them to their moment. Their farm, more like.

The three of us, he could say if he wanted to butt in and be obnoxious. But that's not right, is it? Two Pines Farm is theirs, and all this time Cooper's only been visiting.

Drew and Whit step back, and the moment's gone anyway, carried out under the creak of the hall floor as

Drew walks away, a quickness to his steps that wasn't there last night, and the words left behind on the squeak of the door, *You and me in this together*, that echo through Cooper's head.

"You want a hand with milking?" Whit asks.

Cooper shoves the sock into his bag. His chest is cold, his hands a bit numb. "It's your day off."

His extra shirts, a pair of jeans he doesn't wear that often because of how threadbare the knees are. He puts those in the duffle too.

"Are you okay?" Whit asks.

"Yeah." Cooper stands, dusting his hands off. He wants to go and nurse his sharp pain in private. Grab Whit's shoulders and shake him until something else falls out of his mouth, *You too, it's your farm too, you're important also, Coop, of course, it's always been you.*

How dumb, to wish for something that'll never happen.

"Someone cutting onions in here?" Cooper says. "You and Drew were so touching—especially the big hug. Now excuse me while I go shed a quiet tear with Buttercup."

Outside, the day is already hot and muggy, the wind too weak to do more than stir hot air against Cooper's cheeks. The cows take longer than it feels like they should to amble their way to the barn, and as they're chewing over their breakfasts and the milk is chilling, Cooper strings up the last lines of fencing for the lane. The final fence posts'll need to be pounded in before winter comes, but it's good enough for now, stretching from the far fields up to the side of the barn. Cooper tosses open the barn door and one of the heifers pokes a curious nose out, sniffing at the sunshine.

"Come on," Cooper says, clapping his hands. He grabs a bucket of grain and shakes it. "Buttercup, c'mon, my man. Don't show me up."

It's not gonna work, he can hear in Whit's voice, and no,

he should really be doing this for the first time with Whit and Drew, and even Penny if she's around. They'd help coax the stubborn and unsure herd away from their normal routine and through an entirely different morning. Teamwork makes the dream work, right? And here he is, facing down cows that won't budge.

It's fine. *Fine.* Cooper's just in a crappy mood, and Whit tells Drew everything *important*, and besides, it's too hot for this, sweat already dampening his shirt despite the early hour. His phone buzzes as he stands there, the back of his wrist pressed against his forehead. He thinks about just not answering, sitting down in the shade of the barn and feeding handfuls of grain to whichever cows want to come over and be his friend.

Terry's name is on the screen. She'd understand if he didn't answer. She'd leave a cheerful message for him to call her back, that she loves him, she'll talk to him soon, and she hopes he has a great day.

Though maybe Cooper could use a little bit of that cheer now. He slides his thumb across the screen and says, "Ter, can I put you on speaker and have you help me give these cows a talking-to?"

"Cooper."

"Mom?"

"I missed you yesterday. I was hoping you would stick around more of the afternoon."

"Yeah, no, we had to get back." He squints against the sunshine. He's just so damn hot and the sun's barely above the trees. "Though I did stick around for lunch."

"I know. I had a meeting I couldn't get out of."

Cooper puffs up his cheeks on a breath, and then blows out hard enough it makes a crackling sound into the phone. That meeting was probably important. So damn *important.*

"You know what," he says, "I think I've heard that one before."

Silence.

Don't talk to your mother like that, he can hear in Terry's voice, that gentle firmness she's taken with him only every so often in her years of playing referee between him and Mom.

Normally, thinking of Terry would temper Cooper's ire, but today a fly buzzes too close to his face. He swats but misses, and sweat rolls down between his shoulder blades. "I've been back in New York since April," Cooper says. "Haven't exactly seen you."

"Well, you know you're always welcome to come down here to visit."

"Funny story, I did. Yesterday. For lunch."

The fly buzzes past again. Heat shimmers off the field and the sky's hazy, humidity like a blur between him and the far stand of trees.

"Cooper," Mom says.

"You can't even make it to lunch? Practically downstairs from your building?"

"Cooper. Please."

This is how Cooper's always felt, like he could boost himself up to sit on his mother's desk and still not be seen. There was no real change between the school year when he lived in a tiny apartment with Mom versus when he was up here at Two Pines. Either a handful of square feet to trip over each other or miles of highway were the same too-far distance. All it took was Mom boxing up his bedroom and replacing his childhood bed with a desk, and there he was, wiped away. Not all that different, in the end, than stacks of photographs he's not in.

I tell you everything important, Whit had said to Drew,

and fucking hell, Cooper would like to make that list at least once in his life.

Cooper swallows and his throat is too thick. "Can I talk to Terry?"

"Cooper—"

"Now, please?"

"Kid," Terry says after a shuffle of the phone, the soft murmur of her voice and Mom's.

"The fucking cows won't walk down the lane I built for them."

"Cooper," Terry says, and her voice has all the warmth Mom's never does.

"And Whit's real, real clear there's nothing going on between us."

"Coops, hey, I love you."

"I'm having a shitty day." Days. Weeks.

Though no, that's not right, is it? This has been the best summer since—since forever. Since he was back at Two Pines for this length of time. And then messed up, laying a big goddamn mistake of a kiss on Whit.

Fuck, he thinks when it just makes his chest ache that much more.

"I'm sorry," Terry says.

Cooper drags his wrist beneath his nose. "Everyone keeps saying that."

"Everyone cares about you."

"Funny way of showing it."

Terry lets out a long breath. "Yeah."

Leave her, Cooper used to think, spinning out fantasies of living with Terry in some house with a yard and warm sunlight, no clicking of computer keys to fall asleep to. He might as well have staged that imaginary house here at Two Pines, while he was at it. Maybe he would've made the hallowed pages of Whit's photo albums, though, then again, maybe not.

"What can I say, Coop? You deserve better," Terry says.

He wipes off his nose again. "Whatever."

"You do. That friend of yours, Whit, he—"

"Oh God, don't."

"If you're going to tell me it's not like that, I'm here to say that it should be. If he had any sense, he'd be chasing after you. Your mom would be too. And I know you and your mom have a tough time, but can't help but love the dummy."

"You're the one who married her."

"Happily so, though I know you won't ever believe me. Different strokes."

"Yeah, yeah, different folks."

"You're my absolute favorite, Cooper."

At least I'm someone's, he thinks.

"Thanks," he mumbles.

"I love you so much," she says, and he sniffs as he hangs up, shoving his phone back into his pocket.

It buzzes with a series of texts he ignores, his mom probably apologizing and Terry telling him she loves him again. Same old, same old.

He knows how this one goes: call Terry back tonight, she'll tell him that he's so loved all over again, that he does deserve better but his mom isn't good at this type of thing and that she's so sorry. And then nothing will change, not next time he goes down to the city, not even if he stays here at Drew's for years, for decades.

Oregon is delightfully, wonderfully so far away, such a bright, shining ideal of a transcontinental flight that could've soothed the sting of the lack of visits. Cooper works the heel of his hand into his forehead. The last person who really wanted him around other than Terry was Cheryl, and he just had to go and fuck that up too.

I tell you everything important, Cooper hears in Whit's voice all over again.

So what the hell does that make me? he thinks.

Slowly, he pulls his phone out of his pocket. Sure enough, there are the texts he was expecting. He swipes them away and scrolls through his email until he finds the right number.

Three hours behind in Oregon. Cooper chews on the inside of his cheek as the phone rings, and he's ready to leave a voicemail when Cheryl says, "Hello?"

"Hi, this is Cooper, Cooper Langston. We talked a couple weeks ago, and I'm calling back, uh, now."

"Cooper, of course, it's good to hear from you."

Cooper squeezes his eyes shut. Good to hear from him. A polite line, in all probability. Professionalism smoothing away any irritation with him.

But still. It sounds nice.

"Look," Cooper says, "I know I didn't do a particularly good job with actually heading out west earlier this summer and gave you the runaround, but if you still have any interest at all in hiring me, I could be there by the start of next week."

"To be honest, I wasn't expecting to hear from you again."

"Well, to be honest, I wasn't really expecting to call."

She lets out a gentle laugh into the phone. *Thanks, but no*, he's ready to hear. He'll go up into the loft, scoop up Socks, and hide with him in the fort of Whit's tiny hay bales. Just stay there until he can face today, with its heat and his building headache and Whit's *I tell you everything important*.

"My answer isn't different, Cooper. We need someone

238

who'll work this summer and stay for the fall. If you're here and then gone again come the end of August, I'm not interested."

"That's fair." Cooper takes a deep breath. "I think I'd told you, I have some friends who needed a hand, but that's all wrapped up now. And I—I think I'm really ready for a change. I'd be yours through at least the fall."

"You're sure?"

"Just give me the time to drive out there, that's all I'll need. And look, I get it if you don't want to take the chance, but I work hard, I'm good at solving the problems that come with farming, I really enjoy working with animals, and everything I liked about your farm when I applied still matters. And you liked me as an applicant, which meant a lot. I'm sorry I was an ass and couldn't commit, but I am now."

"You're still an ass now?"

Cooper lets out a short laugh. Oh hell, he might end up liking her. "Well yeah, probably, but I meant, you tell me what time work starts next week and I'll be there."

"You got a place to stay?"

"I'll figure something out."

"There's a cabin we rent out to staff sometimes."

"So, is that a yes?"

"Don't make me regret this," Cheryl says.

"I won't."

"Then I'll look forward to having you here."

Finally, Cooper thinks. He smiles against the pang in his chest as he looks around the barnyard. "Yeah, me too."

———

DREW HOLDS the chain for the fence just out of reach. "No."

Cooper says, "Drew—"

"I can finish your room. I know I've been making a ton of cheese, but you won't have to share with Whit anymore so—"

"The account with the market is all set. Elaina might have some contacts for other places, too, so call and check in with her, okay? And I'm leaving you the number for the shop down in the city."

"But Cooper—"

"Don't let Whit tear down all the fences I just put up. You know he wants to."

"Or you'll come back and fix them?"

"Or you'll have cows running all over the damn place."

"Fuck you, Cooper, you can't just up and leave," Drew says.

"I'll remind you I swung by to say hi—what was it?—oh, months ago now." Cooper grabs the chain and slings it around the fence post to close the gate. "Listen, the next couple days, toss some grain out into the lane here, okay? The cows'll get used to the different routine, but they might need some encouragement in the beginning."

"I'm going to let all the air out of your tires."

"I hate to break the bad news to you, but there's an air compressor in the shop." Cooper steps closer. "Look, pay Whit more, okay? This is crazy for me to be here and you trying to split wages between us."

Drew's cheeks flush red. "I can pay you both. I'll make it work, I—"

"Stop. You'd be running the farm with one hand tied behind your back if I tried to stay, and I don't need you to do that. Get this place into a good spot, okay? And pay Whit what he's worth. I'll deny it to my grave if you tell him I said this, but he's not half-bad." Cooper taps his finger against

Drew's forehead. "Now remember, never, ever repeat that. I gotta go pack."

Inside, Cooper grabs a pair of work gloves off the shelf above the woodstove, but no, they must be Whit's, since they're a size too big for his hands. Gently, he sets them back down as neatly as he can.

"Tell me this isn't what it looks like," Penny says, her hands on her hips. "You've just been suddenly struck by the urge to finally tidy up your shit?"

"Gotta get while the getting's good."

"Farm reg thirteen point four—"

"States I never hang around that long and it's been ages, agreed?"

"What happened?"

"Nothing," Cooper says.

And hell if that isn't the truth. Exactly, utterly nothing happened. It's his own goddamn fault for wishing it would, like he could just hope a future into existence.

Packing takes all of five minutes. Toothbrush, his handful of clothes, his phone charger. He strips the sheets off his bed, leaves the quilt folded and the pillow set against the headboard. *Go, go, go*, he chants in his head as he bundles the sheets into a ball and tosses his towel on top of them, like any hesitation will break this spell, have him sitting on the edge of his mattress, listless and uncertain.

But, no. He should've left ages ago. Whiling away time here, hanging around like if he just stayed long enough, he could force this farm into a shape that fits him.

Force Whit's life into a shape that includes him. He jerks at the zipper on his bag, though it sticks, a fold of T-shirt caught between the teeth.

Footsteps creak up the staircase. Whit pushes the door open. His injured hand's unbandaged, the heel of his palm shiny and red.

Eyes a little too wide, Whit asks, "What're you doing?"

"Getting out of your hair, you're welcome."

"Drew said you're leaving."

"I was always leaving."

"But now?"

"Yes now," Cooper says, "cheese accounts, check, innovative farming solutions, check, you haven't sliced open any of your extremities lately, so check that off the list too."

Cooper keeps his back to Whit, trying to yank the fabric out of the jam he's created. Then he pauses...last night—no, the night before, that was the last time he and Whit will ever have sex, and Cooper didn't even know it. They're never going to fuck again. Oh shit, that's over between them. *One for the road?* he so wants to ask.

Though maybe it's better like this. What else would they do, some sort of horribly awkward, drawn-out afternoon in bed?

It'd be so nice, he thinks. He frowns. *Stop*, he tells himself.

"Don't," Whit says suddenly.

"The farm's going to be fine."

"But wait, though, 'cause..."

Cooper waits. His skin itches, and he wants to bounce from foot to foot. "Wait for what?" he finally asks.

"I just..."

This is your chance, Whit, he thinks. *Lay it all out there, tell me you want me to stay, you're desperate, you can't live without me.*

Whit's mouth opens and Cooper's chest rises on a swell of hope.

But Whit just shuts it again, his lips pressing into a thin line. Cooper turns away.

Of course. That empty, naive *wanting* always leaves him hollow when it rushes back out again. Cooper slings his bag over his shoulder, balancing it so it doesn't spill dirty laundry all over the floor. *Enough*, he tells himself. Whit, chasing after Cooper, like Terry said. What a fucking joke.

"I'll throw these in the washing machine," Cooper says, holding up the bundle of sheets.

"Okay," Whit says softly.

Outside, he tosses his bag into the passenger seat of his truck while Drew glares at him. Penny stands beside Drew, arms crossed. Even Sadie looks miffed, leaning against Drew's knees and refusing to come over to Cooper when he pats at his thigh.

"Bye, baby girl," Cooper says to Sadie.

"She's old and wise and therefore knows you're making a stupid mistake," Penny says.

Cooper kneels next to her, resting his cheek on top of her head. "My puppy would never."

"Sadie, don't talk to him," Drew says.

"Sadie, you be good. You're in charge of the squirrels, okay? You and Socks."

"Socks is mad at you too," Penny adds.

"Socks is my main man." Cooper stands and wraps Drew in a hug. "As are you. I fucking love you, take care, okay? Don't sell the place."

"M'gonna try not to," Drew says, and Cooper squeezes him tight enough he gives a little *oof*.

Penny pushes her mouth to the side, a hard look on her face. "Cooper..."

"Look, I got another job, right? So I'll see you later, gator."

"Fuck you for leaving," Penny says.

He pulls her into a tight, long hug. "Love you, crocodile."

When he lets her go, Whit's there.

"The cows are all set," Cooper says. He shoves his

hands into his pockets. "And the barn's ready for evening milking."

He could stay. Not clear out when Whit's supposed to be enjoying his day off. Though Whit and Drew balanced the chores of milking and the herd before Cooper ever showed up and they will again. Cooper presses his mouth closed over the offer to stick around for another couple hours. He did that once and here he still is, summer edging onward, and where the hell would it leave him this time? Wandering through a life that doesn't fit him well into fall?

Besides, it'll give Whit the joy of one last annoyance if Cooper takes off now. Prove Whit right too, that Cooper can't plan his life for shit when he packs up and leaves at the drop of a hat. Cooper drags his boot backward through the driveway's gravel and says, "Bye."

"Bye," Whit says softly.

Cooper hesitates, then steps forward. He hugged Drew and Penny. What's a quick goodbye to Whit, too?

Whit smells good. Feels good too, the hand he touches to Cooper's back, the strength in his body as Cooper closes his arms quickly, tightly, around him.

Cooper steps back. Jumps up into the cab of his truck and turns the key. *Go*, he tells himself, or he's not going to. He's going to walk right back into Whit's arms and bury himself there, in that soft skin above the collar of his shirt, the spot on his neck that Cooper's grown so used to snuggling into.

He checks his gas gauge to keep himself from staring around. Cooper knows what the barnyard looks like, the house with its maple trees, and the shape of the tractors and trucks parked against the barn. One more glance won't make a difference.

He shifts into second gear as he pulls out. There's a muddy old tennis ball on the side of the road. Sadie must've left it there. That, or someone threw it for her and she never ambled her way over to fetch it. Whit, probably. Cooper works his mouth side to side, pinching it tight enough to nearly hurt.

Take me out to dinner, Whit, Cooper wants to shout from his window. *Say stupid, sweet things to me. Want me.*

But Whit's silence, like ever, would answer him back.

Cooper rolls down the window, sticks his hand out to wave goodbye, turns the corner and is gone.

PART 4

OCTOBER

CHAPTER SIXTEEN

COOPER SETS the latch on the gate and steps back. The doe stares at him from the other side of the fence, her head cocked to one side and her long ears pricked up.

"Stay," he says to the goat, like she's a dog who knows the command. And like she'd listen, if she did.

Cooper takes a step back. She moves one hoof forward. He's hungry. And thirsty. And she's got a feeder full of hay, fresh, clear water, a salt lick, and a dry covered pen full of straw to snooze away the rainy afternoon in, cozy with the rest of her herd. He slowly edges backward.

Rain falls against Cooper's shoulders and the brim of his hat. The doe scratches at her haunch with her teeth, lips curled back and her neck stretched. She's still eyeing him, though. Probably trying to lure him into complacency, so that Cooper'll be back out here tonight, putting up another panel of fencing and coaxing the goat back into her pen while she bleats at him, waking up Cheryl as she prances around the farm, high on the thrill of freedom.

His head hurts. He rubs the heel of his hand against his forehead, but it only smears the dirt coating his palm. He needs a shower. And dinner. And for the damn goat to stay put.

Fuck it. He turns to leave and if she jumps out of her pen as he walks back up the road toward the main house and his cabin tucked against the tree line beside it, the patter of the rain drowns out the tap of her hooves. He can't see her when he glances back, though whether it's from the fence he's reinforced time and again, or that she's gone on another adventure, he doesn't know. If she's gone, she'll be back when she gets hungry or misses the rest of her herd, elegantly jumping clear over the fence as if to drive home the point that she'll be going where she wants, when she wants, with no interest in any input from him.

At least the window above his tiny kitchen sink only shows a small slice of lawn and the woods beyond it, gray and dreary in the cold rain that's falling, and thankfully empty of any wayward goats. There's still no plaintive bleating as Cooper pulls open the tiny fridge, and he eyes the window again, waiting for her to trot by. When she doesn't, he pulls out a jug of milk. Cereal for dinner, yet again, since coaxing the stove to light so he can cook for one is just as depressing as sitting at his minuscule table eating soggy Cheerios.

"Cooper?" he hears from outside.

He drops his spoon back in his bowl. "Is she out again?" He pulls the door open, but it's just Cheryl, her flashlight bobbing in the blue gloom of the evening, and her raincoat held up over her head.

"There's a phone call for you," Cheryl calls over the drum of rain. She ducks under the short porch outside his door, gray hair working loose from her braid beneath her hood. "A friend of yours? Drew?"

Of course it's Drew, not anyone else.

The last time Cooper was in town and had cell service,

he'd received a delayed text message from Drew: *I need to talk to you.* When Cooper called, Drew hadn't picked up, so he'd left Cheryl's landline number. Only later had Cooper remembered that Drew was likely in the cheese room, the three-hour time difference meaning that Drew wasn't eating lunch like Cooper was, grabbing a sandwich after picking up a load of hay.

Cooper trails Cheryl up the stone steps to her house. It looks so cheery on nights like this, golden light shining through the windows and the garden still green and tidy from summer. Even though most of the flowers have died back since he arrived, there's still a certain charm to the well-cared-for beds. *Penny would like it*, he's thought more than once. He even snapped a picture for her, though he still hasn't texted it.

"Thank you." He tucks the phone Cheryl hands him between his cheek and shoulder as he pulls the door shut. "Drew?"

"Coop! What's up, my dude?"

He can hear water running. Drew's in the kitchen, probably. Cooper glances at the clock above Cheryl's stove. It's dinnertime here, so Drew's wrapping up for the day, washing his hands over the sink.

"Everything okay?" Cooper asks.

It's always so awkward to find a place to stand and talk on the phone in the house Cheryl shares with her wife. Nice of them to let him use it, but still, he's left to step out of his shoes, make his way into their living room, and perch on the arm of their couch, his back toward the kitchen as if that's any more private.

Cell service, he tells himself again. So far, that's the only thing on his list of what he wants for his next job. That and maybe a veritable fortress of fencing.

"Everything's great," Drew says. "How're the goats?"

"Opinionated." Cooper adjusts his seat slightly on the arm of the couch. He can hear Cheryl and Kathy in their kitchen, their voices low as if not to bother him. "They're like Houdini, or at least one of them is."

"Escape goat." Drew laughs at his own joke.

He sounds good. Happy. More like himself than he did all summer, that's for sure.

"How's it been going?" Cooper asks. "Everything all right?"

"Sure is," Drew says. "Nice fall so far, the foliage is great. How's it been going for you?"

"Fine." Cooper glances at the window and the smear of rain tracking down the glass. "Raining, so same old. How's the farm?"

"Good, good. Sadie says hi."

"Aw, hi Sadie," Cooper says. "How's she doing?"

"Roasting herself in front of the woodstove. I swear, I'm going to give her an axe one of these days and tell her she's got to help provide if she's wanting us to go through this much wood."

"Can't you get the squirrels to do it?"

"Fucking won that fight, my dude. We ended up trimming back some of the branches on the maples, and without their superhighway to ship acorns in and out, they weren't as excited about being our upstairs roommates."

We, Cooper thinks. "Great job." In the background, the sink runs again. "You busy? We can find another time to catch up."

"Nah, it's fine, doing some dishes."

Don't, Cooper tells himself, but all the same he asks, "Whit isn't on them lickety-split?"

"Whit's in the middle of a week-long battle with our new bull," Drew says. Cooper pulls the corner of his bottom lip between his teeth. "I'm making spaghetti."

"Well, isn't that helpful." Cooper scratches at the back of his head. "How's, um, how's that going?"

"The pasta? Good."

"The bull."

"Oh, yeah, good, it's a real pain, actually, 'cause now he and the old bull aren't getting along and Whit's got the barn, like, partitioned in two."

"You have a second bull?" Cooper asks.

"We kept back a lot of the heifers. Coop, this wholesale thing, I should be sending you a commission, I'm pretty sure."

Cooper realizes he's picking at his pant leg only when a thread comes loose. He smooths it with his thumb. "Send me some more fencing," he says. "These goats are out of hand."

"Can't, we're using it all to pen in that damn bull. But Whit says he can do it, and you know Whit."

Cooper purses his mouth. "Yeah."

"Stubborn asshole, but whatever." Drew shuts the water off again. "I haven't heard any loud noises from the barn lately, so he's probably close to proving whatever point he's trying to make to that poor animal."

"Sales are going well, then?"

"Yeah, yeah, we're still milking and only dried off some of the herd for the fall. Hence the second bull."

"That's great." Cooper's reflection in the window stares back at him, watery and wan. "I'm—I'm glad."

"That's why I wanted to talk to you, Coop." Drew draws in a breath, the sound of it clear through the phone. "I think I can swing the wages for a second position here."

"Awesome." His tone falls too flat.

"I mean you, you idiot."

"Oh." Cooper rolls the thread between his thumb and forefinger, the end of it fraying.

Drew's silence hums down the line. "Is that a yes?"

"Um."

Cooper pulls at the thread, working it a bit looser. Closes his eyes too, and pictures the kitchen and Drew puttering around in it. The maples will likely be shedding their leaves right now, and woodsmoke will be hanging low over the barnyard, crisp and fresh. He's sure Drew's right that Sadie's on her bed next to the woodstove, waiting on the next season to come, and with it, warm sunshine and green grass.

He could be there for it. Settle in, call it home, and put down roots. So fucking tempting. A life full of those fields and that land and Penny and Drew and Sadie.

And Whit.

Does Whit miss me? he so wants to ask. *Think about me at all? Does he bring guys around? Is he dating someone by now and have you met them?*

"You know what, I'm actually good out here," Cooper says.

"What?"

"I'm—yeah, I've got a new best friend. She's a goat, and we don't actually like each other, but we're making it work."

"But I've got a job for you," Drew says. "Is it a money thing? I know I couldn't pay you much before, but now—"

"It's not a money thing."

"Full-time work, Coop. And I finished your room, so you'd have your own space again."

"I've got a job, though." Cooper wraps his arm around himself, over his stomach. "And a cute little cabin."

"The hell? Why aren't you tripping all over yourself already getting packed? Is this Cooper Langston? Please put him on. I'd like to talk to him."

There's a joke in there, he's sure. *No, this is Looper Cangston, so sorry for the confusion.* Something silly and

254

dumb, and Drew would laugh and Cooper would too, and he'd promise he'd be back to Two Pines as soon as he could work out a replacement for himself here in Oregon and not leave Cheryl in the lurch.

"I can't take the job," Cooper says. "Thank you, but I can't."

"Coop." Drew lets out a breath. "The fuck? C'mon, we're your best friends."

"No, I know."

"And you love it here."

"Course I do."

"Say one nice thing about goats. Hell, say one nice thing about Oregon."

Cooper eyes the window. "It rains plenty."

"Coop."

"C'mon," Cooper says softly. "Let it go."

"No, I won't. You've made this farm into what it is. And all the years you put in, everything you did this summer, you know as well as I do that you should be here for when things are finally going well. I can't believe you're not already on your way back, thinking you're sneaky and pulling into the barnyard to try to surprise me."

Cooper rubs his hand across his eyes. "Drew…"

"And it'll be all the better if you jump back into things now and help us get through the winter so we're rocking and rolling come spring or whenever you're gonna come visit."

Drew pauses.

Maybe Cooper should've had something more for dinner. His stomach hurts.

"You are coming back to see us at some point, right?" Drew asks.

"Yeah, at some point."

"Some point…some point when, exactly?"

Cooper forces out a laugh. "Well, you know me, I have no idea."

"But like...this spring? Or summer?"

"I'm all the way out west, Drew. I don't know."

"Cooper."

"I don't," he says, though it sounds weak even to him.

Cooper misses even just the sounds of the kitchen and the picture he has in his mind of Drew standing over the sink. He tips the phone away from his mouth and blows out a breath. Whit's there too, somewhere. Out in the barn, working with that new bull. Of course Whit would think he could manage to get a stubborn bull to stay put in its pen all by himself. If Cooper were there...he shakes his head at his own reflection in the window.

It doesn't bear thinking about. Cooper's not there, no matter that he can imagine it so clearly, leaning against the fence in the barn and giving Whit a hard time for trying to take on the project by himself, before he hops over the fence to help. The two of them could get it done easily enough, though they'd bicker the entire time.

And then what? Spend the rest of the evening fucking each other, with no future waiting for the two of them? Or Cooper would silently go back to his room and Whit would close the door to his own, and they'd play at ignoring how they spent all summer rolling around in bed together?

Maybe that's what he was missing all those years: the clarity that if anything ever did materialize between him and Whit, it'd be just sex and absolutely nothing more.

Ass, Cooper wants to think, but his throat feels thick and he closes his eyes.

"Cooper?" Drew asks.

"Whit and I slept together."

Silence. He can hear Drew breathing. He hunches his shoulders, hoping Cheryl and Kathy aren't listening.

"Oh."

"So," Cooper says. He licks his lips. "I'm not...I'm not sure I'll be back."

"Okay," Drew says. "What?"

"This summer, I don't know. It just happened."

"I don't want the details." Drew's quiet again, and then says, "Okay, I do want the details."

"It was just—" Cooper flaps his hand at the window. "It got, um, weird between us at the end, and it wasn't ever really a thing. So."

"So?"

"So that's that, and I don't really know about coming back east again anytime soon."

"You two slept together?"

"Yeah." Cooper wipes his palm down his thigh. "We did."

"And now you're not coming back?" Drew asks.

Cooper's cheeks burn. No, he can't go back. Whit would likely string him up for telling Drew in the first place. Though it's not like he can unspill the milk now. Beans. Whatever. Whatever Whit wanted over the summer, it clearly evaporated as quickly as it had come. *A couple rolls in the hay*, he thinks and tries to smile like Drew would.

He closes his palm over his eyes and out of his mouth tumbles, "I kind of have a thing for him."

"You do?"

"Whit doesn't obviously—um—care. Or want that—anything, I mean. So I think I'm going to stick around here for a while. And—and you'll find someone to take the job, someone great, I'm sure."

"You slept with Whit? You like him?"

"I should probably go. I think some of the goats are out."

"Whit? Our Whit?" Drew asks.

Drew's Whit, maybe. Some other guy's someday. Not Cooper's.

"Bye," Cooper says. "Hey, good to talk to you."

"Whit?" Drew asks again and Cooper hangs up, pulling in a breath and holding it. He lets it out in a burst. Then, he leans forward, his elbow on his thigh and his forehead pressed to the heel of his hand.

Behind him, the teakettle whistles.

"Sorry," Kathy calls to him.

"Yeah, no, sorry, I was just—"

Carefully, Cooper replaces the phone in its cradle. He feels shaky. It's fine. It's done. Drew knows, and he also knows Cooper won't be back for another season. Cooper'll find something else after his contract here is up, and maybe someday, he'll be in upstate New York again. He can stop by. See the old stomping grounds. And this thing he's got for Whit will have faded. Blown on by like a pesky storm cloud, dumping rain at the exact wrong time. He got over Whit once, all those years ago, and he will again.

"How's your friend?" Kathy asks.

"Oh, he's good, um, calling to say hi." Cooper rubs his hand down the front of his shirt. "I can stay through the holidays. I know you're looking for someone to keep an eye on the place and I—"

"Are you all right, dear?" Cheryl asks.

"Course."

"You don't look all right."

"No, I'm fine, I'm—yeah."

Cheryl pushes out the chair next to her and says, "Come have a cup of tea."

Inside Cooper's chest is too watery and weak. He'd probably sit down and just let it all spill out, and really, he wants to crawl into bed and pull the covers up. Practice forgetting Whit entirely, like he's made any damn progress to begin with. "I should probably check on the herd."

Cheryl pats the chair. "The herd's fine."

"That one doe—I'm thinking, actually, if I built her a shelter? Even just a lean-to against the barn so she'll have some space outside away from the rest of the herd but out of the rain?" *Stop*, he tells himself, but the words flow out just the same. More work to bury himself in, not that it'd take more than a week to get up. "There's some lumber in the back. I'd be happy to give it a try, see if it convinces her to stay put."

"Are you sure you don't want to talk?" Kathy asks.

"You know, I think she's out right now actually." Cooper backs out the door.

He ducks down into his sweatshirt and bends his head against the rain, though his shoulders are still soaked by the time he reaches the door to his cabin. Inside, he dumps his soggy cereal into the trash.

A goat bleats through the pounding of rain. He closes his eyes. Inhales deeply. When he looks again, the damn doe prances by. She stops, turns, and trots back again, tail held high as she passes past his window.

Put your boots on, he tells himself. Coat, boots, flashlight. *Do it*, he thinks as he just keeps standing there. He chose this. It's what he wanted. With a sigh, he slowly gets dressed again and pushes out into the rain.

CHAPTER SEVENTEEN

COOPER FLUFFS a flake of hay and sets it neatly in the feeder. A scoop of grain, a trough of fresh water, and that's that. He gathers up his hammer, the last handful of nails he hadn't needed, and sweeps his arm in a grand gesture to the doe.

She sniffs at the doorway. Icy rain trickles down the collar of his sweatshirt. She pokes her head inside.

"A palace for one," he says.

She struts inside, looks around, and dashes back out into the rain, soaking the toes of his boots with a splash as she goes.

"Of fucking course."

Dramatic, he'd once called goats, and then used the word for them a hundred times more. He blinks as rain drips down his face. He'd told Whit that. Years ago, when Whit had suggested adding a herd of dairy goats so Drew could make chèvre. Cooper shakes his head to whip the rain out of his eyes.

The doe snorts and skips off toward the corner of her pen, her head cocked and her ears pricked with an attitude he's always been sure no other animal can muster. A cat, maybe. Socks had that sort of prance back in the day, but even he never managed that level of sass.

Enough, he tells himself.

Lunch. He needs lunch. Afterward, he'll finish cleaning up the last of the scraps of lumber and feed out the rest of the herd's hay. And then he can change out of his wet clothes and enjoy an evening of dry socks and thawed fingers before he trudges out tomorrow morning to start all over again.

It's probably sunny at Drew's. Crisp but warm in the sun, with autumn's colorful riot of foliage. The barnyard smelling like woodsmoke and the cider Drew makes every year.

Enough. Enough, enough, enough, he thinks as he goes into his cabin.

"Cooper?" someone calls from outside as he tugs off his jacket.

"Yeah?" he shouts back.

He can't see more than a few feet through the window with rain pinging against the glass and a bank of fog sitting beyond it, so he eases his door open an inch, rain splattering over his sopping wet boots, and calls out, "Cheryl?"

"Someone here for you!"

"Who?" Cooper shouts into the rain.

"Just down there, yep, follow that path," Cheryl says and Cooper squints at the two figures, Cheryl's familiar form and someone taller trailing her. "A friend of yours!"

Drew, he thinks, hope leaping in his chest.

But, no. Drew's been on a plane maybe twice in his life, and he's not one to drop in for a surprise, not with his herd of cows and the cheese that needs his attention. Probably just that guy from the co-op looking to buy some breeding does, or maybe the farmer down the road selling off some of the summer's hay that Cooper has been trying to get a hold of.

Cooper takes his hat off and wipes a hand over his face, taking water and dirt with it. "Come in," Cooper calls out and steps back to make room for them.

"Cooper?"

He freezes, a hand on the door and rain splashing over the threshold. "Whit?"

"Hey." Whit hunches under the narrow awning over Cooper's door. Behind him, Cheryl waves, then disappears up the path to her house.

"Hey," Cooper says.

Rain pings against the roof and jumps where it splashes from the eaves to soak the cuffs of Whit's pants.

Whit. Here.

The fuck?

Cooper steps back and widens the door and Whit comes through it, tugging the hood of his rain jacket down, his shoes squeaking against the floor.

"I'm sorry if I'm interrupting," Whit says.

"It's fine," Cooper says. It's not. Or it is. His ears feel like they're buzzing.

"You were working," Whit says.

"I'm having lunch." More water rolls down Cooper's face, and he pushes his hair off his forehead. He blinks once more, and Whit's still standing there, his hands loose at his sides and the hem of his pants damp.

Whit licks at his lips. "I wanted to talk to you."

"Why?" Cooper squints, like it'll bring Whit into sharper focus.

Rain pounds down on the roof and Cooper wishes it would stop, just so he could hear himself think for a second, see if he can figure this out. Whit, standing in his tiny, cramped cabin. No, impossible. Cooper wants to rub his eyes and look again to find out if Whit's really still there.

"I want to talk to you, just for a minute," Whit says.

"A minute?" Cooper sets his hat back on his head, though his hands feel empty without it. He pushes his fingers into his pockets. The nails are still in there, his knuckles bumping against them. Cooper jerks the nails out of his pocket and sets them next to his keys on the small side table. That's right, lunch. He was getting lunch. And then Whit walked out of the misty fog, and here he is, rain splattering down behind him.

"Gonna let me all the way in?" Whit asks.

Cooper gestures him forward with a jerky motion and pushes the door shut. "You on vacation?" Cooper wipes his palms on his thighs, then looks down at them, goat hair clinging to his wet skin.

"No, I wanted to talk to you."

Whit sounds like a broken record. His raincoat looks new, must be new, Cooper's never seen it before.

"Okay." Cooper wipes his hands off again, like his pants are any dryer.

"Is—" Whit pauses. His head tips. Cooper's not sure he's ever seen Whit do that, glance away from Cooper and then back again. "Would that be okay?"

"I guess." Cooper jerks open the fridge. Takes a breath, too. It sounds shaky. Whit, in Oregon. On this farm. Here to see him, apparently. Cooper clears his throat and when he turns back, Whit's still there. "You, ah, hungry?" Cooper asks. That sounds like the type of thing he should say. Someone over to visit. *Whit* over to visit.

"Yeah."

His cabin's even more cramped with Whit taking up so much room. Whit steps out of his boots and Cooper looks down at his own. Normally, Cooper leaves muddy tracks all over, and then gets annoyed about it when he steps out of the shower, the floor gritty under his bare feet. Quickly, he bends down and unlaces his boots, the leather stiff with caked mud and soaked through with rain.

Cooper has bread. And peanut butter. And an old, mostly empty jar of jam that's got dried rings of strawberry around the lip from not screwing the lid back on right. None of his knives are clean, and he rinses one quickly. *Soap*, he tells himself, squirting some onto a sponge. It's Whit. Whit's a soap kind of guy.

"Coffee?" Cooper asks the tiny sink.

"No, thank you."

"What're you doing here?"

"I wanted to talk."

"Right. You said that."

The plates Cooper sets out don't match. Whit's too tall for the table and has to fold himself into a chair. His knee sticks out. And the leg of his jeans is wet, water splashed up on the cuff and dotting his thigh.

"I might have some chips too." Cooper tosses the bag of bread onto the table. He sticks the clean knife into the peanut butter.

"This is fine," Whit says.

Didn't they once get into an argument about crunchy versus smooth? But Whit doesn't complain about the lumps in the peanut butter as he spreads it over his bread. Cooper should've washed a second knife. He'd have something to do if he could be coaxing jelly onto his own sandwich, while Whit spreads peanut butter neatly to all four edges and corners. But instead, Cooper has to wait until Whit holds out the handle toward him. Cooper takes it, keeping his fingers well clear of Whit's.

"So," Cooper says finally, as he folds his sandwich closed.

"This is yours?" Whit looks around as if there's more to take in than just the table, the bed an arm's reach away, and the door to the bathroom.

Cooper didn't make his bed that morning. Of course he didn't, and he suddenly hates that Whit's there to see it.

"Not mine, mine," Cooper says. They can both be pedantic assholes, now can't they? He takes a bite of his sandwich. He doesn't even like peanut butter and jelly. It sticks in his mouth and doesn't fill him up for the afternoon's work to come. "I'm sorry, did you call? I don't have service. Did you tell me you were coming?"

A little warning, he knows he means. *What the actual fuck*, he so wants to ask.

"No, I—" Whit shakes his head. "I, um."

"Cheryl's house has a phone."

"Right."

Whit's chest fills with a breath, and he tears the corner of his sandwich off. Slowly, Whit puts it in his mouth and chews, looking around again like there's anything else to see. Whit's throat works as he swallows. It's not like Cooper offered him water. He could.

"What's this about?" Cooper asks.

"You called Drew," Whit says.

Cooper looks up from his lap, eyebrows raised. "Is that not okay?"

Fuck you, he wants to snap. Months—*months*—of missing Whit and he just shows up here? To what, have a chat? All that careful chinking of a thick wall between Cooper and his feelings, and Whit just drops by?

"No, it's—" Whit's tongue darts over his lips. "It's fine, it's not that, it—"

He shakes his head. Quickly, Whit unzips his coat, stripping the sleeves off his arms and then shaking it out. He folds it, because of course he does, though there's nowhere to put it. Gently, he lays it on the floor, next to the wet cuff of his jeans and his sock, a clean, pristine white against the rain on his pants.

"What is it, then?" Cooper takes another bite and sets his sandwich down. "I gotta go feed the herd."

"No, I know."

Cooper waits, but Whit only tears off another piece of his sandwich. Slowly, he chews it, and only when he's swallowed does he say, "You, ah, you told Drew you weren't coming back? To visit?"

"I know," Cooper says.

Irritation threatens to burn through him. Whit, flying all the way here to—to what? Remind Cooper of a phone conversation that Whit wasn't even a part of? Interrupting his day, his work here, his aching process of forgetting everything about their spring and summer? Cooper's spent enough time trying not to think about him to now have Whit here where he lives, the scent of him filling up the small room. Cooper was doing so well, too. So no thanks, he doesn't fucking want this, Whit here in his space, and the dim, hot flicker of hope that it stirs in his chest.

Stop, he tells himself, hunching forward over his sandwich. It's Whit. Nothing's between them and it never has been.

"So you're not coming back?" Whit asks.

"No."

"Okay." Whit takes a breath. Opens his mouth, eyes on the table. Shuts it again, his lips pursed. "Okay."

"Is this about finding someone for the farm? 'Cause I told Drew, that job won't be hard to fill."

Hell, knowing Whit, he's probably interviewed a half-dozen people already. A dozen, maybe, and has some sort of horribly overdetailed spreadsheet outlining their pros and cons. *Not Cooper,* reads one column, he's sure, a tidy tick next to each and every name.

"It's not about the job." Whit rips off another bite from his sandwich but sets it down. He brushes his fingers together, crumbs falling into the center of his plate. "It's about, well, the job and—and you kissed me?"

"What?"

"That summer? All those years ago, you—" Whit stares somewhere past Cooper's shoulder, deep furrows pinching his forehead. "And then everything this summer, but on the phone you told Drew that you thought I—" Quickly, Whit scratches at his neck. "I don't care about you?"

Blood pulses in Cooper's cheeks. "Drew told you that? That I said that?"

"No, he told Penny, and she—" Whit closes his eyes and pulls in a deep breath. When he opens them, he spreads his hands on the table, his fingers gripping the flat surface until tendons stand out.

"He wasn't supposed to tell you that."

"No, I know, I just..." Whit's throat bobs on a swallow. "I've had this ridiculous thing for you for years and I've been trying to get over you and then this summer was just— I just couldn't believe it, and then—" His tongue presses into his cheek, a bulge under the thin skin. When he looks up, his eyes are bright. "You're really not coming back to Two Pines?"

Cooper blinks. "You don't even like me."

"Cooper," Whit says softly.

"You can barely stand me." Cooper's whole face feels hot. His chest, too. Tight and pounding.

"No, I—"

"What the hell, Whit?"

Whit sniffs. His eyes are red. "I can stand you."

"Since that summer?" Cooper asks. "That was fucking years ago. You've liked me since that summer?"

"Before that," Whit says softly. "Since—since high school. I can go, I'm sorry, I shouldn't have—"

"High school?" Cooper's voice sounds too high.

"Drew said—Penny said that Drew said that you—you don't want to come back again because of me and—" Whit draws in a deep breath, his chest expanding on it. "I wanted you to know."

Whit sits back in his chair, and with his tongue touched to the corner of his mouth, he stares at the window and the drops of rain rolling down. Cooper stares at him. Blinks. Watches Whit swallow again, his thumb rubbing quickly over his knuckles.

"I'm sorry, is this real?" Cooper asks.

Whit nods, still not looking at Cooper.

He got on a plane, Cooper thinks, turning each word over in his mind.

He must've gotten the address from Drew. And just... came. All this way. *I had this ridiculous thing for you,* he hears again in Whit's voice. Cooper's face is burning. It's something he himself would say, not words that should be metered out in Whit's deep, even voice.

Say it again? Cooper wants to ask. He inhales sharply. He can't think right, his mind buzzing and the rain tapping on the windows and Whit so close, right there across the table from him. Cooper blinks. His eyes feel hot. And his nose is tingling. Cooper clears his throat. Then, he clears it again. This room is too damn small. "I need a minute."

"Of course."

Cooper gets up, puts his soggy boots back on, and goes out into the rain. Whit trails after him, head ducked and his hood pulled up. Cooper can still see the angle of his chin, the curve of his nose. Cooper yanks the brim of his hat down. His stomach is twisted over and around, something like hunger sitting deep in his gut.

Whit's here. He came all this way, just to see Cooper. Because Cooper wasn't going to come back again. He wanted...wanted Cooper to know how he felt.

He tugs on the brim of his hat again and turns slightly, and Whit's still there next to him, sloshing through the puddles.

That summer they kissed was so long ago. Years and years and years ago. And Whit, since then...Cooper squints at him. All that time stuck in the same room. In bed together, wrapped up in each other. Whit's hands on him. He'd been...Cooper shakes his head.

In the barn, a goat bleats, impatient for her hay.

"You said to Drew, that I'm not—" Cooper shakes his head. "You didn't even tell Drew about us."

"I thought you didn't want him to know, so I—"

"And you said that you tell him everything and this? Us?" Cooper waves between them. "Of course I didn't fucking say anything to him, you're so goddamn fed up with me all the time."

"I'm not," Whit says. "I'm, Coop—I—"

"You just wanted to hook up with me. That was it."

"No. Cooper, I want—you have no idea."

"Apparently not."

Cooper grabs the sides of the ladder and climbs up to the loft. He needs hay bales. And a second to make sense of everything rushing through his head. He catches his shin on the top rung and winces, bracing himself on the stacked hay.

When he turns to look down, Whit's still there, just standing in the middle of the aisle.

"I constantly annoy you," Cooper says.

"You don't. I get—I get frustrated with myself. Around you. Cooper, I can't think straight."

Cooper pitches a bale down and Whit neatly sidesteps it. Chaff puffs up and clings to Whit's damp pants. "You think I'm a joke. Immature."

"I think you're fun, you're so much more fun than I'll ever be, you bring out this side of me that's—I'm better when you're around, Coop."

"You hate all my ideas. Everything I ever say, you just disagree with."

"I'm not good at change. At new things. You told me that, but I—I can try to be."

"Did you just fly out here to argue with me?"

"I—I guess I did."

"You got a goddamn plane ticket to tell me I'm wrong to have moved out here?"

"I wasn't going to put it like that."

"How were you going to put it?"

Whit licks his lips. He's rehearsed this, Cooper's suddenly sure. On the plane here, before he left. That fact lights up Cooper's chest, warm and bright.

"This summer," Whit starts. Shifts his weight, scrapes his foot against the straw littering the barn. Cooper drinks it in, Whit's uncharacteristic twitchiness, his plain-as-day nerves. "I—it was like out of a dream. You coming to the farm, and ending up staying for so long. I hated it and I loved it and just every day, Coop, you drive me nuts with how into you I am. You're everything I could never be, you're always just going for it. Grabbing life with both hands. And I get it if I'm not—if I'm too different. But you told me I'm too stuck in my ways and you're right, so I came out here to just. . .to just try, Coop. 'Cause I can't stand you thinking I don't care about you, that you're not who I wake up thinking about and that I haven't missed you every damn day since you left."

Cooper crosses his arms. Sniffs once, hard. "Yeah?"

"There wasn't anyone else, Cooper. You kept asking but there wasn't and there hasn't been since you left."

Cooper sniffs again. "Good."

"Good?" Whit asks, taking a small, quick step toward the ladder.

"Yeah, that's good."

Whit seems frozen, staring up at him. Doesn't look like he's breathing, even. His eyes are wide, his fingers working together where his hands hang loose by his sides. Beside him, the goats strain through the fence, sticking their lips out, trying to reach the bale sitting at Whit's feet.

Whit jerks when one of them bleats. Bends down to awkwardly, hastily start pulling the baling twine off the bale. He's really going to help feed the goats. He got on a plane, flew out here, probably rented a damn car, and no matter what Cooper says in response to all of this, he's going to lend a hand around the barn. That's just so...that's just so *Whit*.

Slowly, Cooper swings onto the ladder. Takes a step down to the next rung and peers at Whit. Neatly, Whit folds the baling twine in half and then in half again. He always does that, and today is no different. Each strand, every single time Cooper's ever seen him open a bale. For all Cooper knows, he has a collection somewhere, years and years of farming and neatly folded twine to show for it.

"What's the point of that?" Cooper asks.

"Of what?"

"The—" Cooper jumps down the last rungs and points, his sleeve sticking to his shoulder as he raises his arm. Whit looks at it. And that's...that's something, isn't it? Whit's eyes cutting down to Cooper's arm, then back to his face. It feels good to have Whit's attention on him. "The folding. Why do you always do that?"

"I don't like it when it gets tangled," Whit says.

He's good looking. Hasn't Cooper always thought so? Since that first summer, when they were so much younger. All this damn time, the two of them circling each other.

"You don't like it when it gets tangled."

"That's what I said." Whit puts the twine into his pocket.

"You better fucking mean all of this," Cooper says. "I can't, I've—" God, this is hard to say. Easier too, than he might have guessed. Might have expected, if he ever even thought to dream any of this. "I've been trying to get over you too, asshole."

"You have?"

"So fucking hell, Whit, tell me this is real."

"I mean it," Whit says softly.

"You do?"

"I love you," Whit says. He's half-mumbling and he clears his throat. "I love you," he says, louder this time. "That's what I wanted to tell you. And I came because I wanted to know if there was a chance that you might come back home."

Home, Cooper thinks. Drew and Penny and Sadie. Sunshine. Autumn. Cheese. *Whit*.

"I want that," Whit says. "And Drew said...I think you might want that too."

Whit's really here. Standing in front of him, hopeful and looking nearly as miserable as Cooper's felt all these months.

"Whit," Cooper says softly and Whit's eyes snap to his, that soft, deep brown. Cooper's always liked Whit's eyes. He likes them all the more now focused on him as he walks closer. Whit's face is wet, his cheeks cool under Cooper's hands. Cooper looks at him for a long moment, touches his thumb to Whit's cheekbone and then leans in and kisses him.

A sound rises from Whit. Soft and surprised, and Cooper tips his face and kisses him again, slow and hard, Whit's cheeks in his hands and his mouth so warm. Whit tastes the same as Cooper remembers, and beneath the rain and hay, he smells the same too. All these fucking years, and Whit right in front of him the whole time.

"It's baling twine," Cooper says when he pulls back. "It gets tangled anyway."

"But less so."

"Maybe." Cooper kisses him again.

Whit's hands close over the back of Cooper's neck and Whit's mouth opens for his. He pushes Cooper's hat back and presses closer, until Cooper's T-shirt sticks to his chest, Whit gathered up against him. And that's better, isn't it? A firmer hold on each other. Whit sucks at his lower lip and Cooper lets him, opening his mouth for Whit's tongue and tipping his head to the side as Whit shifts the angle of their kiss. Cooper wants to laugh. Or cry, maybe. He pulls back enough to open his eyes, just to make sure Whit's still there, no matter the fact of his body held tight in Cooper's arms.

"You're sure?" Whit asks, his lips brushing over Cooper's.

"No." Something's tugging on Cooper's pants. It's a goat, the edge of his pocket caught in her teeth. Cooper nudges her away and Whit kisses his chin, his jaw, down his neck. "But you are, and you're stubborn enough for the two of us."

"Me?"

Whit's even warmer when Cooper tucks his hands up under Whit's jacket and the shirt beneath, and his pulse shoots through his stomach at the flex in Whit's back, how his spine moves.

"Yes, you, you asshole," Cooper says.

"Your hands are cold." Whit reaches back for Cooper's wrists and cups his fingers, blinking at Cooper, his eyes soft. Cooper could twist away if he wanted to, with how loose Whit's grip is.

Cooper swallows. Whit's watching him so gently. It's a new look on Whit's face. Though isn't all of this new? Something full and aching wells up in Cooper's chest.

"Don't you know how to feed a goat?" Cooper asks.

"I think I can figure it out," Whit says.

He drops his hold on Cooper, and Cooper readjusts his hat. His hands feel shaky. All of him does.

Cooper just watches as Whit finishes opening the bale. He's allowed to look, he realizes dimly. And he does greedily, his eyes on how Whit's pants tighten over his thighs and his jacket pulls up his back.

"Don't fold it." Cooper grabs away the baling twine once Whit tosses the hay to the goats.

"It's easier that way," Whit says.

He grabs the twine from Whit. Easier would have been one of them saying something years ago. But they're here now and he shoves the twine into his own pocket. Whit's probably right that it'll make a mess.

"It's absurd," Cooper says. "Come on, let's go."

Whit follows him across the yard, a half-stride behind, nearly stepping on the heels of Cooper's boots. Cooper finds Whit's wet fingers and holds on, and when Whit squeezes, Cooper squeezes back.

Inside his cabin, Cooper grips the zipper pull under Whit's chin. *This isn't real*, he wants to say, but Whit's standing there in front of him, his ears a little red, his lips shiny and wet, and his warm hand on Cooper's elbow.

"You came all this way for me?" Cooper asks softly.

"You could've picked a farm in Pennsylvania," Whit says. "It certainly would've been easier."

Cooper smiles. "Shut up."

Cooper works Whit's rain jacket off and drops it on the floor. Their boots leave muddy, wet tracks and Cooper's knees hit the bed, Whit's tongue in his mouth and hands tight in his hair. Cooper's shirt lands on the table next to a half-eaten sandwich. They left the peanut butter out, he realizes, and the rest of their lunch.

"Don't you want to stop and clean up all the food?" Cooper whispers, hot into Whit's ear. He touches three fingers to the small of Whit's back, up underneath his shirt.

A soft nip at his jaw, all teeth and then the wet press of lips. "Get on the bed," Whit says.

"But what about mice?"

Whit just sits on the edge of Cooper's bed and Cooper laughs out loud, the sound startling him. He's about to have sex. With Whit. He tries to hold on to that thought, like he can make it all the realer for thinking it harder.

Cooper settles on Whit's thighs, straddling him. Tugs Whit's shirt off too, and then there's the planes of pecs to rub his hands across, the stacked muscles of Whit's abs. Cooper bends and drags his mouth over the hard ridge of Whit's collarbone. Hauls him closer too, fingers biting into the hard muscle in Whit's spine. Gets Whit's hips between his knees and squeezes, holds him there, fumbling for his belt.

Whit loves him. The power of that thought surges through Cooper, and he stands and kicks his pants off and shoves Whit's boxers down over his thighs. Cooper's got a condom somewhere. Lube, too. He gets them, and there's Whit, lying back on his rumpled quilt. They're both naked and Whit's so fucking gorgeous. All tight skin over muscles, and the sharp points of his hipbones, and his hard cock that Whit grabs. Cooper kneels next to him and watches as Whit strokes himself once. There's a scar on the heel of his hand. Cooper leans down and presses his forehead to Whit's, his palm pressed to his breastbone.

Closing his eyes, Cooper whispers, "Fuck you, I missed you."

He's not sure he could really say that out loud if he had to look at Whit, too. Cooper rubs his thumb over the slope of Whit's pec. Hasn't he lain here so many nights, curled on his side and thinking of this? Whit lifts Cooper's chin with a finger and gently draws him close for another kiss.

When Whit rolls them over, Cooper moves with him, letting his legs fall open, and Whit settles between them. Cooper touches his fingertips to Whit's cheek.

"You got my bed all wet," he says.

"So sorry." Whit fumbles with the condom wrapper. He finally opens it with his teeth and Cooper grabs the lube.

"You're not," Cooper says.

His eyes close as Whit pushes a gentle finger inside of him. Whit's knees shift and *he's looking*, Cooper realizes, watching his own hand between their bodies.

"I'm not." Whit sounds breathless.

And *oh*, that touch inside him is nice. Whit's cock is, too, big and blunt as he slowly pushes in. Cooper didn't appreciate that enough before, the stretch inside of him, how Whit so perfectly hits that spot—"Oh, *fuck*."

"Too much?" Whit asks, his back locked tight, all ridges of muscle.

"No, fuck you, I got it," Cooper gasps. It's too fucking good is what it is. *I could tell Whit that*, he realizes. Just throw his head back and let Whit know exactly how good he's making Cooper feel.

Though, Whit kisses him before he can and hooks an

arm behind Cooper's knee. It's so slow, that drag out and ease back in.

"C'mon," Cooper says against his mouth.

"I don't—" Whit laughs. Cooper presses his head back into his pillow. He's never heard that sound before from Whit and he stares. "I don't want to come."

Cooper lets out a laugh of his own. "Well, I do."

"You can wait—*ah*—wait a second."

"Are you going to let me know when?" Cooper rubs his hand up Whit's back and into his hair. "What'd I say about that itinerary?"

Whit laughs again, a breathy, quick sound. "Fuck you."

"Please. Finally," Cooper says, and Whit does.

Cooper tries to squirm closer, draping an arm behind Whit's neck, mouth open against his collarbone. Whit holds him like that, hips pounding, the sheets jerking beneath Cooper. It's going to be over too soon and Cooper's wanted this, waited for this.

"Whit," he groans, head back and heat blooming through his stomach, down his thighs until they shake.

"I told you," Whit says, and Cooper grabs his own cock, and when he comes, Whit grunts and follows him.

Cooper turns his face into Whit's neck. Whit's skin is sweaty, and Cooper tastes salt when he presses a soft kiss to Whit's throat. He passes his fingers through Whit's hair, scratching gently at his scalp.

"Since that summer?" Cooper asks softly. "You've liked me this whole time?"

Whit pushes his nose into the dip behind Cooper's ear. He's still breathing hard. "I tried not to."

"Good job with that, apparently."

Whit huffs a soft breath. Cooper's skin is too sensitive. He tips his head and Whit kisses him, slow and wet and precise as Whit always is, all of that attention turned on

Cooper. He slides his foot up Whit's calf and presses into it, humming with how good it feels. How right.

"I kissed you that summer because I couldn't get you out of my head," Cooper whispers when Whit draws back. "It didn't help any."

"Sounds like kind of shitty planning," Whit says, his lips on the corner of Cooper's mouth, the side of his nose, beneath his eye.

"Well, I thought I'd give it a try at least, you giant fucking genius. Were you ever going to say anything?" He turns his chin and Whit's right there and they kiss softly.

"I did say something," Whit says.

Cooper smiles into their kiss, and whispers back, "You did." And he's smiling through their next kiss and the one after that too.

PART 5

JANUARY

EPILOGUE

THE HIGHWAY WHIPS past the windows of Cooper's truck and as he drives, his knee bounces. He makes himself still, pressing his lips together, and then starts tapping his fingers on his thigh. Two exits left. Then one. He presses harder on the gas, only to slow down when he has to wind his way around another corner, slick with ice and the roadside banked with piles from the snowplow.

Good and tired of winter, Drew had texted him. But the snow's gorgeous, all that white clinging to the trees and covering the fields.

Cooper's stomach rumbles, but he doesn't pull off to stop for a snack. Just steers around the familiar turns in the road, the outer limits of the suburbs around Albany giving way to the woods. He passes Whit's parents' old house, the high school, and finally Caroline's house comes into view—and beyond it, Two Pines' farmhouse.

It looks a little different covered with a deep layer of snow, smoke curling up from the chimney, and holiday lights still up on the porch, twinkling in the gathering evening.

There's an extra parking spot plowed next to Whit's

truck. Cooper parks, grabs his bag from the passenger seat, and jumps down.

But before Cooper can even climb up the porch steps, the door to the farmhouse swings open and Whit comes out.

"Hey," Cooper says.

"Hey," Whit says.

Cooper's stomach flutters, though it's been doing that all damn day. Whit's steps crunch across the ice and gravel, and Cooper lifts his face for a kiss—which is too short. And it's too cold out here, but Cooper pulls a hand out of his pocket anyway, touching a fallen snowflake caught on the curl of hair over Whit's forehead.

"There was bad traffic," Cooper says. "The roads are a mess. Sorry I'm late."

"And I'm sure you're starving."

"I'm absolutely starving."

Whit kisses Cooper's palm and Cooper's stomach flips over. Whit's voice is so much better in person than on the phone. Deep and rich and smooth.

"Drew's making dinner," Whit says.

"Good," Cooper says but doesn't move toward the door, just lifts his arms to tuck around Whit's shoulders and kisses him again, slower this time. More thorough, just like he's been waiting for. Cooper tightens his hold as Whit kisses him back. It's nearly embarrassing, how that kiss zips straight through Cooper.

I love you, he thinks and presses closer and kisses Whit again and says, "I love you."

"Good," Whit says and pulls back. He's hiding a smile, and Whit never smiles.

"Good?" Cooper tucks his fingers down into Whit's collar, his shirt soft and his skin warm. "That's it? Good?"

"I'm glad you're here."

"With that welcome, I should've just given you a handshake."

It's been too damn long. Cooper used to go months without seeing Whit. Without talking to him, driving all the way to town for cell service and staying late enough he had to make his way back to his cabin in the dark. Cooper kisses Whit again, softly this time.

"That's not how you shake hands," Whit murmurs, his lips moving against Cooper's.

"Say, 'I love you too, Cooper.'"

That's a smile against Cooper's lips. A real one. Small and gentle and so sweet.

"I love you too, Cooper," Whit obediently echoes back.

"Hmm, perfect. Again, please." He's smiling too, he knows, and his stomach's still flip-flopping over itself. It hasn't stopped, has it? No, Cooper's been a twisted tangle of happy, flushed excitement for so long now.

Whit takes Cooper's bag from him, setting the strap over his own shoulder, and Cooper follows Whit into the house where Drew is standing near the woodstove, grinning, and Sadie is lounging. For months, Whit claimed that Sadie perked up every time Cooper called. All he gets from Sadie now, stamping snow from his boots as he follows Whit inside, is a yawn and a thump of her tail as she rolls over on her back, her short legs sticking up.

"Sweetie," Cooper murmurs, scratching over her stomach. The fur on her side closest to the woodstove is warm from the heat. "Nobody else knows how to give belly rubs, do they?"

"I like to think I've managed all right," Whit says.

"There's a technique." Cooper scratches up between her front paws and down her sides. "Whit doesn't know, does he? No, he doesn't."

"Hi," Drew calls loudly.

"Hi," Cooper says without looking up.

Sadie snuffles into his wrist when he rubs the top of her head, her ears falling this way and that, and her mouth opening in another slow yawn.

"Welcome back, good to have you, hello to me too, your best friend, I'm Drew, since apparently you don't remember."

When Cooper stands up, Drew lifts him off his feet in a hug, squeezing until Cooper coughs, and only then setting him down again. Behind Drew, Whit's still holding Cooper's bag. Cooper's chest fills up warm and tight and he smacks Drew on the back.

"Hi," Cooper says again.

"Hi yourself." Drew finally lets Cooper go. "Good trip?"

"Good to be back."

And it's so damn true. He glances toward the door and Whit's still there, bent over to take off his shoes with Cooper's bag balanced across his back. Cooper wants to hold Whit's hand again. It's weird, isn't it, with Drew in the room? He takes a breath. Cooper's going to get used to this. Someday, it'll be old hat.

Cooper grasps the cuff of Whit's sleeve and tugs at it. "I'm going to go put my stuff down."

Drew raises both eyebrows. "Is that what the kids are calling it these days?"

"You wouldn't even know, you cheese-making monk," Cooper says.

"Go unpack"—Drew makes air quotes—"and then we'll eat."

The stairs squeak the same as they always do beneath his and Whit's feet. Cooper wants to walk up, back down, and up again, just to get to listen to it. In his room—his old room—the bed is set up. It's where it should be, the headboard pushed up against the far wall, and the nightstand sits in its proper place. Though still, the room looks different. Odd, with fresh, new paint. Drew must've redone the floors, too, because they're brighter and far less scuffed.

"Nice," Cooper says. He runs his hand over the door trim. "Damn, Drew."

"He's going to do the rest of the house too," Whit says. "Not all at once, but room by room."

"He said he's working on Penny's?"

"He's almost done," Whit answers.

The view from Cooper's window is even prettier with snow coursing down, the sky the deep, dark blue of late evening, the moon shining over the barnyard and the bare, snow-lined branches of the maple trees.

Cooper opens the drawer of his dresser and closes it again. Slowly, he sets his bag down and turns around again, taking the room in. The bed's already made, he realizes. Neatly, too. He smiles.

"My, ah, parents were asking about you," Whit says.

"Yeah?"

"They want you to come by for dinner sometime," Whit says. He's talking just a touch too fast. "If you want."

They're really doing this, him and Whit. That warm, soft hum rises through him, same as he's felt whenever he's seen Whit's name on his phone screen. *Focus*, he spent weeks telling himself, but more than once, he'd been feeding the herd and realized he was staring into nothing, goats nibbling his boots and his mind far from the barn he stood in. "That'd be nice."

"And—" Whit pauses, his eyes on the snow falling past the window, as if it's really that interesting. "Well, Drew wants to redo my room too. I told him it didn't matter to me how it looks, but insulation, and heating costs, and all."

Cooper takes Whit in, standing in his socks and a

flannel shirt. It looks so good on him. *It'd look good on the floor too*, Cooper lets himself think.

"How practical," Cooper says.

"He wants to do it soon, before spring comes, and we're all that much busier."

Yeah, that shirt would look real, real good on the floor, Cooper thinks. "Oh, really?"

"So."

It's cute that Whit's even asking. "So?"

Whit finally looks at Cooper, a slight twitch at the side of his mouth. "So maybe I could crash in here?"

"Hmm, maybe," Cooper says. *Fuck yeah,* he thinks. Whit in bed next to him, snow falling outside the window while they lie skin-to-skin under quilts and blankets. He drapes his arms around Whit's shoulders and steps into him. "My room's kind of small, I don't know."

"Think about it."

Cooper drags his nails up the back of Whit's neck. "I am thinking about it."

"There's always the couch," Whit says.

"Sadie snores," Cooper says. Softly, he kisses the corner of Whit's mouth.

"Like you don't."

"Coop?" Penny calls out. She pokes her head in, cautiously peering around. "Oh, good, everyone's wearing their pants."

"Ha," Cooper says. "Hi to you too. Are we going to be getting a lot of this?"

Penny holds her arms out to him, and when he hugs her, she squeezes him tight. "Absolutely," she says. "Hi, you're back, I'm so happy."

"I am too," Cooper says.

"Yeah?"

"Yeah."

"Food!" Drew shouts from downstairs.

"I'll help him out." Penny ducks out, her hand finding Whit's wrist and squeezing gently.

Cooper wants to lean into Whit's chest, given Penny's footsteps retreating down the hall. Or maybe see just how well the two of them fit in his old bed. Take that shower he needs, after yet another day on the road, and watch water run over Whit's neck and shoulders, pool in the dip of his collarbone and slide downward.

The smell of dinner wafts in the door. Food first. Dinner with Drew and Penny, and Whit there, close enough to squeeze Whit's thigh and lace their fingers together. Cooper and Whit will have time together, afterward. So much of it. More than Cooper could've ever imagined.

"That's my side." Cooper tosses his bag toward the nearer side of the bed.

"Fine," Whit says.

Cooper nudges his shoulder into Whit's arm.

"Hey, lovebirds, time to eat!" Drew calls upstairs.

"Where's the argument from you?" Cooper asks.

Whit's hand trails over Cooper's back. It feels so nice to be touched like that. "Maybe that's just the first thing you've ever agreed with me on."

"Agreed with you?" Cooper asks. "Nah, second." He leans up and kisses Whit just once, softly. "This was the first."

TRANSLATIONS

Chapter 1

1. "Tell him it'd make a difference if he stuck around tonight and besides, we need the help"

Chapter 5

1. "You're as dumb as you are pretty."

Chapter 7

1. "Tell him how you feel."
2. "Whit, you're just as dumb as he is."

Chapter 12

1. "This is painful to watch."

Buy Now!

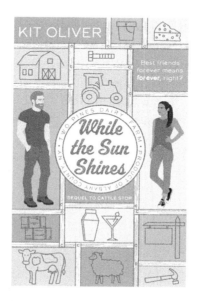

Best friends forever means *forever*, right?

Joined at the hip since high school, Drew and Penny live together, hang out together—and now, commiserate together about their other roommates falling in love. With their foursome suddenly shrunk to two, Drew has to double down on his one rule: never *ever* let Penny find out he wants more than friendship.

Keeping his secret is easy enough with his focus on his family farm, but when a handsome stranger visits, Drew learns he isn't Penny's only childhood friend—and that they might not be as close as he thought. As Drew juggles summer on the farm and his hidden feelings for Penny, he's faced with not just missing any shot he has at romance but losing her friendship too.

While the Sun Shines is a steamy, m/f romance novel that follows Cattle Stop. If you enjoy best friends finding true love with each other, the joy of inside jokes and the wrench of years long pining, then this heartwarming story of found family, friendship, and the bonds between two people is the perfect romance novel for you.

Grab your copy of While the Sun Shines to watch Drew and Penny grow from best friends to lovers and learn how much they mean to each other - and how desperately they'll work to make sure they get to share their lives.

www.kitoliver.com

ROLL IN THE HAY
A FREE NOVELLA

Get your free copy of Roll in the Hay, along with info on new releases, glimpses behind the scenes, and upcoming projects!

Find your copy at www.kitoliver.com/cs-rith

One of the best parts of writing is getting to know you.

When you sign up for my mailing list, you get: first looks at new stories, exclusive access to ask behind the scenes questions, the opportunity to join my Reader Team, and FREE novellas and short stories that aren't available for download anywhere else.

ACKNOWLEDGMENTS

What a long and winding road Cattle Stop took from a spark of an idea to becoming a finished novel! First and foremost, I'd like to thank Elle Maxwell for her gorgeous design work. She brought Cooper and Whit to life and humored me fitting both a squirrel and a spigot onto the piece of art that is the book cover. Sarah Calfee, my editor, did a fantastic job coaching my writing, finagling the plot structure, and fine tuning the dynamic between Whit and Cooper. Jules Hucke provided the final polish that makes this manuscript truly shine. Thanks to each of you for your continued hard work, support, and enthusiasm for these projects I bring to you.

As ever, Erin provided endless rounds of feedback and encouragement in the many years it's taken for this novel to reach this stage. Sam, my imagination partner, Cooper and Whit's biggest cheerleader, translator extraordinaire, and fellow cow appreciator, you've been everything this story needed and more. The two of you are invaluable and irreplaceable. And finally, Ali for the long-ago suggestion that I give this manuscript a try. It very much would not exist without you and for that, you'll always have my thanks.

Deep appreciation to the original Sadie for lending her name, and to Russell for lending his spirit. We miss you, bud. Most of all, thank you to my husband. I promise that in all the adventures I suggest as we live our lives together, none will ever include running a dairy.

ABOUT THE AUTHOR

Kit Oliver's days are spent writing, thinking about writing, having just written, or preparing to write. When not mulling over plot points and dialogue, Kit can be found reading or outdoors - or reading outdoors - often with one or more of the family dogs for company.

Kit writes contemporary queer romance novels full of bantering, bickering, pining, and kissing (and then some) that always end in Happily Ever Afters. Kit may take writing seriously, but believes that above all else, books should be fun to both create and consume. Kit's stories are based around a strong sense of humor, a deep love of complex characterization, and the joy of two people finding each other and falling in love.

ALSO BY KIT OLIVER

The Place Between

A Place to Go

Another Shot

While the Sun Shines

Roll in the Hay